DALE DYE

Dale Dye is one of the acknowledged masters of military fiction. His previous novels of the U.S. Marine Corps, OUTRAGE and RUN BETWEEN THE RAINDROPS, combined his sharp storytelling skills with his own combat experience in Vietnam and Beirut. A retired Marine officer, Dye authored the bestselling novelization of Oliver Stone's award-winning PLATOON, in addition to serving as a technical advisor for the film. Now he presents his most controversial novel—the story of an officer accused.

CONDUCT UNBECOMING

. . . is the most explosively powerful novel of a military trial since THE EXECUTION OF PRIVATE SLOVIK. It is a journey into the intensely charged soul of the modern military—the labyrinthine moral code that separates civilian from soldier.

DALE DYE PROVIDES "FIRSTHAND KNOWLEDGE . . . AN INSIDE VIEW."
—*Kirkus*

This book contains a preview of the exciting new novel *Sons of Glory* **by Simon Hawke**

CONDUCT UNBECOMING

Dale Dye

BERKLEY BOOKS, NEW YORK

CONDUCT UNBECOMING

A Berkley Book / published by arrangement with
the author

PRINTING HISTORY
Berkley edition / April 1992

ISBN: 0-425-13236-6

A BERKLEY BOOK ® TM 757,375
Berkley Books are published by The Berkley Publishing Group,
200 Madison Avenue, New York, New York 10016.
The name ''BERKLEY'' and the ''B'' logo
are trademarks belonging to Berkley Publishing Corporation.

PRINTED IN THE UNITED STATES OF AMERICA

10 9 8 7 6 5 4 3 2 1

For

The Rock and Debbie,
who inspired it . . .

Kathryn,
who cheered me while I wrote it,

and for . . .

Adrienne Kate,
who just loves her Daddy

"If e'er my son follow the war,
   tell him it is a school
   where all the principles tending to honor
   are taught, if truly followed."

Phillip Massinger, 1583–1640

"The man who devotes himself to war
   should regard it as
   a religious order into which he enters.
   He should have nothing,
   know no concern other than his troops,
   and should hold himself honored
   in his profession."

Maurice de Saxe: *Mes Reveries, iv,* 1732

CONDUCT UNBECOMING

I.

Forward, March . . .

Sheets of Atlantic rain rinsed the Outer Banks free of a cloying cloud cover. In the muggy wake of the shower, a blazing sun appeared to announce the arrival of another broiling bastard of a North Carolina summer day. Sturdy patches of sawgrass began to wilt and wisps of steam rose from the greasy macadam road surfaces that intersected the sprawling Marine Corps base at Camp Lejeune.

Major Rodney Claiborne, Stanford Law '70, braked his battered Chevy station wagon to a halt near the main PX and switched off the windshield wipers. He rolled a window open and labored to fill his lungs with damp air. What a shithole, he thought. What a bullshit, backwater place for a guy with my talent and brains.

Washington would also be hot, Major Claiborne mused as he unwound from the front seat and straightened his summer service uniform, but the heat emanating from that city was the kind that could be used to forge a bright, shining future. Claiborne blinked and double-etched the bottom line in his mind once again. He had chosen the military over a lucrative civilian practice because he liked being a big fish in a small pool, but he was not myopic. Washington was the goal; the place where a smart fish from any little pool could become a powerful shark.

He plucked a bulging briefcase from the car and headed for a stairway at the side of the Base Legal building. As Staff Judge Advocate for the 2nd Marine Division, he rated a private entrance that led directly to his office. It was a petty perk and an irritant to the other military lawyers who labored at Base Legal, but Claiborne didn't let that keep him from exercising the privileges of his rank and position.

It was all about power and the trappings of power. He smiled as he keyed the lock and stepped into the dark inner sanctum of his office. In the mirror mounted on the back of the door he saw the same tight, enigmatic smile he used on trial judges and court-martial boards. The practiced expression said: Sorry to bother you with these banalities but . . . well, it's the law, you know.

Claiborne liked to let people think he had a wry, self-deprecating view of his place in the hierarchy of the modern Marine Corps. The reality was another thing entirely. He was a man who knew exactly what he was worth in the moribund, post-Vietnam market for military talent. He knew exactly where he was headed and what sort of timetable was feasible for attainment of his long-range plans.

Taking advantage of the lull before the storm of office business that would begin right after morning colors, he poured coffee, sat down, and slid his secret roadmap out from under the government-issue green blotter on his desk. It was a foldout calendar and personal planning schedule that he'd begun keeping the day he was accepted at law school. Graduation, OCS, and The Basic School, Military Law Course, promotion eligibility points, State Bar exam schedules, transfer dates, publication deadlines, major cases he'd managed to discover and handle . . . it was all there; an admirable record of travels and turnings throughout his chosen career.

At the end of one page was a box outlined in red. By the end of the year, he'd have served his minimum thirty-six months on-station at Camp Lejeune. His triple underlined note read: "Trans to HQMC!!!" It would take an organized, orchestrated, and persistent effort to get himself selected over more senior men and transferred to the seat of power, the Office of the Judge Advocate General of the Marine Corps. Claiborne had thought he might manage it in a year or so of concerted ass-kissing. And then, unexpectedly, he hit leverage paydirt: the kind of case that would grease the skids; mark him as a True Believer who should be making policy rather than defending it.

He picked up his phone and punched a series of buttons as the 2nd Marine Division band, mustered by the headquarters flagpole just down the street, struck up the National Anthem. The commanding general's staff secretary blurted his rank, name, and title into Claiborne's ear.

"John, this is Rod Claiborne over at SJA. How's the CG's schedule looking this morning? Uh-huh . . . sounds tight. Listen, can you work me in ASAP? I'll need about thirty minutes."

The staff secretary was a man who understood the burgeoning power of military lawyers in a Corps that was being forced to rely more on the Uniform Code of Military Justice than the first sergeant's fist for maintaining discipline and standards. If the division's senior counsel wanted a private audience with the Old Man, it had to be something important. Still, he was the official gatekeeper and there wasn't much flextime built into Major General Tobrey's busy schedule of command briefings.

"Can't discuss it on the horn, John. Just tell the general it concerns a matter of . . . oh, call it moral turpitude. Yeah . . . that ought to get his attention. Thanks. See you later."

Major Claiborne hung up the phone, snapped open his briefcase, and began to meticulously assemble all the elements of a high-explosive blockbuster.

First Lieutenant Rebecca Campbell reached under her pillow to silence the muffled clang of the alarm clock she kept there to avoid disturbing her lover's deep sleep. She didn't have to look at the luminous dial to know it was 0430 and time for the man at her side to begin the morning ritual of another duty day.

He'd asked her to hold an early reveille. Captain Thurmond Becker was due to take his infantry company to the field for a week of live weapons firing. The early alarm would give him time to pack and plan. It would also provide Becky with a good chance to make it back to her own room in the women's wing of Bachelor Officers' Quarters without having to answer questions about her business in a senior male officer's room at zero-dark-thirty.

No big deal, she thought, deciding to give Becker another five minutes of untroubled sleep. Four hectic months of nocturnal visits provided good escape-and-evasion drill. She knew shortcuts through the passageways of the rambling BOQ that kept her out of the path of early-risers stumbling from their rooms to use the communal head facilities. Becky didn't particularly care for playing charades with morning shadows, but Mother Corps had yet to recognize any moral reality outside her own picket fences. Maybe when Becker returned from the field, she'd resurface the question of getting a place of their own . . . off base and away from the unblinking eyes that registered no shades of grey in a black-and-white picture.

Becker would balk at the thought of being more than five minutes away from his precious command. If she pressed, his mood would swing through towering snit to blue funk as it had on an earlier date when she'd told him she was married. Legally separated under North Carolina law, but married nonetheless. When he walked away from that revelation, delivered after a passionate good-night kiss on the steps on the BOQ, Becky thought she'd heard and seen the last of the man everyone called Buttplate Becker.

Cursing her nagging, passionate attraction to an older man so wholeheartedly engaged and enmeshed with the Marine Corps, she wrote an angry letter to her estranged husband asking, pleading with him to sign the necessary papers and grant her an uncontested release from their failed marriage.

There was no reply from the young second lieutenant cruising with the Amphibious Ready Group somewhere in the Mediterranean, but Captain Becker got back in touch.

He said he was nervous and uneasy about continuing their relationship under the circumstances. He also said his gut told him it was the right thing to do . . . and his gut instincts had kept him alive in much more dangerous situations. Each moment they spent together produced sparks like flint on steel. And now, Becky realized, she was totally, irresponsibly in love with the flinty boulder of a man who snored softly at her side on this hot summer morning.

Becky trailed her fingers across Becker's naked thigh, softly circling the two puckered scars punched into his left leg by AK-47 rounds. She slid her hand upward and felt him stir under her caress. Becker grinned and groaned, coming awake slowly. Burying her head under the coarse sheets she took him in her mouth and let passion battle with reason.

It's got to work out in the end, she told herself. They can frown and bitch . . . but even the Marine Corps can't legislate love.

Major General Darwin Tobrey, commanding the 2nd Marine Division of the Atlantic Fleet Marine Force, ran a round plastic brush through his thatch of slate-grey hair, freshly leveled into an outdated flattop, and smiled at the tingle of the bristles on his scalp. He always felt better on mornings when he could face the day with a fresh, high, and tight haircut. The way he saw it, close-cropped hair was part and parcel of the Marine uniform. You put it on—or cut it off—as a sign of your commitment to the *spirit* of the Corps.

Spirit of the Corps, he thought, savoring the concept. It's damn well time we got back to it. That meat-grinder of a war in Vietnam had left the ranks strewn with rubble. There was trash all over the area these days, but sweepers were manning the brooms. After many traumatic years, it was time for a clean and sweep-down fore and aft. The *real* Marines had survived to take the helm again and the trash would be swept to the leeward side of the fantail for dumping.

General Tobrey slid the brush into a desk drawer and squinted at the scrawled note the staff secretary had left in the center of his daily calendar. The SJA was waiting outside. A matter of moral turpitude? That's interesting, he thought, reaching for the buzzer on his desk. Maybe my little reminder rattled the bones in some of the closets around here.

Major Claiborne entered at a brisk pace and stood at attention until the CG motioned him to a padded chair near his ancient oak desk. Tobrey eyed the large manila envelope lying in the lawyer's lap and frowned.

"Morning, Judge. From the sound of things I'm probably not gonna like what I'm about to hear."

Claiborne painted on his courtroom smile. "I'd think not, sir, given your recent command guidance concerning the sanctity of family and . . . that sort of thing."

The general leaned forward on his elbows and stabbed the air with a stubby finger. "You know I stand four-square behind what I said in my letter to Commanding Officers, Judge. I'm not gonna tolerate this Peyton Place business anymore. Like it or not, it's a married Marine Corps these days . . . we've got a responsibility to our Marines *and* their families . . ."

Major Claiborne squirmed and glanced at the nautical brass clock over the general's desk. It would have to be quick and dirty. He started to speak but Tobrey was up from his desk and pacing like a caged lion.

"I'm damn serious, Judge. While we were playing in the Southeast Asia war games, it was WestPac Widows, fooling around with all the young studs while their husbands fought in Vietnam. That's not bad enough? Now we shift focus back to regular deployments in the Med and the Caribbean and we got people hot-bunking all over the housing areas. Soon as the ships single-up to get under way, this demoralizing game of musical beds starts.

"The 2nd Marine Division is a family, Judge, and the way I see it, illicit relationships within the family are nothing more than *incest*! I'm not gonna have the morale and readiness of this command threatened by a pack of horny home-wreckers!"

Claiborne waited while the CG regained his seat and his

breath. "Yessir. I believe everyone is aware of your feelings on that whole subject . . . which is why I asked to see you this morning . . ."

He felt his stomach churn violently but he was on final approach to the bomb-release point. There was no turning back from the target now. "Perhaps I should brief this in chronological order, sir. On or about 18 March of this year, I received a call from the CO of Battalion Landing Team 1/6 out in the Med . . . the amphibs were in port at Naples at the time. He was concerned with a domestic situation facing one of his platoon commanders . . . a Second Lieutenant John B. Stewart. Seems young Stewart got a letter from his wife asking for an immediate divorce . . . ."

General Tobrey craned back in his swivel chair, crossed his hands over his stomach, and shook his head. "Familiar story, Judge. Probably got married right out of The Basic School . . . dress blues, arch of swords, the whole shot. Then reality set in and she decides it's just not what she wanted. Am I right?"

"Generally speaking . . . yessir." Claiborne shifted in his seat and glanced again at the clock. "Those elements are all included in this case, but it's more sticky than usual. Lieutenant Stewart's wife is another Marine officer. Her name is Second Lieutenant Campbell . . . she's in the S-1 over at Camp Geiger. She has filed for a divorce—which young Stewart apparently does not want—and is now pestering him to waive his rights and cut her loose."

Glancing at his watch, the general straightened in his chair. "Doesn't sound too sticky to me. I'll have him brought home from the Med. They'll either patch it up and continue the march or become another sad statistic for the status board over at the Family Services Center."

Claiborne recognized the bomb-release point and punched the button. "Too late for that, sir. Lieutenant Campbell has been, uh, consorting . . . carrying on an illicit affair with another officer from this command. In fact, the evidence is that they've been, uh, shacking up together . . . over in the Hadnot Point BOQ—and elsewhere—ever since Lieutenant Stewart deployed to the Med."

The general's serene countenance screwed into an ugly mask. His eyes narrowed and Claiborne saw a vein throbbing at his temple. He punched the intercom button on his desk and growled at the staff secretary. "No calls. Back the briefings off for an hour." His voice was thin and tight when he glared up at Major Claiborne. "Fire for effect, Judge. I want the whole story."

"I did some unofficial checking after the phone call from Naples, sir." Major Claiborne reached into the envelope on his lap and pulled out a sheaf of carefully prepared briefing notes. "In an effort to advise Stewart's CO, I did some checking out in town. Lieutenant Campbell filed for and was granted a legal separation from Lieutenant Stewart citing irreconcilable differences. While he's deployed, no action for dissolution of the marriage can be taken under the Soldiers and Sailors Relief Act. I advised the CO of this in a separate phone call.

"That was followed by a letter from Lt. Stewart himself that arrived at my office the third week in March. Lt. Stewart was convinced—apparently from rumors he'd heard from fellow officers—that his wife was carrying on an affair with another Marine back here at Camp Lejeune.

"Given your letter on the subject of marital infidelity, sir, I initiated an unofficial investigation into the situation on 30 March by personal inquiry and through the offices of the Naval Investigative Service."

Claiborne stood and carefully laid the manila envelope in the center of the general's desk. "These are the results, sir. Lt. Stewart's allegations are entirely true. Lt. Campbell is, indeed, carrying on an illicit affair with another officer of this command."

General Tobrey's stubby fingers toyed with the flap of the envelope. Claiborne waited until he slid the typed report and a selection of eight-by-ten glossy prints onto his desk blotter. Tobrey seemed to be suppressing some seething inner emotion; not at all anxious to delve into the sordid details of the case.

"Two things prompted me to bring this to your personal attention, General. On the one hand, BLT 1/6 has been extended on deployment for patrol duty in the Indian Ocean. That means it will be three months or better before Lt. Stewart can return to address his grievance on his own behalf. Secondly . . . the identity of the other officer involved with Lt. Campbell . . ."

The bomb exploded on target. General Tobrey stiffened in his chair and grabbed for a pair of reading glasses. As he examined the photos, his jaw dropped open and his breathing became clearly audible in the still room.

"Good Lord! Is this . . . it's Becker! This man here is Captain Becker! Isn't it?"

Claiborne passed on his courtroom expression and locked his features into a neutral mask. "It is, sir. Captain Thurmond Becker, the most highly decorated officer in the division; a genuine mustang, up from the ranks and extremely popular with . . . well, with practically everyone in the Marine Corps the way I hear it."

The general began to shuffle through the stack of photographs that had been carefully arranged to run from merely incriminating to clearly damning. Captain Becker and Lieutenant Campbell were caught, in the grainy format of a long lens and ultra-high-speed film, through the progression of their love affair; from innocent hand-holding in restaurants to a naked tryst on a beach at Emerald Island.

General Tobrey finished scrutinizing the final photograph and then shoved the pile away from him with a grunt of distaste. Claiborne waited nervously for the bomb-damage assessment.

"A Navy Cross and whatever else Captain Becker wears on his chest don't cover his ass when he chooses to display it in public. Your opinion, Judge?"

Claiborne couched his words carefully. A hiccup at this point could sweep the case under a very heavy rug. "It depends on how you want to proceed, General. From a purely legal point of view, she's still married. That means her relationship with Becker—assuming he knows her status—constitutes what can be construed as conduct unbecoming an officer, conduct prejudicial to good order and discipline, all the standard UCMJ Article 134 specifications.

There's even some possibility we might be able to float a charge of violating the spirit of a general order, given your command guidance on this very subject. As a company commander, Becker was an addressee on your letter. Naturally, Becker would be the defendant in any legal proceeding since he's the senior officer involved. We'd waive charges against Lt. Campbell and force her to testify against him. Of course, all that presumes we go for court-martial . . .''

General Tobrey clawed his reading glasses off his nose and blinked. "Why wouldn't we go for a court-martial, Judge? There's enough evidence of immoral conduct here to sink a battleship."

Claiborne realized his bomb had hit the mark. Now it was time to insure he was well out of the shrapnel fan. "General, there are a number of things to consider in this case beyond the simple preferring of charges and subsequent court-martial. Relationships like this one—repugnant as they may be to us—go on all the time outside the gates . . .''

"So what? This isn't a civil matter, Judge. It's a Marine Corps matter best handled by Marines. Becker is guilty as sin and I can't think of a better way to illustrate my point about punishing the home-wreckers in this outfit!"

"Yessir. I couldn't agree more. But we'd never be able to bring this to trial in a civilian court. Given Becker's reputation and notoriety, there's bound to be press interest. We might wind up pitting the Marine Corps' version of morality against the less stringent view of such things taken by the rest of the world."

The general rose and stood gazing out his office window. "That's a battle I am prepared to fight, Judge."

Claiborne also got to his feet and glanced at the clock. He was only two minutes over the allotted time for the start of the biggest event of his career. "Yessir, I was just trying to look out for the welfare of the Corps."

Tobrey nodded and favored the SJA with a rare smile. "I understand that, Judge. You are to be commended on your handling of this matter. I'll see the word gets passed along to the right people."

"Shall I proceed then, sir? Along official lines? Article 32 investigation and the whole shot?"

Major General Darwin Tobrey leaned on his desk, supporting his massive shoulders with both arms. He put his hands together and closed his eyes for a second, as though in prayer. When he looked up his expression was fierce. "Judge, you will make the following things happen in short order. Formalize that investigation. Make it bulletproof and bring it back to me through official channels. When everyone's satisfied that the *t's* have been crossed and the *i's* have been dotted, we'll prefer charges and I'll personally convene the court-martial. Now let's get on with it."

Back at Base Legal, Major Claiborne savored a rush of adrenaline coursing through his veins. He paced and jinked around his office, battle-ready as he organized the necessary paperwork to formally present his case against Captain Thurmond Becker through the chain of command. There was little doubt the flash and crash over a high-profile trial would cover his minor step over an ethical line. So what if the story he told the CG was a little out of order? So what if *he* was the one who told Lt. Stewart about his wife's ongoing affair with Becker? So what? From this point on through the high-profile crucifixion of Buttplate Becker, the school solution applies. Just don't lose the momentum of the attack.

Captain Thurmond Becker grinned at his blurry image in the polished aluminum square he used as a field mirror and began his patented four-stroke shave: from the top of one ear, down across the chin and up to the top of the other ear. He'd perfected the method somewhere out in the bush, where he ingrained most of the habits in his life, so he could be ready in a hurry for a full day of training or combat or whatever Mother Corps might demand.

He was excited about the mission at hand. A week's worth of rock and roll, the kind of stuff Marines love. Pack 'em up and pump 'em out. All of his heavy machineguns, mortars, and antitank weapons on a distant range where the kids can let it rip. For once Becker's company had no restrictions on ammo and no senior officers from regiment standing over his shoulder, ever ready to cluck disapprovingly if he should decide to place his boot firmly in some errant gunner's ass. There it is, he thought, jamming his old canvas shaving kit into his field pack. The way it oughtta be all the time.

He reached for a wall locker where his clean camouflage utility uniforms hung like well-tended hedges. Jamming his feet into a crisp pair of trousers, Becker felt exhilarated. This is the only way of life for a Marine, he told himself. If only Becky could understand that. God knows, she ought to understand. She's a Marine. Becky knows how important . . . how addictive it can be. Money can't buy the thrill, the sweet agony of laying it all on the line where mistakes can result in death or serious injury.

Becker swung his pack onto his shoulders and headed for the BOQ entrance where he was scheduled to meet his jeep and driver. He inhaled the pine-scented air and barked at the dawn. Aaaaaa-oooooo-rah! Another hot-shit day in this hot-shit old Marine Corps. Ain't it great?

Becker's driver was late but that didn't foul his mood. He sat down on the BOQ steps, lit the first smoke of the day, and smiled at the pale pink sliver of sunlight that peeked through the trees. It was Becker's favorite time of day and he loved the pastel color of it no matter what part of the world happened to be home. He remembered the icy blue-greens of dawn above the Arctic Circle in northern Norway, the seering yellows of daybreak in equatorial Africa, the bloody reds of first light in Southeast Asia.

Dawn glowed a glorious springtime pink on the day he met Becky, right here outside the BOQ. He'd been cleaning mud off his combat boots with his well-worn K-Bar fighting knife. Distracted by a thorny tactical problem involving mortar fire on reverse-slope defenders, he didn't notice her arrival. She was walking toward the BOQ with an armload of clean uniforms when he tossed his knife at a familiar old tree without looking and damn near sliced off a very attractive kneecap.

He heard the satisfying thunk of the blade penetrating

moist pine. And then he heard an irate shriek. There she stood, hands jammed onto her hips, staring at a pile of clothing she'd just dumped into a mud puddle. Becker chuckled as he remembered her first words.

"Goddammit! This is every clean uniform I've got!" She glared at him and stabbed the air with a polished fingernail. "Do you work for the Base Laundry . . . or are you just some kind of homicidal maniac?"

Becker stared at the sopping pile of women's Marine uniforms and then shifted his gaze upward, pausing to appreciate slim, athletic legs emerging from a pair of running shorts. She wore her auburn hair bobbed short to form a halo around an aqualine face. A pair of emerald-green eyes locked Becker in place until he was able to recover from the sight and mumble through an apology.

On his way over to make amends, Becker noticed lush breasts distorted the eagle, globe, and anchor on her Marine Corps T-shirt. He stooped and began to pick up rumpled clothing. She grabbed a uniform blouse from his hands. "I'll take care of it, thank you. Jesus, I hope this isn't an omen."

Becker smiled at her. "Just checking in, huh? Didn't they teach you in Basic School to expect an attack from any direction?"

She squinted into his blue eyes. Grey at the temples and the lines of hard service in his craggy face. Shit, she thought. Probably some senior officer. "Sorry . . . sir. It's just that . . . well, I'm due to report for duty tomorrow . . . and it wouldn't be a good idea to look like a soup sandwich."

Becker reached for more uniforms and examined the damage. She noticed the faded Marine Corps emblem tattooed on his right forearm. Death Before Dishonor. She'd never seen a tattoo on an officer.

"No big problem here, Lieutenant. I can fix these up in a hurry. You'll be A. J. Squared Away by reveille."

"That won't be necessary, sir. I can handle it by myself."

Becker flashed a disarming, lopsided grin. "You could probably care less right now, but my name is Becker, captain type, one each . . ."

Becky nodded, forgetting to introduce herself, just glad
she hadn't tangled with some stiff-necked bachelor colonel.
This guy seemed humble enough . . . and he was apolo-
gizing. She decided he must be a mustang, up from the
ranks with painful memories of what it's like to be jammed
down on the bottom of the totem pole. She hesitantly
returned his smile.

"I guess I can salvage a UD out of all this . . ."

Becker scooped up the soggy pile of clothing and headed
for the BOQ. "I have some lengthy experience with this
kind of thing. Let me help you get your gear moved into the
Q and repair the damage."

He stormed up the stairs and into the barracks before she
could protest. She grabbed a suitcase from the trunk of her
car and followed him. When they had her gear stowed in a
second-floor room of the women's officers' wing, Becker
paused on his way out the door.

"I see by the markings on your seabag and the insignia
on your uniforms that one Second Lieutenant Campbell has
arrived at Swamp Lagoon. Congratulations. Meet you in the
laundry room down below on the first deck."

He was gone before she could protest. Becky rattled
around her room for a few minutes thinking about Captain
Becker. Had she heard that name before . . . somewhere?
At The Basic School? A class on history and traditions?
Probably not. There was just something . . . familiar,
magnetic about him. Maybe a knee-jerk reaction to a man so
different from the one she married. She picked out the
uniform items she'd need for duty the next morning and
headed down the stairs.

Becker was waiting, testing the temperature of a well-
worn travel iron, when she arrived. He popped her muddy
skirt and blouse into a washer and then set up a footlocker
ironing board that he covered with an issue blanket. He'd
changed into running shoes and a pair of tattered sweatpants. She sat on a warm dryer and watched the rippling
muscles in his upper back, wondering about the wormlike
scars that marred his skin.

"So, Lieutenant Campbell . . . you got a first name? Or

did they tell you it was a military secret?'' He really did seem to want to be friendly. She relaxed a bit and began pulling her wet clothes from the washing machine.

"It's Rebecca, sir—or Becky—whatever . . .''

Becker took the wet clothes from her and chunked them into a nearby dryer. He wiped his hands on the legs of his sweatpants and reached for her hand. She was caught unawares by the move and missed the grip.

"Better learn to grab 'em firm and fast, Becky. There's people around here who'll make judgments about you based on a handshake . . .''

She adjusted and squeezed his hand. They smiled at each other from close range. "That's better,'' he whispered. "Don't let 'em catch you shaking hands like a girl.''

They sat side by side on a pair of warm, whirling dryers. She was beginning to feel comfortable with him and he was certainly making no move to take care of business elsewhere.

"Are you assigned to the division, sir?''

Becker frowned and crossed his legs. "Listen, I get sir'ed to distraction all day long. How about you and me drop it off-duty? People tend to call me Buttplate. I've got one of the infantry training companies out at Camp Geiger.''

"That's where I'm headed—according to my orders anyway. Assistant adjutant at Infantry Training School.''

"Good deal. Good duty out there . . . away from the flagpole. Just watch your step with Major Spencer, the adjutant. She's a hard case.''

There was a tingle in Becky's memory banks. She'd heard his name before. She was certain of it. "Did you say your nickname was Buttplate?''

"Yeah. I tell people it's because I used to be a pretty fair hand with mortars. There are others who'd say it's because I'm like the buttplate on a rifle, you know? Just a dumb piece of metal that gets banged around a lot.''

He retrieved her uniforms and began to iron, expertly flipping and folding to nail the necessary fore and aft creases in a blouse. Watching him, she recalled the stories about his heroism in combat. The Navy Cross and about a zillion other decorations for bravery in Vietnam and Beirut. A minor legend in the Marine Corps was sweating over her rumpled uniforms.

"I believe I heard about you . . . in Basic School . . ."

He looked up from his ironing and shook his head. "If you did, it was mostly bullshit. I can promise you that. I can also promise you some chow over at the O Club tonight. Interested?"

Becky was interested. They talked and laughed through a first informal dinner date. Pleasant, very pleasant, Becker remembered as his jeep came snorting up the road. Ain't this a bitch? He chuckled as he stood and shouldered his pack. Damn near cut off one of her legs, fuck up her uniforms, get 'em unfucked . . . and then fall in love. Shit, you couldn't sell that to the soap operas on TV.

Riding the base shuttle bus out to Camp Geiger, Becky felt her stomach rumble. There had been plenty of time for breakfast but she'd puttered around her BOQ room at dawn trying to think of a way to force a response from John Stewart. Why was the man being so uncommunicative, so obstinate?

Why couldn't he just shrug it off as a bad move before things got messy? What made him think—in a time when the majority of young marriages ended up in divorce—that there was some sort of dishonor about an amicable separation?

"You can do whatever the hell you want," he told her on the phone from Norfolk just before his ship sailed for the Med, "but I've got a career ahead of me and the first entry in my service record is not going to be a goddamn divorce!" Becky screamed at him to consider *her* life, *her* career, but he slammed the receiver home and shot her a jolt of irritating dial tone.

At least the cards were faceup on the table, she thought as the bus slid to a stop. She got off, returned the salute from a pair of passing lance corporals, and began to walk toward the Administration building. The oppressive heat had forced most of the classroom work outdoors. She could hear the bark of instructors as they pounded out facts and prodded sleepy privates. Becky remembered rubbing thighs with Candidate John Stewart as they sat in similar school circles at Quantico.

They married in a fever; full of themselves after OCS and that magical, mystical rite of passage when slime-sucking civilians become Marine officers. They'd seen the Holy Grail. They'd proved their mettle in a demanding quest. It seemed so right. Two eager, college-educated Marines pooling their resources to push and pull each other along the road to success in the Corps. And it was hard—in those glory days, flushed with initial success, blinded by the glitter of brass and braid—to separate one passion from another.

They made love constantly for the first few weeks on practically every semiflat surface available in a tiny efficiency apartment just outside the gates. Coarse, crude, near-violent lovemaking is what she remembered most from those days. They attacked each other at odd moments with a groaning lust; snarling, sweating, pumping, and pushing as they had on the Obstacle Course.

The bottom dropped out of the thermometer when she went to Parris Island for Admin School and he went to Camp Lejeune to join an infantry unit. Whiney phone calls turned into shouting matches. She wanted him to come and visit her. He wanted her to stop bothering him so he could focus on making the right moves in his first assignment. Without a steamy sex life to cloud the mirrors, they began to see themselves as prisoners of their own designs.

She felt cut out of an active, attractive social whirl that seemed to be part and parcel of life as a Marine officer. She'd been socially active and popular in college. Now, when all the social graces should pay dividends, she felt frumpy, crippled by a relationship that seemed empty and unreasonable considered from a distance. It came to her that she didn't know much about John Stewart and didn't care much about him either.

He found himself shackled, watched by family men who expected him to behave like the little woman was waiting for him each night with open arms. He couldn't run and gun with the other exuberant young officers in his battalion or be seen in the company of unmarried women. John Stewart revelled in his life, his own rifle platoon, his upcoming deployment overseas, his young stud status in a world where such things constituted the brass ring on a high-speed merry-go-round. For his money, the marriage was a mistake. Still, you had to guard your six if you wanted a spotless record. They could deal with the situation later, after he'd cut himself a groove in the fast track.

Frustration fueled anger. They spat and hissed over the phone until he arrived at Parris Island one day on a flying weekend trip in a borrowed car. No dice on the divorce business, he said. He was in predeployment training and not about to beg off for embarrassing court appearances. That would mean he'd have to explain to his company commander why he'd married some "WM bimbo" in the first place. They frowned on things like that up at 2nd MarDiv. But she could fuck whoever she wanted to. That's sure as hell what he intended to do.

She'd asked for orders to Camp Lejeune out of Admin School so she could be with her husband. When they arrived, she circled an ad in the base newspaper, made a phone call, and paid a North Carolina lawyer running a Jacksonville divorce mill $250 to file legal separation papers. John Stewart was gone by the time she arrived. And along came Buttplate Becker.

Holding a man like Becker at arm's length was no mean feat. When he attacked it was with all weapons registered; bayonets fixed, hey-diddle-diddle, right up the middle. She tried to be honest. After a few dates, after too little pizza and too much wine, a shuddering passion swept over both of them. Becker wheeled his muddy Toyota Land Cruiser into the parking lot of a motel and grinned, challenging her to the duel they both knew was coming.

She sat rigid in the blue neon glow of the vacancy sign; balking, talking, fighting a rearguard action until he got the wrong idea. "Can't say I haven't paid for it a bunch of times in my life," he growled, jamming the truck into reverse, "but I never took something that wasn't being made available for the taking."

That was all he said until they arrived at the BOQ. He stopped her before she could enter and took one of her hands gently into his own. "Listen," he said in a quiet voice, "I want you to know I don't blame you for shutting down tonight. I ain't no bargain by a long shot. I'm old, ugly, horny, and hitched to the Marine Corps . . ." She tried to disagree, but he waved her to silence.

"For the past twenty years, I've avoided any kind of permanent relationship. I guess because I figured a woman would want me to think about her before I thought about the Marine Corps. Can't do that. Never could. Anyway, I'm getting long in the tooth. If I stay, they'll promote me out of leading troops and I just don't want to do anything else. That means I'll probably punch out in the next year or so. I'll choose a partner then . . . and I'll want her to be someone like you."

It was the longest speech she'd ever heard him make, full of open, honest sentiment, and each word hit her like a jackhammer. For the first time in their burgeoning relationship, Becky realized she could have this man. He was making himself available to her for the taking. And there was no danger in it. No harm. She knew instinctively, staring into his pale eyes, that Thurmond Becker was the kind of man she wanted in her life. He was strong, steady, sexy, considerate, and long past trying to prove anything to her or anyone else. Becker was seething with repressed emotion, and she could trigger it. That moment, on the steps of the BOQ, was frightening. It sparked and sizzled like a fast-burning fuse. Becky pulled him down beside her and told him she was married.

He simply lit a cigarette, smoked, and listened while she spilled it all in a gushing, confused sequence of events. She was panting softly, very near tears, when she finished. Becker nodded and turned toward her. His face was a mask.

"That shyster out in Jay-ville would probably say it's OK to go ahead and crawl in the rack. No harm, no foul. The way I hear it, civilians on the rebound do more fuckin' than they ever did when they were married. But we ain't civilians, are we?'' He stood and breathed deeply of the pine-scented night air. ''I'm gonna have to chew on it for a while.''

He disappeared from her life and Becky spent most of her off-duty time writing a series of letters to John Stewart that alternated between emotional appeals and irate demands for freedom. She never mentioned a new love. Nor did she speculate about Stewart running around with hookers in Mediterranean liberty ports. Her arguments concerned correcting a mutual emotional mistake in both their lives. There was no response.

Becky stepped gingerly across a rutted field on a shortcut to her office. A Camouflage, Cover & Concealment class was under way near a thatch of pine woods. She paused to watch as the instructor loudly and lewdly painted a buzz-cut private to look like a bush. The ghoulish green, brown, and black paint smeared on his skin made her tremble slightly and she smiled, remembering how Buttplate Becker reentered her life.

There was a note tacked to the door of her BOQ room. Her name was scrawled across an envelope embossed with the Marine Corps emblem. Inside was a note: ''Command Performance. My room. 2030. Utility uniform. Tremble and Obey. The Buttplate.''

She knocked nervously on Becker's door that night, feeling the sweat begin to pool in her armpits when a bachelor major paused to ask if he could help her find someone. Just delivering a message, she said with a smile. The major arched his eyebrows, but continued his march to the head carrying the Sunday newspaper.

The door whipped open and Becker bowed her inside his room for the first time. He was dressed in camouflage utility uniform and every inch of exposed skin was a tapestry of camouflage warpaint. He looked evil, dangerous . . . like some sexy version of the Swamp Creature. Becky thought for a moment he was clad for combat; suited up to beat the hell out of her for starting something they couldn't finish. Before she could stammer into all the things she'd decided to say, he violated camouflage discipline with a wide white smile.

He took her hand and led her toward a pile of sandbags arranged around his footlocker. An old artillery shell casing held fresh wildflowers. There was some sort of odious concoction bubbling in a steel helmet suspended over a scorch-streaked field stove. Sandalwood incense burned in the belly of a porcelain Buddha. C-ration meal components littered the makeshift tabletop. Apparently he had in mind some sort of field-expedient dinner date.

He sat silently across from her, expertly carving the top off a can of peach slices with a P-38 ration can opener. She looked around, soaking up the strange atmosphere lit by guttering candles. She imagined it was like sitting in some dank bunker on a disputed hilltop. Her heartbeat pulsed and pounded in her chest like incoming artillery. A giggling fit came coursing up from her nervous stomach.

"Hey," he said, laughing along with her, "whaddaya want? I'm a bush beast. I always do my best work in a field environment." He took a deep breath and pondered the tiny can opener in his hand.

"See this? Sometimes I wish we could take this little P-38 and pop off the top of my head. There's lots of things in there that just won't come out, you know? Like that good, greasy stuff at the bottom of a can of Ham and Mothers . . ." She nodded in silence, hoping for the best out of what was coming.

He chewed on the inside of his cheek for a moment, frowning, and then waved his hand around the room. "All this stuff . . . it makes me feel comfortable. Hell, this has been my life in one form or another since I was sixteen. I don't know from bulldog doodley-squat about any other kind of life . . . and I don't want to know.

"If I wanted to be a civilian and live by their code, I coulda done it, a hundred times over the past twenty years. But this is my way—no bullshit, clear priorities, life or death, clean and simple. It's like being in a monastery, see? You got a uniform that subs for a clerical collar, you got self-sacrificing service to mankind, you got foreign missions, you got daily devotions, you got poverty for damn sure . . ."

He chuckled deep in his chest and shook his head at the picture he was trying to paint for her. "What you ain't got is a clear picture of relationships outside the Corps. You know how to handle your superiors, your subordinates, your outfit, the Corps in general . . . all that's spelled out. Where you get your dick in a crack is when you fall in love . . . or think you do. You can't tell Marines not to get laid and you can't order 'em not to get married. You can own their brains and most of their bodies . . . but when you get right down into the crotch, you're dealin' with a whole different set of values.

"Now . . . here's the nut of it, see? The Corps knows that, but it won't admit to it. You choose to marry somebody besides Mother Corps, well, you'd better find a way to live your life by two differents sets of rules. Civilians say something is OK; the Corps says it ain't. You got a case of different values, see? You got a choice to make and it ain't easy if you're a good Marine on the one hand and in love with somebody on the other."

Becker moved to kneel between her knees. He pressed the palms of his hands to her cheeks and stared into her eyes. "It takes an instinct to make it work. You got to get down to the spirit of a thing—what the Corps intends—what it really means. Now there's been some heat on around here lately about married people havin' affairs—sanctity of the family, stuff like that . . ."

He pulled her to her feet and held her tightly. "But you ain't got a family beyond a piece of paper that's about to be canceled for lack of interest. And I think, after all these years, my family will understand how much I love you."

The flickering candlelight made it hard for her to read what was in his eyes. It seemed to be hunger and longing when the light washed brightly over his features. When the shadows returned, a soft sadness seemed to lay beneath the spooky camouflage pattern on his face.

Her breathing sounded like the roar of storm-driven surf in the still room. Becker lovingly ran his tongue down the side of her neck to feel the pulsing artery there. He sucked lightly on the vein causing an exquisite stab of pain. She began to fumble with the buttons on her uniform blouse. He backed away and helped her lift a green skivvy shirt over her head and then pushed her down into a sitting position on his bed. Becky started to strip the rest of her uniform, but Becker pinned her arms to her sides.

"Don't rush the cadence," he whispered. "When it's time, it's time . . ."

She hugged his head to her chest as he ministered to each bare breast. Much of the warpaint on his face rubbed off onto her body. She closed her eyes and swam away, an Amazon queen locked in primeval passion with a pagan warrior.

Their lovemaking was a thrilling combination of brutal energy and tender compassion. It ebbed and flowed, eddied and swirled, until Becky felt herself drowning in a long, shuddering orgasm. Still Becker nursed and nudged her with his tongue and hands until he finally exploded with a primal growl. She felt the heat of his ejaculation flow into her. It was beyond her experience, beyond even her secret masturbatory dreams.

Covered in smudged camouflage paint, she lay panting on the coarse wool of his GI blanket, feeling warm, protected, fulfilled; drifting in the sensual, tactile memory of the experience. Becky shoved at him while they worked to steady ragged breathing. She wanted to stare into his eyes and tell him how she felt. He winced in pain as the heel of her hand ground into a great welt of scar tissue near his right shoulder.

"My God . . . I'm sorry . . ."

"No sweat. Old war wound. Still gives me a twinge every once in a while . . ."

She trailed her fingertips across the mangled flesh between the deltoid muscle and the right nipple. "How did it happen?"

He rolled over beside her and reached for a battered plastic cigarette case. "Little commie bastard tried to kill me. Damn near pulled it off . . ."

She clicked open his engraved Zippo lighter and examined the waxy ridges of the wound scar in the flickering light. "Tell me about it."

He inhaled and grinned at her. "Nah . . ."

"Yes," she insisted. "I want to know all about you. The truth . . ."

II.

By the Right Flank, March . . .

When it came time for his men to pick up the bloodstained machetes, Sergeant Becker wished he had gloves to offer them. Another of Vietnam's little ironies, he thought. Sweating like hogs in a hot box and wanting another article of clothing to wear.

He nodded to the point squad leader and collected the machetes. Wordlessly, Lance Corporal Leon Kramer and Private First Class Tyrone Douglas squeezed past him and took one of the blades from his hands. Before long their hands would chafe and blister, adding another coat of blood to the sticky handles. There'd be no complaint from either of them. There never was.

Kramer, the bright young black man from Dee Cee, and Douglas, the thick farmboy from Oklahoma, would hump the load, hack the distance, and bitch about it later. That's the way they'd been since the day he picked them up at the III MAF Transient Facility in Danang to begin their tour in Vietnam. Becker took a special interest in them. He'd maneuvered around the demands of shorthanded infantry platoon commanders and hauled both of them into his 60-millimeter mortar squad.

They lined up abreast and began to methodically hack at

the dense wall of creepers, vines, and leaves that blocked the route of advance through the dripping rain forest. They'd rigged the main components of their small mortar to pack frames before taking their turn in the point rotation but the oversize loads made swinging machetes an ungainly exercise.

"Jesus Christ!" Becker hacked viciously at an arm-sized vine. "How the fuck do the gooks move rockets through this crap?"

"Good question," Kramer grunted. "They probably get about six zillion of the little motherfuckers on line and each one moves the rocket about an inch. The dude on the end of the line just lights the match. Boom. Quang Tri takes another round right between the runnin' lamps."

Becker felt the sting of blisters forming on the palm of his left hand. "Why the hell don't they send the Rangers out here? It's a National Forest, ain't it?"

Douglas wiped sweat out of his eyes and growled. "Fucking Hai Lang National Forest. Ain't that a crocka shit? We'll run up on Smokey the goddamn bear before we find gooks in this mess."

Operation Osceola brought the entire 2nd Battalion, First Marines, into the dense forest, dedicated by prewar decree as a preserve for the indigenous tropical flora and fauna of Southeast Asia. No one in the Vietnamese government objected to the Marines going in there on a hunting expedition because everyone in Quang Tri Province suffered from the impact of 122mm rockets launched from the Hai Lang.

Behind the launchers were North Vietnamese Army regulars of the 44B Independent Rocket Artillery Battalion. Aerial photos revealed a number of launch sites had been cleared in the lush foliage that covered the area. The Marines hoped to surround several of those sites and pinch inward to catch the NVA in a fatal trap.

The estimated three hundred or so enemy troops in the target area were not supposed to be aware of the American effort, but Becker knew there was little chance for surprise once the entire battalion began to crash and thrash through the jungle. The slow, noisy progress of overburdened Marines through the clawing vegetation could probably be heard in Hanoi.

They'd been at it for two days without much progress and the battalion commander knew his plans were bound to bust unless he could speed the movement of his unit through the jungle. When they broke for chow, he called his company commanders together to change strategy.

"Here's the highway," he told the officers, indicating a meandering blue line on his plastic-coated map, "it looks like a good-sized stream. We'll find it and walk in the water in this general direction until we reach a point parallel to the launch sites. Then we get out, assemble, and tie in for a sweep."

The infantry commanders mulled over the plan in silence for a while, toting up the pros and cons. "Sir, it looks good," commented the Foxtrot Company skipper, "but in this bush we'll have to replot direction to the sites every thirty meters or less once we come out of the blue. It's an ass-kicker of a land navigation problem."

The battalion commander nodded. "Yeah, it's a bitch out there, I know. We need some kind of guide, but air ain't worth a shit while we're under this canopy . . ."

From his position on the perimeter of the circle, the weapons CO had a different perspective on the map. He could see the tightly bunched circles indicating a piece of commanding high ground that was roughly equidistant from all of the marked launch sites in the area.

"Look, sir . . . how about this?" He shoved his way into the circle around the battalion commander and jabbed a grimy finger at the map. "The problem is moving quickly without getting lost once we come out of the water. What if we had some kind of route marker to keep us on track? Something like Willy Pete rounds from our mortars."

"It's got possibilities," the colonel admitted, glancing around the circle. "The gunners would need an exact fix on their own location and the grids of our assembly areas. But they could compute the line of march and fire rounds along the track to keep us moving in the right direction . . ."

Golf Company's CO was unconvinced. "All those rounds popping off will alert the gooks that something's coming for damn sure . . ."

"Not if we mix and match at random with Harassment and Interdiction fire," the weapons CO responded. "We can get the long-range arty at The Rockpile to fire H&I missions to cover the mortar fire. The gooks couldn't tell the difference. I think it'll work if we can get a tube up onto that high ground."

The battalion commander nodded, his decision made. "We gotta give it a try or write this whole deal off. Weapons, it's on you and a damn good mortarman."

"Yessir, I'll pass the word for Sergeant Becker."

Becker scrutinized the battalion commander's map, staring at the contour lines, turning his head, pondering the proposal. He indicated a hill mass marked simply "513" to indicate its rise above mean sea level. "It's steep and green as hell, which probably means triple canopy. I make the range from here at a little under two klicks. We'd need all afternoon to get there and have to make the climb to the top in the dark. You'd have to set-in somewhere along the stream tonight and move in the morning when I'd be set up to shoot for you."

Feasible, the battalion commander realized, but a bitch-kitty of a map, compass, and precision-gunnery drill. "What do you think, Sgt. Becker. Can you do it?"

Becker pondered briefly over the complexities. "Yessir, we can pull it off. Just hold the H&I fire until we're up on top."

The battalion commander nodded at his artillery forward observer and then turned his attention back to the map. "The zips won't know one round from another by the time you start to shoot. Now, how about the route to 513?"

"Looks like there's a branch of this stream that runs almost right to the base of it, sir. We'll do the same thing you're gonna do . . . move in the water to make some time and then get out and head for the high ground."

"OK, saddle up. I'll send a platoon from Echo along for security."

Becker shook his head and hitched at his pack straps. "Negative, sir. We'd travel too slow and make too much noise. I'll take a short rifle squad and a machine gun. If the gooks spot us, they might think it's a recon patrol and let us pass. They don't want to give their positions away any more than we do."

"Good deal. Pick your people. Take all the Willy Pete we've got. Mortar, map, compass, and radio . . . they've all got to be squared away before you leave. You'll be Walleye. Push 75.85 and call Bushmaster. We'll be monitoring that frequency on a dedicated radio. Stay in contact . . . with us, not the gooks."

The water in the stream that meandered through the dense jungle of the Hai Lang was cool, clear, and swift. Becker's unit of ten heavily loaded men—including Douglas and Kramer as his handpicked mortar crew—moved as quickly as the resistance of the water would allow. He walked point, consulting his compass and map regularly. Becker calculated another klick or so to go, noting the high, hot orb of the sun—visible through the jungle roof only as shafts of pale yellow light—was moving toward a western rendezvous with the earth.

Walking was difficult with heavy loads of mortar ammo strapped onto each man's pack. They sloshed in the stream—alternately bathed from ankles to midstomach—searching for footholds on the rocky bottom. Becker decided they could afford a five-minute break and the pathfinder team sprawled wherever they could find space on the bank.

Doc Jarvis, the hospital corpsman, splashed over to him, holding his Unit One medical kit up and out of the water. "Sgt. Becker, we've got to start checking for leeches. They're gonna eat these guys alive."

Becker had been too distracted to think of leeches. He stared down at his boots, dangling in the silky rush of the water. All he could see were leaves and twigs cascading over his toes. Doc Jarvis pulled the liner out of his helmet and dipped the steep pot into the stream. In the confined pool, Becker spotted four or five wriggling creatures that looked liked flattened roofing nails.

"Fuckers'll suck you dry, man. I had enough of 'em on me to know . . ."

Becker nodded. Nobody who ever humped a flooded rice paddy came out the other side unfamiliar with leeches. "OK, Doc. We take five more right here. Have everyone check for leeches. Use the bug juice. I don't want anyone lighting up to burn 'em off with a cigarette."

Becker waved a hand at the departing doc and began to struggle with wet bootlaces. His feet were wrinkled from immersion and there were two leeches, bloated like fat link sausages, one on his ankle and the other on his instep.

He reached for the plastic bottle of insect repellant stuck in the elastic camouflage band that circled the base of his helmet and squirted several drops of the oily substance on the point where the leeches latched onto flesh. The bloated worms arched into a horseshoe shape and reluctantly gave up their place at the dinner table. Becker tossed them over his shoulder into the bush.

They walked for another hour as quietly as possible, letting the roar of the rushing water cover the sound of the inevitable stumble, cough, fart, or mumbled curse. He was plotting their progress on the map when Tyrone Douglas caught his attention and passed the word. "Doc says he needs you right away . . . back there."

Becker gave a hand signal and the patrol members fanned down and out of the water. He struggled back along the line of march hoping he wouldn't find anything more serious than a sprained ankle. As he rounded a bend in the stream, pushing through tangled mangrove roots, he realized it was bad news. Someone was down hard with Doc Jarvis bending over him. He recognized the casualty as a machine gunner named Grimm but details of the situation were blocked by Jarvis's broad back.

Jarvis heard Becker approaching and splashed into the water on an interception course. Several other Marines stood around Grimm, staring in disbelief at the man's exposed crotch.

"You're not gonna fuckin' believe this shit." The Doc looked worried and that worried Becker. "Grimm's been bitching for the past hour about not being able to take a leak. I thought he was shittin' me and told him to keep drinkin' water, you know? He did . . . and now his belly's bloated like a goddamn pregnant water boo . . ."

"What's the problem?" Becker calculated they were within five hundred meters of the base of Hill 513. Dusk was approaching fast and he didn't want any delays.

Jarvis suppressed a nervous giggle and then ran a water-wrinkled hand over his face. "I seen some shit in my time . . ." The doc shook his head and swallowed a deep breath. "Listen, I think Grimm's got a leech *inside his fuckin' dick*, man. It's the only thing I can think of that would cause him to swell up and turn blue . . ."

Becker made a move to check the implausible story for himself, but Jarvis caught his elbow. "Look, he's scared shitless. It's the family jewels, for Christ's sake. Don't go fuckin' around or he'll go into shock. Either that or his bladder will rupture if we don't get him out of here in a hurry."

"Goddammit! We're almost there . . ." Becker grabbed Douglas and pointed at the tableaux around the injured man. "Get over there and tell those people to get away from Grimm. Get 'em spaced out along the stream and tell 'em to keep their eyes on the bush."

Jarvis stared up at the darkening canopy. The gloom of a deep jungle night was descending like a thick blanket. In another thirty minutes he'd have to work by flashlight. "We got to get him out of here, Becker. We can call a chopper and blow an LZ or we can turn back . . . but I can't treat no leech in a guy's dick!"

In the drippy dark under a teak tree, Grimm lay squirming with his ankles drawn up toward his bare buttocks. His knees were spread and he ran his hands nervously up and down hairy thighs. His frightened gaze was fixed on his swollen, distorted penis. He was moaning softly, in obvious pain and confusion.

Becker put a comforting hand on Grimm's shoulder and

knelt to take a closer look at the man's crotch. Jarvis illuminated the area with a red lens on his flashlight. Grimm's penis had swollen to a turgid bloat. It seemed to vibrate under pressure from swollen kidneys and the urinary tract. The head of his penis was the size of a crab apple, the opening distended into a gaping oval. Grimm screamed when Doc Jarvis prodded at the organ to give Becker a better view.

Becker clamped his hand over the struggling man's mouth. "Christ, Doc, give him some morphine or something."

"Can't do it, man. He stops resisting the pressure and something's bound to rupture inside." Becker glanced quickly at Grimm's distended belly and made a decision.

"Sit him up, Doc."

"What for?"

"Just sit him up, goddammit . . . and take his helmet off." Becker stood and peeled the pump shotgun off his shoulder as Jarvis carefully lifted Grimm into a sitting position with his back propped on the tree. Becker stepped around behind Grimm and reached to cant the man's head forward.

Jarvis cradled Grimm and stared up in wonder. Becker flipped the shotgun around and hit the moaning man a precise, glancing blow on the back of his skull. Grimm slumped silently into the corpsman's arms.

"What the fuck are you doing?" Jarvis reached for the carotid artery to see if Becker had murdered his patient. A thready pulse beat against his fingers. "Blow a fuckin' LZ, willya? We gotta get him outta here!"

Becker flipped the shotgun again and let the muzzle dangle near his knees, pointing in the corpsman's general direction. "We ain't beat yet, Doc. Let's see if we can get that fuckin' leech out of his dick."

Jarvis was incredulous. "How the hell we gonna do that? You want me to *cut* in there? I can't do that. Even if I did, we'd still have to medevac him. Fuck this mission, man. Call a chopper."

Becker knelt by the unconscious Grimm and whispered,

"He'll be out for thirty minutes or better. We got that much time to work on it. If we can't fix it, we call the medevac . . ." Jarvis nodded. Arguing with Becker was pointless.

"Go up and down the line. Collect everyone's insect repellant. Tell 'em to dig in their packs and give you all they've got. Take off."

Jarvis splashed into the stream and Becker went to work on the only plan he could formulate. He disassembled a helmet, stripping the camouflage cover and washing it thoroughly in the rushing water. When the doc returned cradling a dozen bottles of bug juice, Becker instructed him to pool the contents. The yield was a helmet nearly three-quarters full of foul-smelling liquid. Becker moved it into position in the vee of Grimm's crotch and immersed the man's swollen penis.

"The fucking leeches back off when you hit them with bug juice, right?" Becker stared hard at the corpsman. "We'll try to massage his dick and work some of this shit up in there. If we can get the thing to let go, maybe we can just milk it out . . . like a short-arm inspection."

Doc Jarvis pondered. "Shit, I don't know. Maybe." He grasped Grimm's distended member and began to squeeze, working the skin back and forth along the shaft. "Join the Navy, run around the jungle, and give some fuckin' grunt a hand job."

Becker grinned and patted him on the shoulder. "No sweat, Doc. He'll still respect you in the morning."

Jarvis prodded and massaged for ten minutes. When he finally lifted Grimm's penis out of the bug-juice bath and squeezed delicately, a few drops of ugly yellow urine dripped into the helmet. "I'll be goddamned," he whispered. "Might just work . . . but it's gonna be a slow process."

"We ain't got time for a slow process, Doc." Becker reached for the corpsman's medical bag and began to rummage under the red glow of a flashlight. He held up a small glass pipette used to syphon off blood samples. "You squeeze on his dick. I'm gonna put this tube up there and squirt some of the bug juice inside.''

As Jarvis got a firm grip on his penis, Grimm began to moan and sob. He'd be conscious again before long. Becker inserted the glass tube into the liquid and placed a finger over the open end. About three inches of insect repellant remained in the pipette. Pinching the head of Grimm's penis, Becker began to insert the glass tube. He twisted to work it well up in the urinary tract. Doc Jarvis grimaced in sympathy with the patient but held on until the tube was lodged in place.

Becker put his mouth on the end of the tube and began to blow gently, forcing the liquid inside Grimm. ''OK, you got most of it in there . . .'' Doc Jarvis plucked the tube out and began to massage more vigorously. He squinted and moved the flashlight closer.

''There it is, Becker. Right there's the little fucker's tail. It's gonna work!'' Jarvis began to pinch and pull on Grimm's penis. Another quarter inch of bloated shape emerged. It was a hideous sight and Becker watched bug-eyed. ''Grab hold of it, Becker. Try to pull while I squeeze.''

He grabbed the tail of the slug between two fingers and gingerly tugged while Doc Jarvis pinched, milking the parasite out of Grimm. More and more of the leech began to appear. Becker began a steady, straight pull to the rear.

Suddenly, a jet of urine blew his hand away from Grimm's crotch. The leech disappeared in an evil yellow spurt that thoroughly hosed both Becker and Doc Jarvis, then steadied into a majestic yellow arc that ended with a loud, gurgling splash in the jungle stream. Grimm groaned and moaned in an eerie, orgasmic ecstasy of relief.

They stood and stared, fascinated by the high-pressure fountain of piss that poured from Grimm's rigid dick with no sign of abatement. ''Look at that, willya?'' Doc Jarvis shook his head and aimed the beam of his flashlight. ''He's pissin' five feet straight up and ten feet out into the water. I never seen nothin' like that . . .''

Becker checked his watch and compass. ''Can he walk?''

"Don't see why not. I'll bring him around soon's he stops pissin'. Sore dick and a headache don't get you no light duty in this lash-up."

Becker nodded, slipped into the stream, and waded out to brief his patrol. They'd have to cover the last stretch up to the bottom of the hill in full dark.

Grimm was ambulatory—his only complaints a bellyache and a throbbing knot on the back of his head—when they emerged from the water less than an hour later, nose-to-tail like elephants stumbling through the inky darkness. Now comes the hard part, Becker thought, squinting into the dense jungle that rose away from the stream bank. He motioned the radio operator to his side and put Douglas to work with a fifty-foot length of rope.

"I'm gonna let battalion know we made the hill. You get everyone lined up on me and tie us all together. I don't want anyone wandering off while we climb this sonofabitch."

Becker took the handset and depressed the transmit key. "Bushmaster, Bushmaster . . . Walleye, over . . ." A response crackled down the long whip antenna and into his ear. "Bushmaster, be advised I am at the base of 5–1–3 and on my way topside, over . . ."

Another voice. "Walleye, Bushmaster Six . . . we are at phase line Alpha . . . say your status, over . . ." The battalion commander, in place and waiting for his high-explosive roadmap.

"Bushmaster, Walleye . . . negative contact en route. We're about to start climbing. Unless you have further traffic, we need to move . . ."

"Negative on your last, Walleye. Good luck . . ."

Lashing the leading end of the rope around his own waist, Becker whispered to the tightly clustered Marines at the base of the hill. "We're gonna have to feel our way up and try to keep quiet. It's gonna be slow. Don't pull each other off balance and stay tight."

Becker stepped into the vegetation and began to climb. Unseen vines, creepers, and thorns tugged, clawed, and scratched at clothing and equipment. God help us, Becker prayed, feeling the umbilical rope twitch and snatch as people below fought through the thick bush. Don't let the gooks have an arty OP up on top of this bastard.

For the first two hundred meters of rugged climb, Becker jerked and jinked, involuntarily swatting at the leaves and creepers that fell across his face. His mind fed false images to blind eyes. Vines became slithering rock pythons. Fragile night flowers felt like hairy banana spiders. He slowed his pace and fought the panic lurking just below the thin veneer of his self-control.

There was literally nothing to see during the cloying, claustrophobic climb. Becker kept his eyes open but he might as well have given them a rest. His hands and feet found the tiny keyholes through which he could lever the next man and his heavy load closer to the top of Hill 513.

And then, suddenly, he could see. A pale point of light bobbed in the gloom. He had to study it carefully for a while before he realized it was the moon peeking through a hole in the canopy. Cool night air turned sweat to ice water as they emerged onto a high level portion of slope just above the jungle roof. Becker coiled in the slack line until everyone was sitting, snorting and gasping, on the edge of a clearing.

Above them a bright sniper's moon silhouetted the bald cap of Hill 513. That made the clearing at their feet on or near the military crest. He found Tyrone Douglas, who had a country boy's feel for the lay of land, and slithered off on a reconnaissance while the remainder of the squad caught their breath.

They lay on their bellies and waited for a clutch of dark clouds to scoot across the moon. It was 0130 by the luminous dial on Becker's watch when they got a panoramic view of the clearing. It was about fifty meters wide and surrounded by jungle on all but one side. The open portion of the clearing tapered toward a tall rock formation. Behind that, Hill 513 rose nearly straight up to the topographical crest.

"We'll climb toward that point of rock over there." Douglas glanced where his squad leader was pointing and easily made out a triangular spike of stone overlooking the clearing. "If it looks good, we'll set up the mortar and use the rock as an OP. That finger running off to the right should be easy to spot on the map. When it's light enough, we'll get a grid on our position by shooting an intersection on the surrounding peaks."

In the soft silver glow of the full moon, Becker set his men in motion. He spotted a mortar position at the base of the rocky pinnacle, putting Kramer and Douglas to work scraping out a pit for the tube. He sited the machine gun to one side of what he thought must be the easiest approach for an attacker climbing the hill, then slotted riflemen in a fan around the clearing, slightly downslope from the mortar.

When he was satisfied with their dispositions, Becker climbed to the mortar pit with his radioman trailing. "Get Bushmaster on the horn and tell him to send grids on their positions. Kramer, rig a hooch so we can use a flashlight to copy the dope they send. Douglas, police up all the Willy Pete rounds and make sure everybody's awake. We start to shoot early in the morning."

In the first fulgent glow of daybreak over the Hai Lang, Becker stood perched atop the rocky pinnacle near the mortar pit. He raised his binoculars and scanned the mottled carpet of green stretching to the edge of the horizon. He saw the dark blossom of bursting 155mm howitzer rounds long before the roar of their detonation reached Hill 513. The random H&I fire was rolling in right on time. Closer to home, his Marines were digging in, improving their ability to defend the clearing on Hill 513 should that become necessary. He scanned the smaller, surrounding peaks, blinking as he slid the binoculars across the flare of a rising sun. Full dawn; great visibility. Not a creature stirring. Not even a gook.

Opening his lensatic compass, Becker spread his map and settled into a comfortable position among the rocks. He laid the compass flat and aligned the straight edge with a north-south grid line. Then he shifted the map until the compass needle swung onto magnetic north, relating the real direction to the arbitrary direction represented by the top of the map sheet. With the map oriented, he spotted hilltops to his left and right and then located them by general direction and shape on his map.

Aiming through the compass, he shot magnetic azimuths to the peaks and recorded the data in a notebook. Adding or subtracting 180 degrees, he computed back-azimuths representing the direction from the selected hills to his own position. Checking the margin data of his map, he subtracted the magnetic variance from true north listed for this part of Asia and plugged that figure into the equation to obtain a set of grid azimuths, which could be plotted on the map.

Then he pulled a plastic protractor from his pocket and centered it over the first hilltop he'd spotted. He read the back-azimuth from that hill to his position and drew a straight line. Becker repeated the procedure to obtain a line along the back-azimuth from the second peak. Where the two lines intersected was a point on Hill 513 just below the crest. Becker smiled. Right where he thought he was. He computed a six-digit grid coordinate and had the radio operator pass the numbers to Bushmaster. Battalion's overnight positions were already plotted on his map. Now everyone's address book was current.

Becker measured the rough isosceles triangle he'd constructed with a practiced eye. Some of the old-timers who watched his work said no one since the legendary Master Gunnery Sergeant Lou Diamond was as good at setting up and reading this sort of gunnery problem. For a moment he watched the rising sun melt the mist hanging over the jungle and wondered if the Corps' greatest mortar magician was somewhere out there, tugging at his nonregulation goatee, ready to mark center of sector and adjust.

From the OP on Hill 513, a line to the targeted launch sites represented one leg of the triangle while a line to the battalion's positions along the stream formed another. In theory, all he had to do was dump mortar rounds along the hypotenuse of this triangle and the good guys—marching toward the white phosphorous blossom of his rounds—should run into the bad guys.

Becker noted that Douglas and Kramer were finished

seating the mortar tube and laying an aiming stake along a rough direction of fire. They could fine-tune the gun-target line after the first round went downrange. Sitting on the edge of the mortar pit, his radio operator waved the handset. Bushmaster was ready to move. They were asking for a round every hundred meters or so along their route of march.

Kramer quickly flipped through a plastic-coated stack of firing tables for the 60mm mortar, calling elevation and deflection numbers to Douglas who dialed them onto the sight. Becker watched with pride as they operated. Good gun crew. No wasted motion as Kramer peeled powder increments off the tail of a WP round and jerked out the bore-riding safety pin. Douglas displayed a deft touch on the tiny mortar's elevating and traversing handwheels. He had the sight laid on the left edge of the aiming stake and the leveling bubbles locked up dead center in less time than it took Becker to let Bushmaster know they were ready to shoot.

A battery salvo of H&I rounds screamed in from the self-propelled guns on The Rockpile and Becker nodded at Kramer who was holding the first round at the muzzle in a half-load position. Kramer dropped the round and shied away from the muzzle blast. The mortar clanged and coughed the round up into the muggy air over the Hai Lang. Douglas immediately went to work at the sight, correcting the effects of firing a first "seating round" from a new position.

"Bushmaster . . . Walleye, shot, over . . ." Becker eyed the jungle below, searching for the fall of the mortar projectile. "Walleye . . . Bushmaster, roger shot. Continue mission. Next round on call. Bushmaster, out."

Becker scanned with his binoculars along the gun-target line. The dazzling starburst of sizzling white phosphorous was fairly accurate. He sensed the deviation and made a mark on his plotting board. "Long, left. Drop one hundred . . . right five-zero . . . charge three . . . at my command . . ."

The radio crackled and Becker grinned at his crew.

"Bushmaster says they saw the splash. They're walking to it now."

By noon it was oppressively hot on Hill 513. Becker and his crew had fired nine more rounds since the first of the morning. The rifle companies were having no trouble keeping on track but movement was still dead slow through the dense bush. He passed the word to eat chow and climbed up on the rocky pinnacle with his binoculars. He could see and hear the rumble and crash of the H&I missions going in on the outskirts of the forest. It would take a damn smart gook with a good grasp of the Big Picture to realize the irregular rounds moving steadily closer to his position were anything more than dumb luck.

Becker rechecked his map. All three rifle companies in the assault had made more than half the distance to the objectives. Four or five more rounds ought to do it. He was scrambling down off the rock when he heard a booming echo followed by the throaty cough of a heavy machine gun. A crackling crescendo began to build somewhere under the jungle canopy below and he scrambled back up to the high vantage point. There was nothing to see in the sea of green but the sound was familiar, all too familiar. He closed his eyes and tried to compensate with his instincts for the confusing Doppler effect of a shifting sound source at long range. There was contact below . . . major contact.

Becker listened hard, scanning the jungle for smoke or tracers to spot the contested area. His radioman crawled up on the rock and flopped down beside him. "I'm up on battalion tac. Echo, Fox, and Golf have all stepped in the shit. Six is tellin' everyone to stay off the net. They're gonna try to shift the H&I onto the gooks."

Becker nodded. "Stay on the net but don't bother 'em unless they call for us. Lemme know what you hear."

Nothing human was visible below their perch. He caught the occasional flash of tracer arcing into the air, but not much more than a cloying pall of dissipating smoke and staccato noise indicated what everyone on Hill 513 knew. Men down below were dying.

Terse radio transmissions indicated the battalion was

tangling with a sizable NVA force along a wide front. The
CO was trying to control the ebb and flow of a wild melee
with no visibility and very little room to maneuver. Becker
had been in that sort of mess before. Marines were measur-
ing the world in feet and inches down there. In that kind of
fight over that kind of terrain, your entire focus narrowed
down to the width of a gnat's ass. You lived or died
depending on your ability to get a rifle round or a grenade
into the tiny firing slit somewhere on the front of a
practically invisible enemy bunker.

They watched and waited in silence. An hour, maybe
two; and still the firing continued. Becker easily picked the
sound of heavy machine guns and rocket-propelled grenades out of the distant din. They couldn't monitor the
artillery net, but the big guns had clearly shifted onto direct
support for the infantry battalion in contact. Becker and the
rest of the Marines he allowed up on the rocky OP for an
occasional look into the valley below could hear the crack
and see the dirty black puffs as airbursts broke over the
canopy.

"Don't sound good." The radioman stiffened out of a
slouch and passed the handset to Becker. "Bushmaster is
telling everyone to blow LZs and get the medevacs out.
Hope to Christ they don't forget to pull us off this fucking
hill."

Becker waved him to silence and listened to the crackle
of radio traffic. Battalion was trying to consolidate before
dark. They'd let the artillery pin the gooks in place and then
bring on the air strikes. Good, he thought. Don't beat your
head against a brick wall. In terrain like that, the defender
just multiplies his advantage. He caught a quick transmisson
from Echo Company about heavy casualties but didn't share
the information with the rest of the Marines huddled around
the radio. Twisting the dial to battalion command frequency, he shoved the handset at his radio operator.

"Try to push Bushmaster when the panic dies down. See
if they're ready to bring us down off of here." Becker faced
the worried Marines who drifted toward the mortar pit and
the radio, their only source of information.

"It looks like this," he said, kneeling among them, trying to keep his voice level and confident. "They hit some kind of big-ass ambush. Coupla things could have happened. Most likely, the gooks heard us coming and dug in along the route to defend their turf. Whatever they hit down there stopped them cold. The CO is gonna try to beat 'em up with air and artillery. You know the rest of the story. The gooks will either lock in so close we can't hit 'em with the big guns . . . or they'll disappear right after dark."

Kramer spoke for the rest of the Marines. "Where's that leave us?"

"Right up on top of Hill 513 for now. Soon as we can get a word in edgewise, we'll find out what they've got in mind. They're gonna run medevacs before dark, so we'll probably get picked up by chopper somewhere along the way."

Shortly before dusk, Bushmaster finally came up on their frequency. It was not the news Becker wanted to hear but he'd half expected they were stuck on Hill 513 for the night as he watched the creepy fingers of fog begin to roll upward from the humid depths of the jungle. All the helos were committed, hauling resupply and reinforcements into battalion and ferrying out casualties. Dig in, they said. Be cool. We'll get you down off that hill at first light.

While radar-guided air strikes alternated with the crash of artillery fire in the valley below their hill, Becker briefed his men, predicting a quiet night. He pointed out it was better to be sitting up on 513 high and dry than down in the shit with the rest of the battalion.

It was hard to tell in the dark, but the riflemen might have bought that story. Becker certainly did not. Back in the mortar pit, he pulled Douglas and Kramer close and expressed his fears. "I think the fucking gooks are gonna run. They kicked some ass today and they'll be wanting to break contact before they get hurt too bad. If I were them, I'd head for high ground . . ."

Douglas nodded. "Yeah. Right up the side of this hill. Quickest route out of the Hai Lang . . ."

"There it is." Becker checked his watch. Dawn was eight hours away. "I'm gonna check the holes. Kramer, you set the 60 up to fire on the tree line. Douglas, you get me a count on ammo and frags.''

Becker felt the wet compress of fog on his face as he lay on his belly near the machine-gun team. Despite a bright moon, clouds and fog were reducing visibility rapidly. He ordered the gun moved back to a higher, more commanding position. As the gunner dragged his weapon and ammo away, Becker studied every roll and twist in the terrain between the jungle surrounding the clearing and the ring of fighting holes.

They'd muster in the trees. There was a steep, three- or four-foot rise in the ground about twenty meters in front of the old machine-gun position. That would be the final assault line. The key would be to spot them early and hit hard when they tried to cover the open ground between the jungle and the rise.

It was just after midnight when they came. A rifleman on the left flank of their position passed the word for Becker. He slithered to the man's hole and jumped in beside him. PFC Hardy was relatively boot to The 'Nam but not prone to panic. Becker included him on the pathfinder team because the squad leader said he was steady.

"I think I seen something out there," he whispered. "At first I thought it was fireflies or some shit like that. Now I think it's movin' toward us . . ."

Becker stared out into the dark, searching for the points of light Hardy described. He moved his eyes in steady sweeps across the white wall of fog, trying not to stare at anything, letting his peripheral vision work. He caught movement and focused. An eerie greenish blob of light, moving left and right. He stared and detected four or five other glowing orbs.

He'd seen it before . . . last year, during the monsoons in Antenna Valley. The NVA honchos tied little squares of wood covered with luminous paint to their packs so the troopers following them through the bush at night could follow the leader. They were coming. But how many? Do they know we're up here? Do they want to fight?

Becker decided he could not afford to let the bobbing

lights get any closer to his leaky perimeter. He'd test their resolve and then call battalion for a ring of artillery fire around the hilltop. Hardy silently plopped an M-26 fragmentation grenade into his outstretched hand. Twisting and pulling on the pin, he armed the frag and hurled it deep into the bush.

The grenade made a dull crack in the wet air. When Becker and Hardy popped their heads back up out of the hole, the green orbs had disappeared. Becker picked up another grenade and waited.

Suddenly, a rifleman to his right opened up, spitting three rounds into the dark. There was an immediate and violent response from the bush. AK muzzles flared and winked. Green golfballs pulsed through the night. The M-60 shifted and hammered a burst into the dark. Becker rolled out of the hole screaming against the rattle of weapons.

"Cease fire, cease fire . . . hold it up!" The machine gun spit two more bursts before he could reach the position. The NVA were peppering the hillside, searching for defenders, but the fire was sporadic. They hadn't decided what they were facing yet.

He gathered up an armload of ammo and shoved it at the assistant gunner. "Move the gun . . . quick! Two holes down to the left. Send the guy in the hole to me."

They scrambled out as the tempo of incoming fire steadied into a rhythm. He heard the rattle of equipment as the displaced rifleman sprinted for his new hole. Rounds slapped into flesh and the man went down hard. Becker screamed for the doc. Rounds were cracking close over his head but he kept his eyes above the edge of the fighting hole. He spotted at least six weapons banging away at them in the dark.

Doc Jarvis pitched into his hole while Becker was heaving grenades at the muzzle flashes. "What about the guy who got hit?"

Jarvis struggled to catch his breath. "Dead . . . but that ain't the worst of it. Kramer and Douglas both caught ricochets off the rocks . . . and the fuckin' radio is shot all to shit. They told me to find you and let you know . . ."

The news hit Becker like a buttstroke. No comm with battalion, for Christ's sake! No way to call for supporting arms. And the gooks showed no sign of wanting to detour around his position. They were out there in enough strength to risk a fight. It occurred to Becker that he was probably at the end of the string he'd played out over the last eighteen months in Vietnam.

No, goddammit! Not yet. Not for a while anyway. He shoved a rifle at Jarvis, grabbed his shotgun, and crawled back toward the mortar pit.

Kramer and Douglas were slumped near the tube, their freshly applied battle dressings clearly visible despite the drifting fog that spilled like molasses over every indentation in the rocky ground. Becker bumped the mortar as he rolled into the hole. "Be careful, goddammit! We got that fucker leveled and ready to fire." Douglas had his wounded right leg stretched out beside the weapon. Kramer was dripping blood from a scalp wound but ready to drop rounds as soon as he got the word.

"Wait till I call for it. Ain't that many rounds left and I don't want 'em to know we got a mortar just yet. Get out of the hole and use your rifles." Becker reached for a LAW antitank rocket and slung it over his shoulder. "I'm gonna try to back 'em off before they decide to rush."

Two riflemen in forward holes opened up in a rapid volley as Becker lurched back toward the perimeter, spotting two more of the ghostly green lights bobbing out in the bush. He crawled from hole to hole under sporadic, grazing fire, urging his people to wait for clear targets, save their ammo, use their frags. At the machine-gun position, he spoke with Grimm and Hasford, his assistant.

"You guys are the pivot point. Don't get goosey and waste ammo. Displace the gun if you have to, but don't move backward . . . go right or left. Got it?"

Hasford nodded. "Everybody OK so far?"

"Godfrey and Ault are dead. We got a couple more wounded . . . but we can hold. Just hang tough. It'll be dawn in a couple of hours and they'll come looking for us."

Becker pulled the retaining pins and extended the light

antitank weapon into firing position. When it was ready he jacked a round into the chamber of his .45 pistol and crawled out of the hole. "Watch out for the back blast. I'm gonna crank this fucker right out there."

As Grimm and Hasford ducked below ground level, Becker crawled thirty meters to the berm between the perimeter and the tree line. Rounds snapped overhead and he realized gook grunts also tended to fire high at night. When he reached the wrinkle in the ground, Becker paused to listen, picking a target with his ears. He heard heavy breathing and guttural whispers to his left front and shouldered the long plastic tube.

Before he could press the firing switch, the perimeter to his rear erupted in a wall of fire. Too soon, he thought. Too soon. Wait for a target. He peeked over the mound of dirt making the edge of the berm and saw plenty of targets. They were coming, headed for the berm to group for a final rush. Dark figures were slinking out of the jungle wall, slithering through the patchy fog.

Becker swung onto a clutch of crouching figures and squeezed the trigger bar. The LAW barked and spit its high-explosive rocket round at the charging enemy. Becker rolled onto his back and dug in the cargo pockets of his trousers for a grenade. He was looking up when he saw the looming figures rise over him. Two NVA troopers stood shoulder to shoulder, whipping their SKS carbines up into firing position. They spotted him at their feet and Becker saw both muzzles swing toward him in perfect unison.

Rocking back onto his shoulder blades, Becker grabbed for the pistol tucked into his cartridge belt and brought it to bear on the NVA. The weapon popped and bucked in his hand but Becker was blinded by muzzle flash as the enemy carbines barked back at him. He kept hauling back on the trigger until the slide locked to the rear over an empty magazine. Both of the looming NVA soldiers were down when his vision returned but there was a swarm of angry replacements rushing out of the bush.

Becker heard Doc Jarvis screaming his name and began to crawl back toward the perimeter just as the mortar began to clang and bang. He hadn't called for it, but Douglas and Kramer knew it was time for their firepower. If the ammo held out, they just might be able to cut the assaulting shock troops off from their reinforcements.

He found Jarvis bleeding into the side of a hole near the machine-gun position, lung-shot but still trying to man a rifle. "Two dead that I found before I got hit. Don't know how many wounded . . ." Becker could still hear M-16s spitting into the jungle from holes on his right and left, but the sound was diminishing. Kramer was reducing the rate of fire on the mortar, probably trying to conserve a dwindling ammo supply. The machine gun was barking in fits and starts. Still three hours until dawn and the NVA were being cautious.

Got to pull back, Becker thought. Got to tighten the perimeter. He was halfway out of the hole when a close blast tore the helmet off his head. Three more explosions detonated around him and he realized the gooks were inside grenade range. Becker felt the warm ooze of blood from a scalp wound. He shook his head to clear his vision and reached for Jarvis. The doc was dead. Shrapnel from the incoming ChiCom had lanced into his brain through the right eye.

Blood ran in rivulets down his forehead and congealed in his eyebrows but Becker had no time to assess the extent of his injury. He spotted three NVA charging on the right flank of the machine gun and screamed a warning. Grimm and Hasford died before they could react. He killed one of the attackers and drove the other two back with M-16 fire but the machine gun was out of action. That was a deadly serious liability.

The berm was crawling with NVA troopers and the terrain advantage made grazing fire from their AKs and SKSs more deadly. Becker was desperate to reach the abandoned machine gun and get it back in action. He was heaving grenades, trying to buy some breathing room, when he heard pounding footsteps at his back.

Tyrone Douglas was plummeting downhill as fast as his wounded leg would let him run. "I got the gun," he screamed. "You get everybody else and pull back." Somehow Douglas made it to the machine-gun position and got the M-60 back into the fight. Under cover of its steady rattle, Becker pulled his dwindling band of defenders back toward the mortar pit.

Only two men were able to make it back with Becker. Everyone else was either dead or about to be when the wave of NVA attackers spilled into their abandoned holes. They splashed 60mm Willy Pete all over the berm area and put out a withering blanket of covering fire that allowed Douglas to make it back with the gun and a pitiful supply of remaining ammo. During a lull in the sporadic exchange of small-arms fire, Becker realized he was sleepy. Bone-weary, in fact. It was probably a result of blood loss. The flap of scalp loosened by grenade shrapnel was still leaking steadily.

Douglas and Kramer were also weak from loss of blood. Over the past hour they'd been peppered with shrapnel and shale from ricochets. Neither man bothered to bandage the bloody puncture wounds. At this point, their entire focus was narrowed to the mortar and seven remaining rounds. No grenades were left anywhere on the hill except for the long-handled ChiComs that still sailed through the mist. A rifleman named Bayer was about to pass out from pain and the resulting blood loss when a bullet carried away most of his lower jaw. Wyatt, the other rifleman, had the remaining two HE rounds for the M-79 grenade launcher, four spare magazines, and a mangled right arm full of grenade shrapnel.

Becker ran his hand along the last belt of M-60 ammo. Less than one hundred rounds, he estimated. No supporting arms throughout the night; no arty, no air, nothing but the pissant 60 mike-mike. The enemy would assume they were out of contact with fire support. And they were conserving ammo so desperately now that gooks on the other side of the berm were getting brave. They'd rush before long. It was nearly over.

He twisted away from the machine gun and stared up at the rocky crest of Hill 513. Pale light leaked around the pinnacle. Thirty minutes until dawn. Thirty minutes of darkness left to slip away . . . if only someone could provide covering fire.

"Douglas . . . Kramer, break down the sixty. Leave the tube and all the ammo in the hole. I'm going forward with the gun. When I open up, you guys take Bayer and Wyatt and get the hell over onto the other side of the hill as fast as you can. Just hide out until the choppers arrive . . ."

Kramer shook his head. "Fuck you, Sergeant Becker. It ain't over. We ain't gonna di-di on you . . ."

Becker crawled to his side and stared directly into the black man's dark eyes. "Yeah, you are, Leon. You and Douglas are gonna do exactly what I tell you to do. You're gonna take care of each other and the wounded . . . and you're gonna live through this shit. You don't want to die and I don't want you to die. Now get ready to move."

He grabbed the M-60 by the bipod and began to drag it toward a pile of enemy bodies, stacked up during a flanking attempt on the left side of the tiny perimeter. He could deliver ninety rounds of enfilade fire from behind the corpses. When the ammo was gone . . . well, he'd just have to think of something else to do . . . that's all.

Becker rested the barrel across the bloody stomach of an NVA trooper and glanced over his shoulder. He could see shadows moving around the mortar pit. Warm air from the rising sun was pushing the fog downhill. He rested the front sight blade on the edge of the berm and pressed the trigger. His initial burst attracted a wave of return fire that thudded and thumped into the dead meat on his barricade of corpses.

When the last round rattled through the M-60 there was a moment of eerie silence. Then he saw NVA troopers rushing from the tree line. Up and running for the mortar pit, Becker caught a fleeting glimpse of assholes and elbows scrambling uphill. They'd need just a few more minutes to make the summit and safety.

He tumbled into the hole and grabbed the mortar tube. Jamming the knoblike spherical projection on the base of the cylinder into a pile of rocks, he dropped in a Willy Pete round and lowered the muzzle nearly parallel to the ground.

Becker bowed his head and depressed the manual firing lever. The mortar clanged and recoiled in his hand, showering him with dirt and rocks. He shook off the shock and loaded another round.

The impact was spectacular. The shell detonated among the charging enemy and burst into angry white stars. Hot, pulsing chunks of white phosphorous spewed in all directions, knocking several NVA to the ground where they writhed and screamed in agony. The momentum of their final assault staggered and slowed as Becker sent another round into their midst. More attackers tumbled down the slope, bodies distorted and smoking from the seering heat of the burning chemical.

Deafened by the concussive blast of the mortar, Becker kept firing, oblivious to the incoming rounds that pounded all around his position. Concentrating on the swarm of bodies flowing out of the jungle, he completely missed the sound of heavy rotors beating through the morning air. A relief force was inbound to Hill 513 but Becker was too busy defending it to notice.

He fired the final 60mm round just as a bullet ricocheted off the tube and smashed into his left thumb. He was pumping blood from the mangled digit, nearly in shock, when it finally registered that the NVA were running in the other direction—away from him—back into the jungle.

Becker stood and reached for a rifle with his good hand. He was fumbling with a magazine when a steel-jacketed 7.62mm parting shot tore into the right side of his chest and dropped him, leaking what was left of his life's blood into Hill 513.

The earsplitting roar of bomb-laden aircraft diving on NVA positions throughout the Hai Lang National Forest made hearing difficult on top of Hill 513. The lieutenant colonel commanding 2/1 had to ask for the number twice when his sergeant major reported the body-count on the slope.

"There's thirty-seven dead right around here, sir." The sergeant major stood shaking his head and scanning the area with a veteran's critical eye. "About twice that many back in the tree line and a whole bunch of blood trails. The radio must have got shot up early on . . ."

In the valley below 513 they'd heard the fighting and tried to raise Becker's beleaguered command on the radio with offers of fire support. "Lucky the choppers weren't available. We found two twelve-point-seven machine guns back there in the bush."

The CO ignored the rest of the report, silently watching as corpsmen worked over the casualties preparing them for evacuation to a hospital ship offshore. He was thinking about what the surviving Marines told him when they were plucked off the reverse slope of the hill. He was wondering why Becker would do what they said he did. Somewhere in the mainstream of American society, he realized, there is a tiny pool of men like Thurmond Becker. Every once in a while—usually in the most desperate situations—they bob to the surface and save everyone's ass.

"If you'll give me your thoughts on the matter, sir . . ." The sergeant major appeared at his elbow. "I'll insure we get the decorations rolling."

He strolled behind the CO toward the line of stretchers bearing the survivors. Douglas, Kramer, Bayer, Wyatt . . . and Becker. Five survivors. Fifty percent casualties. And they held the hill—killed something like a hundred NVA in the process. Jesus . . . where do we get them?

Watching the first medevac helicopter claw up into the air, the battalion commander turned to his senior enlisted man. "Silver Star for all of them . . . dead or alive. And I want no less than the Navy Cross for Sgt. Becker."

"Are you still gonna recommend him for a field commission, sir? He might not come back in-country, depending on what the docs find . . ."

"Becker?" The CO headed for his own helicopter pulling the sergeant major and an entourage of radiomen behind him. "You can bet he'll be back, Sarn't Major. Guys like him quit when you kill 'em . . . not before."

The sergeant major was proud of Becker but even prouder of the fact that it was a sergeant—not an officer—

who held Hill 513 against formidable odds. He was a man who believed in the preservation of his species. "Becker's a damn fine NCO, sir. He might not be interested in a commission."

Both men turned their backs to the stinging rotorwash of a departing helicopter. "Hide and watch, Sarn't Major. The system dotes on men like Becker."

"Yessir. I guess it does . . . as long as we got us a war to fight."

III.

Left Oblique, March . . .

"Yessir, we're aware of the publicity angle, but it's difficult to hide a general court in a town like Jacksonville . . ." The caller seemed to understand. Major Claiborne drummed his fingernails on a thick file folder, stealing glances at himself in the office mirror. "General Tobrey is quite confident, sir. And I'll be handling the prosecution personally."

That seemed to satisfy the full colonel in the SJA office at Fleet Marine Force Atlantic headquarters in Norfolk. He hung up with the admonition that headquarters had heard about the case and was watching events at Camp Lejeune very closely.

Couldn't be better, Claiborne thought as he hung up the receiver and treated himself to an ice-cold can of Coke from the minirefrigerator in his office. He patted the file again and smiled. This baby is a silver bullet, a launch-pad, a career builder.

He crossed his legs and scrunched down comfortably in his swivel chair. The complete case against Becker—neatly, unerringly typed into boiler-plated legalese—sat in the center of his desk ready for presentation to the CG in just under one hour.

He toyed with the idea of tying it all up in a pretty piece of symbolic ribbon, but General Tobrey would fail to see the humor. No, he'd run it down hard and fast, strictly professional. Check all the boxes and give the general the warm, fuzzy feeling he wanted about the case.

With Second Lieutenant Stewart out there drilling holes in the Indian Ocean and Tobrey bound and determined to slaughter a scapegoat, there was no way he could be tied in to the case outside that dreary courtroom down the hall. The anonymous letter, typed on his wife's beat-up old portable, would be untraceable if the source of Stewart's complaint ever became an issue. Claiborne was fairly certain that wouldn't happen anyway.

He wasn't the only officer to see Becker and Campbell carrying on like a couple of hounds in heat. The alarm bells started to ring just after he'd spotted Becker having a candlelight dinner with a pretty young woman at that seafood place out on Emerald Island. One of the young lawyers having dinner with Claiborne recognized the woman and said he wished they'd been making second lieutenants that good-looking when *he* went through The Basic School.

Claiborne ignored it at first. Figures, he thought, ordering a second round of after-dinner drinks, if a dinosaur like Becker would be seen in public with a woman, it would have to be a woman *Marine*. About a week later, Claiborne got a call from a civilian attorney out in Jacksonville—a man he'd met briefly and given his card at some social function—to inquire about specifics of the Soldiers & Sailors Relief Act.

Could action be taken in an divorce case, the civilian attorney wanted to know, when one of the parties was a military officer on duty outside the United States? Claiborne could have given a simple answer but his curiosity was piqued. As a professional courtesy to a fellow member of the North Carolina bar, the civilian named the officers involved and outlined the basic situation.

It took Claiborne until noon chow to connect the dots drawn by the phone call. Second Lieutenant Rebecca

Campbell . . . wasn't that the name of the woman mooning over Becker at dinner? And she's married to another
Marine officer! He researched case law, the Uniform Code
of Military Justice and the Manual for Courts-Martial long
into the night. By the time his wife arrived at the office with
his dinner on a tray, Claiborne realized he was onto a
precedent-setting situation. And setting precedents was
something that got lawyers noticed in high places.

He'd have sicced the ghouls at Naval Investigative
Service onto the case anyway, but General Tobrey's puritanical screed, blathering on about morals and morale,
cocked Claiborne's pistol. This was one high-profile case
that would not get buried.

Major Claiborne finished off his Coke and reached for the
phone. He got an outside line and dialed the desk number of
a reporter on the local newspaper.

"Jim Payne . . ."

"Hey, Jim . . . Rod Claiborne. I've got something for
you . . . something hot. You can have it early and exclusive if you promise to protect the source."

"You know me, Rod. How long we been friends, for
Christ's sake? I always protect the source."

"No, I mean *really* protect the source. It's either that or
you get nothing . . . stone-walled out here."

"Yeah, right . . . OK. Who the hell is the source?"

"I am. Can't talk now. Search your files on a guy named
Thurmond Becker and meet me at that place down on Court
Street tomorrow night . . ."

Major General Tobrey stared balefully at the thick file
centered on his desk and chewed on his lower lip. His Staff
Judge Advocate sat quietly across the room waiting for a
cue.

"OK, Judge. How do we stand here?"

"Rock solid in my opinion, General. Claiborne steepled
his fingers under his chin for dramatic effect. "The verdict
will be as a general court-martial directs, but I don't see
how they can return anything other than guilty on the face

of the evidence and under the nominal interpretation of the UCMJ.''

"What are the charges?"

Claiborne ticked them off on his fingers. "We're going for failure to obey a lawful order, wrongful cohabitation, and conduct unbecoming."

"How do you intend to proceed?"

"I'll grant immunity for Lieutenant Campbell and force her to testify as the principal witness for the prosecution."

"You expect her to do that? Nail the man she's been sleeping with?"

"She'll do it or face her own court-martial for failing to testify as a material witness in a federal case. That's chargeable under Article 133 of the Code and carries a maximum penalty of dismissal, forfeiture of all pay and allowances, and confinement at hard labor for a period not to exceed five years."

General Tobrey began to pace, pausing occasionally to stare at one of the framed pictures or certificates that covered the walls of his office. "I don't like it, Judge. A young second lieutenant like Campbell hasn't got that much to lose. If she refuses to testify and it comes to a court-martial for her, she'd never get the max sentence. You know that and so does she."

Claiborne rose and gripped the back of a padded leather armchair, couching his words carefully. "I believe Lieutenant Stewart *will* testify, General . . . because Captain Becker will force her to testify."

Tobrey arched an eyebrow and folded his arms across his chest. "The man may be an immoral pig, Judge, but he's not suicidal."

"No, sir, he's not suicidal. But he *is* a firm believer in the system that's protected him and rewarded his, uh, irregular behavior for the past twenty years . . ."

"The same system that's bringing him to trial at a general court-martial?"

"One and the same, General. Look at it from Becker's perspective. He's seen essentially similar cases ignored or swept under the rug before. SOP for this kind of mess has been to separate the parties quickly and quietly . . . keep the dirty laundry from flapping on a public line. At most one or both of the Marines involved gets a letter of reprimand or some other nonpunitive nonsense.

"Given his experience—not to mention a rather superlative combat record—Becker is bound to believe that the court-martial board will vote to dismiss or simply slap him on the wrist. A man like Captain Becker believes he's bulletproof, General, but he sees a young officer like Rebecca Campbell as very vulnerable. Becker knows we could—and would—go after Stewart if we miss him. He'll urge her to testify."

Tobrey walked toward his senior attorney and nailed him with a cold glare. "Judge, I want some assurances here. I want to feel that your strategy isn't based on something you picked up in Psych 101."

"I'm basing my assumptions on Becker's track record, sir. He's a troglodyte . . . a throwback to the days of Chesty Puller and all that macho nonsense. But he knows the rules as well as you and I do. He knows Stewart is still married in the eyes of the Corps. Yet he continues to keep company with her, to sleep with her . . ."

"Meaning what?"

"Meaning Becker must be in *love* . . . with something besides the Marine Corps for the first time in his life, General. He won't let anything happen to the woman he loves, no matter what happens to him."

General Darwin Tobrey pondered for a moment and then returned to his desk. When he was seated, he took a pen, flipped open the folder, and began to scrawl his signature on a number of paper-clipped pages. He finished, replaced the pen, and stabbed at a button on the intercom connecting him with his chief of staff.

"Chief, I am ordering a general court-martial for Captain Thurmond Becker. Major Claiborne will brief you on the particulars of the case. Notify his CO, then have Becker and Second Lieutenant Rebecca Campbell arrested and confined to quarters."

The 2nd Marine Division chief of staff was finishing a

cup of coffee with the division sergeant major when the order sizzled into the receiver on his desk. Both men frowned and stared at each other in disbelief. They knew and respected Buttplate Becker. There had to be some mistake. The chief punched his intercom.

"Did you say Captain Becker, sir? Company commander out at ITS?"

"That's the man. Put him in hack pending court-martial." With an angry electronic snap, the general cut communication without waiting for confirmation of his orders.

"Gahd-damn . . ." The chief of staff had personally promoted Becker back when they served together in the 3rd Marine Division on Okinawa. "What the hell could he have done to rate that?"

The sergeant major had been a platoon sergeant in Becker's battalion back in '67 during the fight for Hill 513. "The SJA will probably be here in a few minutes to fill you in, Colonel. Meanwhile, I'm gonna slip out to the mortar range to, uh, check on the troops."

"Take my vehicle, Sarn't Major. And tell him to stand by for a ram. Whatever this is about, the CG is dead serious."

Gunnery Sergeant Tyrone Douglas stood on a hillside observation post forward of the 81mm mortar firing line and focused his field glasses. The skipper had just put the third round from Gun 2 smack into a 55-gallon drum at a precise range of 2,140 meters. He grinned and picked up a field phone to inform the line of their success.

He could hear a faint echo of cheering as he turned to watch the gun crews congratulating themselves and Captain Becker, the man on the sight for the precision gunnery demonstration. Christ, he thought, after all these years Buttplate still can't keep his dick-skinners off a mortar.

At the gunny's back, a clutch of enlisted forward observers in training began to pay off bets won and lost on the fall of the round. He listened to the losers bitch for a while and shook his head in despair. "Some of you assholes are gonna go broke before you learn Captain Becker don't miss."

Down in the mortar pits along the firing line, Douglas could see Becker forming the troops into a school circle. A pall of pale white cigarette smoke rose over the cluster as the skipper lit the smoking lamp. There'd be a sea story to get their attention and then Becker would roll right into the technical stuff. They'd listen and they'd learn.

The young Marines worshiped Buttplate Becker . . . because he doted on them. And because he had a rugged reputation for no-slack training that produced the finest mortarmen in the Marine Corps. From personal experience—from Vietnam to Beirut and points in between—Douglas knew Becker was a very special, endangered breed of cat. The skipper was the kind of guy who would have no qualms about listing his occupation as "professional soldier" on a job application. He was proud and protective of all the arcane images the term conjured up these days.

Guys like Thurmond Becker stood tall and traditional, while everybody else slouched around wearing a shit-eating grin and trying to turn the Marine Corps into a big green version of IBM. Douglas had done a lot of bolt-working in the system to stay with Becker over the sixteen years it had taken to become what he'd always wanted to be: the Buttplate's company gunnery sergeant.

He broke the student FOs for a C-ration meal and went to draw his own chow. If I never sew another chevron on my sleeve, he thought, at least I'm one guy who traveled the right road and wound up at a good destination.

Lance Corporal LaBella—one of the losers who thought the skipper's bracket was too wide for a third round bull's-eye—approached with a cigarette dangling from his lips. "Got a light, Gunny?"

Douglas pressed his battered Zippo out of a trouser pocket and handed it to LaBella. The young Marine lit his smoke, snapped the ancient lighter closed, and then turned it over in his hands.

"This thing's been around some, ain't it, Gunny?"

"Sure has. Skipper gave it to me in Vietnam back in '68. He's got one just like it . . ."

LaBella squinted at the engraving of the Marine Corps emblem and the words below it. "What's it say here?"

"Nobody ever taught you to read, LaBella? It says Tubes. That's what they used to call me. Skipper's lighter says Buttplate. We had another guy—he's out now—his lighter says Bipod. But we never called him that. Name was Kramer. Went to law school after 'Nam."

LaBella handed the lighter back and sat cross-legged in front of Tubes Douglas. A number of the other FOs joined him in a ragged circle. "So you guys were together in Vietnam?"

"Hope to shit in yer messkit. Then Beirut. Me and the skipper's been around the horn together a few times."

"What was the skipper like back then?"

Tubes Douglas used the Zippo to light a smoke of his own and smiled. "It was buck Sergeant Becker in them days, but it didn't take me and ol' Kramer long to figure out we were dealin' with something special . . ."

IV.

To the Rear, March . . .

The scene inside the huge Quonset hut reminded Private First Class Douglas of pictures he'd seen—those old black-and-white shots of Marines sprawled all over troopships headed for the South Pacific during World War II. Sweaty bodies reclined wherever there was clear space on the dusty concrete deck. Outside, a monsoon rain rattled into an annoying roar on the tin roof of their temporary home.

They'd been seventeen hours on an airplane. Douglas, Kramer, and about eighty-five other replacements were bleary, dreary, and confused on their first day in Vietnam. Kramer sat on his seabag and tapped Douglas's knee. The hand he offered was pale chocolate on the palm. "We still got a deal?"

Douglas shook and offered a stateside cigarette. "Damn straight, Leon. Just like in boot camp. You watch my back and I'll watch yours."

Kramer struck a match and held it to their smokes. "Your momma recover yet?"

"What?"

"Did she recover from that picture you sent her from Oceanside, man? You standin' there with your arm draped around a splib dude?"

"Shit. C'mon, Leon. Ceiling, Oklahoma, ain't Selma, Alabama. We got Indians and shit . . ."

"Izzat a fact?" The litany that began between them at Parris Island survived the long trip to Southeast Asia. "Well, let me tell you, mah man. We got white folks in Dee Cee, but we don't treat 'em worth a shit."

Douglas blew a gout of smoke at the roof of the Quonset hut, wondering when they would be assigned to a unit and get to work on the job of war. "Listen to that fuckin' rain, willya? Sounds like a double-cunted cow pissin' on a big, flat rock."

They stretched out, resting on their damp seabags, glad to be inside something called the 15th Aerial Port Squadron rather than out in the monsoon rain that was pelting down over Danang in South Vietnam's northernmost sector. Kramer crapped out, but Douglas was too excited to sleep. He closed his eyes and listened as the rattle of rain on corrugated metal receded into the background, like the croak of frogs and the chirp of crickets near the pond on his grandparents' farm.

He began to isolate other sounds, grunt sounds, the sounds of Vietnam: NCOs barking orders, asthmatic snores from bone-weary men, the clink and scrape of lighters, a hollow belch, a warbling fart, colorful strings of profanity, the squeak and scrape of combat equipment, the keening scream of jet engines on afterburner, the snort and whine of unmuffled diesels, the bass rumble of distant artillery. Tyrone Douglas would never admit to it, but the entire symphony thrilled him to the marrow of his bones.

A wet wind howled through an open door and whipped through the building. The replacements sensed their time had come and began to sit up slowly, blinking in the dim light that filtered through filthy windows. A soggy lump stood silhouetted in the open door, rock-still, making no move to enter the terminal. Gusting breeze wrapped a tattered poncho tight around his body. Where his hips and elbows should have been, there were only mysterious lumps.

Behind the cascade of water that sloughed off the man's

helmet Kramer spotted a pair of intense green eyes. He looked like a lanky lizard recently emerged from some muddy jungle pool. One of the Air Force clerks behind the passenger desk raised his voice over the weather. "In or out, goddammit . . . in or out!"

Dripping rain in puddles around a pair of disreputable jungle boots, the apparition entered and slammed the door behind him. Douglas spotted a strong, square jawline covered by a stubble of sandy beard. His complexion was in the midst of fading from a bone-deep tan to monsoon pallor. A wicked-looking twelve-gauge pump shotgun dangled from his left hand. He squished past Douglas and Kramer without looking down, tiny fountains of water squirting out the vent holes in the arch of his boots.

They followed him with their eyes all the way up to the Administration desk where he reached under his poncho and handed a bored clerk a sheaf of papers. There was a shattering squeal of electronic feedback as the clerk snapped on his PA system.

"Following named personnel are assigned to Task Force X-Ray, 1st Marine Division. When your name is called, report to the desk for transportation to your final destination. Alvarado, Anderson, Behrman, Beehler . . ."

Douglas and Kramer were on the list. They dragged their seabags toward the front of the building and stood looking around as the sodden Marine eyed them carefully. Douglas thought he looked shrewd, keeping his own counsel, like a breeder at cattle auction. Eventually, fifteen new guys were gathered around him. He accepted the endorsed orders from the clerk and stuffed them inside the liner of his helmet.

Something resembling a lopsided grin split his face and he ran a wrinkled hand through a crop of copper-colored hair. "Welcome to The 'Nam . . ." His voice was strong, friendly but not patronizing. "I'm Sergeant Becker from 2nd Battalion, First Marines, up at Quang Tri. They sent me down here to police you up and move you north sometime tomorrow."

He swept the assembly with his eyes, chewed on his lip for a moment, then nodded and continued, "We'll be staying here in Danang tonight. Nothing flies until the rain lets up. From here we go to Task Force X-Ray at Phu Bai . . .''

Several of the replacements waved their hands or shouted questions. Becker just cradled his shotgun like a squirrel-hunter and motioned for silence. ''Hold on. I know you've all got questions. Right now all I know is that I'm supposed to deliver thirteen of you to Phu Bai and then take two with me on up to Quang Tri. The ones who go with me will wind up in 2/1. The rest will get their assignments from the pogues when we get to Phu Bai. Now police up your gear, break out a poncho or raincoat if you've got one, and climb into that deuce-and-a-half parked outside.''

Aboard the open-topped truck, Douglas and Kramer wiped at the water that blew into their eyes and tried desperately for a first look at Vietnam. They couldn't see much but the sounds and smells were enticing, exotic . . . enough to fire a load of adrenaline into their systems. As they rattled and swerved up a potholed road through an area Becker called Dogpatch, Douglas and Kramer sat quietly, cataloguing sensations.

There was an incessant honking and a babble of strange language from people jammed like market-bound chickens into odd three-wheeled conveyances. Over the diesel whine they heard the rap and snap of small gasoline engines. They caught snatches of stateside rock and roll blaring from windowless shacks.

When the wet wind shifted the truck's acrid exhaust, they smelled fecund incense and woodsmoke laced with the tang of camphor oil. Layered under it all was the basic scent of shit. They followed their noses to the flooded fields on either side of the road and saw rice paddies, the bread baskets of Asia.

Becker stood leaning over the canvas cab of the truck when they swung through a perimeter gate guarded by white-helmeted Marine MPs. ''This is Hill 327,'' he shouted at the replacements. ''First Marine Division head-quarters.'' The truck lurched to a halt outside a plywood shack with screen walls and a tin roof. Becker waded toward the rear of the truck and vaulted to the ground. Pointing at the building, he motioned with his shotgun.

"Inside the hooch and pick yourself out a rack." As they jumped down, dragging wet seabags after them, Becker chased them inside with instructions. "Be sure and get your wet uniforms off. Towel down real good."

They stumbled, fumbled, and bumped into each other trying to select a cot away from the rain that blew in through the screens. "Just grab a rack. Ain't no such thing as dry inside a hardback hooch when the wind's blowing. Take your boots off and break out a dry pair of socks. We got a lot of ground to cover tomorrow and you don't want to get sick."

"Hey, Sarge . . . I'm already sick . . ." The replacements paused in midstrip to stare at a Marine sitting on his seabag in a corner of the hooch. He was a lanky man with a hooked nose and eyebrows that formed a firm, furry bar over squinty eyes. When he'd finished wiping the rain from a set of issue eyeglasses, he put them back on his face and stared around the room. "I wanna go to sickbay . . ."

Becker slung his shotgun muzzle down over his shoulder and walked toward the seated figure. He stared for a moment, turning his head, first one way, then the other.

"And just who might you be, Ace?"

The replacement stared up through his glasses. He didn't seem at all impressed with Becker's authority.

"Name's Behrman . . ."

"What Behrman? Shitbird Behrman? Asshole Behrman?" The hooch burbled with snickers and chuckles as the replacements stopped to watch the confrontation.

"Kevin Behrman . . ."

"You got a rank to go with that name, Ace?"

"Lance corporal . . ."

"What seems to be your problem, Lance Corporal Behrman?"

"I've got a cold . . ."

"Uh-huh. Well, let me tell you what we do about colds in The 'Nam, Ace. We live with 'em and we hope they become pneumonia or malaria. Because colds ain't shit . . . but pneumonia or malaria? That's worth a week's light duty.''

Behrman uncoiled from his seabag and put his hands on his hips. Becker backed up a step and looked him up and down with a sarcastic grin splitting his face.

"I got a right to go to sickbay!"

"Ace, what you got is an attitude problem. You figure on keepin' that attitude for thirteen months in The 'Nam?"

"They never should have sent me here! I'm on an aviation guarantee . . ."

"We got all kinds of aviation here, Ace. We got helicopters, we got fixed wing. Take your pick."

"I want to request Mast . . ."

A small muscle began to twitch along Becker's jawline. Kramer nudged Douglas and whispered, "That asshole is about to get his fucking head ripped off his shoulders . . ."

"OK, Lance Corporal Behrman . . . start talking."

"I mean I want to see the commanding officer!"

"Well, here's your predicament, Ace. You ain't got a commanding officer right now . . . except for me. So what's on your mind?"

Behrman glanced around the room. The replacements just grinned back at him, sensing the first instance of bloodshed they would see in Vietnam. "I'm supposed to be going to tech school . . ."

"You *are* going to tech school, Ace . . . right here in The 'Nam. You're gonna learn all the technical aspects of being a grunt and wasting gooks."

The snorts of laughter from the other replacements tripped Behrman's trigger. He made the mistake of leaning into Becker's face and shouting. "You can't treat people like this! Who the fuck do you think . . ."

Becker brought the muzzle of the shotgun up hard between Behrman's legs and shoved. The replacement found himself painfully suspended by the scrotum, his toes barely touching the plywood floor. Becker's voice was a guttural snarl.

"I've got more time on a medevac slab than you got in the Corps . . . so listen up! You weren't drafted so you got no bitch comin'. This is *Vietnam,* ass-eyes! This is where the *real* Marines are. You owe me and the rest of them real Marines a hundred percent. You keep bellyachin' and one of us is gonna blow you away long before the gooks get a chance.''

Behrman struggled against the prod jammed painfully into his crotch, but Becker increased the pressure, lifting him even higher. ''You get the picture, Ace?''

Behrman's voice was a painful squeak. ''Yeah . . . yeah.''

''Good.'' When Becker jerked the shotgun free, Behrman collapsed in a huddle. ''Now work on adjustin' that piss-poor attitude.'' Becker's face was placid and unaffected by the confrontation when he turned and walked toward the door. ''The rest of you people hit the rack. There's bunkers at the front and rear of this hooch. Anytime during the night you hear somebody yell incoming, you head for one of those bunkers . . .''

He paused at the door, removed his helmet, and checked the paperwork he'd picked up at the transient facility. ''There's two of you people carryin' an O341 MOS. Who's mortars?'' The replacements stared around at each other, shrugging until Douglas and Kramer stepped into the center aisle.

''That'd be us, Sarge.'' Kramer pointed at himself and jerked a thumb at Douglas.

''You two police up your gear and come with me.'' Becker smiled, the confrontation with Behrman apparently gone from his mind.

They scrambled into wet boots, shouldered their soggy seabags, and followed Becker out into the night. He led them about fifty meters from the relative warmth of the hard-back hooch and pointed to a culvert that marked the entrance to a sandbagged bunker. ''Inside. We're gonna spend some time together.''

There was no room to stand inside the dank cavern. Douglas and Kramer sat on their seabags and waited for orders. A match flared in the gloom as Becker lit a candle and stuck it into an empty ration can. ''This is home. Find a flat spot on the deck.''

Kramer eyed the pools of muddy water at his feet. "Sarge, we ain't been issued ponchos . . ."

Becker dug around in a dark corner and hefted several C-ration cases into the center of the dugout. "We'll eat and then you can sleep on the ration boxes. I got an extra poncho and poncho liner in my pack."

He popped the wire binding on the rations with his K-Bar knife, tossed each man a meal, and then held up a handful of small paper packages. "String these John Wayne can openers on your dogtags. You'll be using them regularly."

Douglas began to lay out his meal. "Are we the ones goin' with you to, uh, that place you mentioned?"

Becker dug in his pack for hot sauce and onion powder, placing them on the ration boxes beside two canteens he pulled out from under his poncho. "Yep. Quang Tri. I run a mortar squad in 2/1. We were up on the DMZ at Con Thien, then they ordered us back to operate out of the provincial capital. We get attached to whatever company needs the tube. You been trained on 81s, but we're usin' 60 mike-mikes over here because we can hump 'em easier in heavy bush and bring fire quicker when the shit hits."

"So we're gonna be in your squad?"

"You are if you don't turn to instant shit . . ." Becker grinned around a mouthful of pork slices. He seemed inclined to talk, not at all haughty about his rank or their lowly status as new guys.

"I believe in mortars for the kind of fighting we're doing over here, see? They ain't like artillery or air or naval gunfire. You don't have to ask everybody up to and including God for clearance to fire. With the tubes along out in the bush you can bring smoke in a hurry . . . before the gooks break contact."

Kramer cut a look at Douglas and raised his eyebrows in an unspoken question. Becker didn't miss the signal. He swallowed a chunk of pork and pointed with his spoon.

"I know what you two are thinking. You got a mortar MOS out of ITR and it looked like a skate, right? Riflemen and machine gunners hump. You guys crap out behind 'em and wait for word to shoot. Am I right?"

They snickered and nodded. He'd read their minds precisely. Becker put his ration can down and reached for a canteen. "Lemme run it down for you. We use plenty of 81s for support over here. Great weapon, no doubt about that. But it's too heavy to hump in heavy bush most of the time. Small units on patrol are always walking out of the range fan and the 81s can't advance fast enough to follow. Arty takes forever to clear through the ARVN sometimes and air is spotty depending on weather and shit like that.

"The answer is a mortar that moves with the grunts, ready to shoot as soon as we make contact. So, the Corps broke out the 60 mike-mikes from Korea and sent 'em over here. We learned to use 'em in a hurry. Now everybody wants good mortarmen who can hump and dump rounds—on time, on target."

Douglas finished his meal and began to arrange ration boxes on the wet floor of the bunker. "Are the 60s hard to learn?"

"Nah. Piece of cake. Same principle as 81s. What's hard is to *think* when the shit's hittin' out there and don't lose your cool. You can't just start tossin' HE into the bush. You got to make every round count for something . . . and that means you got to forget the incoming and concentrate on good mortar gunnery."

As they stretched out in the clammy, cramped bunker the bump and rumble of distant artillery added a base note to the night sounds of Vietnam. Becker snuffed the candle, prodded his haversack into a pillow, and reclined on a poncho with a deep sigh. They were drifting into sleep when the eerie owl hoot of a falling flare canister caused Kramer and Douglas to bolt upright.

"Relax . . ." Becker never moved from the prone position. "It's just an illum canister. You'll learn to love it. Illum freezes the gooks, gives you a good sight picture even in the dark. Go back to sleep."

After an hour of fitful tossing, trying to turn off his mind, Kramer sat up quietly and lit a smoke. He just couldn't keep the questions on hold. There were so many; so pressing now that he was actually in-country; actually facing the devil.

And there was no one to ask. Even Douglas wouldn't understand his ambivalence about Vietnam. He'd never tried to explain, even in their most intimate conversations. A white guy wouldn't understand.

"You ain't gonna know until it happens . . ." Becker's voice was a soft purr from the corner of the bunker.

Kramer cupped his smoke and stared at the sergeant's prostrate form. "Ain't gonna know what?"

"You ain't gonna know how you'll act under fire until you get under fire. Relax and forget about it."

"I ain't worried about that. I'll be OK . . ."

Becker sat up with a groan and hooked the cigarette out of Kramer's fingers. "You got something rattling around in your seabag, now's the time to shake it out." He took a drag and passed it back. In the flare of the smoke, Becker's eyes narrowed into a squint. He looked old and wise.

Kramer decided to take a chance. Becker didn't seem to be a cracker or an overbearing lifer. If his ass was going to belong to this white man for the next thirteen months, they ought to have an understanding . . . for better or for worse.

"I was thinkin' about how many black men I saw comin' over here . . ."

Becker reached for the smoke again and Kramer saw a smile creasing his unshaven face. "Have we got a race relations problem here, Lance Corporal Kramer?"

"I don't know. Have we?"

It was a while before Becker answered. His voice was serious and intense. "If you mean are black men carrying too much of the combat load, the answer is yes. If you mean do they resent it sometimes—yes again. If you mean is the Marine Corps trying to kill off as many black men as possible, the answer is no."

"That's hard to believe with some of the shit we hear back in the States."

"I expect it is, but look at it this way, Kramer. There's got to be a reason you joined the Marine Corps rather than wait around to get drafted in the Army. Most of the black Marines I know say they wanted to be something special, to be with guys who gave 'em the best chance of survival if they wound up getting sent to Vietnam. Guys like that ain't stupid and they ain't suicidal. You don't turn guys like that into cannon fodder, I don't give a fuck what color they are . . ."

"That's one white guy talking . . ."

"It's one white guy who believes in the system, Kramer. There's lots of us around . . . especially here in The 'Nam. Most of us have survived long enough to know the system is at its best in combat. That's when all the other bullshit disappears and things get real basic. Let me tell you something, man. I don't know how this fuckin' war is gonna come out in the end, but I do know there's a lot of white guys and black guys who are gonna come away from it with a different attitude about the races."

"Back where I come from, you believe in the system and the system tears your guts out."

"Like I said, Kramer. Lots of guys are gonna come home from this war ready to change all that."

"You gonna be one of those guys?"

"Yep. How about you, Kramer?"

"The GI Bill ought to help me through college. I been thinkin' about law school. Seems like the fuckin' lawyers got all the heavy artillery these days."

"There it is . . ." Becker chuckled, stubbed out a smoke, and collapsed back onto his poncho. "You go on and go to college and law school, Kramer, but for the next thirteen months you keep your mind on the law of the jungle."

Listening to the whispers, Douglas scrunched nearer to the muddy wall of the bunker, giving Kramer a few more inches of floor space. Right up until the day he arrived in Vietnam, the whole experience had played for him like the setup of a John Wayne movie. Now people he liked and respected—even the man he expected to watch his back out in the bush—were asking questions that took the edge off the great adventure.

The morning monsoon had drizzled down to a fine mist by the time they cleared the C-130 ramp at Phu Bai and finished initial processing for further assignment to combat units. Becker hustled Kramer and Douglas through the morass. He had them wait outside while he hand-carried their orders through a bevvy of clerks and infantry officers looking to shanghai replacements for undermanned units out in the bush. By noon they were clutching Willy Peter bags full of field gear and standing along a muddy road lined with parked trucks.

Becker had a word with the convoy commander and then motioned them aboard an idling six-by. "Be about twenty minutes before they get rolling up to Quang Tri." He hopped into the truck, eyed the sky, and then spread a poncho liner.

"Take a look over the cab and see where we are in the convoy." Becker began to disassemble his scattergun, placing the parts carefully on the poncho liner in a precise row from left to right as he peeled the weapon apart.

"Lesson One . . . we are in the fifth truck back from the convoy lead vehicle. There's a reason for that. Never ride on the first through the third vehicles. The first one catches the mine or rocket to block the road and the next two get hosed first in an ambush. The rest have time to turn around or we have time to bail out if we get hit. Also, never ride in the last vehicle. Smart gooks will hit it to block retreat."

Kramer and Douglas studied the convoy configuration and then sat down on their canvas bags. They watched Becker's hands move with practiced precision. The weapon seemed to lurch into pieces at his touch. No wasted motion, no fumbling for button or catch as he worked.

"Lesson Two. In bad weather, take advantage of every opportunity to clean your weapons. Your feet and your face can wait, but you can't afford a weapon that malfunctions when the shit hits the fan. Any questions?"

Douglas glanced at Kramer and then back at Becker. The sergeant seemed in an expansive mood. He shrugged. "I heard you guys talkin' last night . . ."

"Sorry if we disturbed your beauty rest." Becker ran an oily rag over shotgun parts and began to slide the weapon back together in a rhythmic series of clanks and metallic snicks. "What's on your mind?"

"Well, you know—I don't know too much about all this—just what they told us in staging battalion and all—but what's the score, you know? Some guys said we were stoppin' the communists, helpin' the South Vietnamese and all that. But—I mean, shit—it's hard to see why we gotta be over here messin' in other people's business."

Kramer hooted and punched his buddy in the ribs. "Sheee-it, fuckin' Douglas is turnin' into a peace-freak on me!"

"No I ain't, man! I ante'd up to play the game just like you did. You know what they said. We're over here helpin' the Vietnamese to be free, but I read the papers. It's just that it don't seem that fuckin' simple anymore."

Becker racked the bolt of his shotgun, holding it to his ear, listening for the telltale scrape of sand or dirt in the mechanism. Satisfied, he propped the weapon against a knee and lit a cigarette.

"Listen, I don't want you people getting your skivvies all wound up in a knot over politics. You got more pressing problems to worry about—like learning your trade and staying alive—but there's something you ought to understand from the git-go.

"Wars are simple. It's been that way since the first son-ofabitch picked up a rock and went after the second sonofabitch. No matter what you hear, it's all about power. The guys who own the most land generally have the most power. That's why wars are fought on land. You don't win by droppin' a nuke and turning the territory into a fucking parking lot, see? That wouldn't bring you any more power. You got to beat the shit out of the other guy and then park on his property so he can't come back and claim it. You do that and you win. You don't do that and you lose.

"Now, the Air Force can't occupy land and the Navy can't float their ships on land, so there come the grunts to take the high ground and hold it. That's you and me, doing what they ask us to do."

Douglas was starting to feel better. He grinned at Kramer. "Seems pretty straightforward to me . . ."

Kramer studied Becker's face for traces of sarcasm. The gaze that met his was open and honest. "What happens if what they ask us to do turns out to be wrong?"

Becker smiled. "You qualified to judge that, Kramer? I'm not. I figure I'm doing good just to get the job done. We ain't gonna know if anything is right, wrong, or indifferent for a long time yet. Meanwhile, nobody ever promised me a light pack and a downhill grade."

V.

Platoon, Halt . . .

"Damn . . ." Lance Corporal LaBella stood as Tubes Douglas finished his story. "I don't remember no buck sergeant ever talkin' like that." His buddies added their comments until Douglas finally raised a hand.

"Like my grandpa used to say, still waters run deep. Just because the skipper sets his sights on one thing, it don't mean he ain't thinkin' about a whole lot more."

Douglas raised his field glasses and saw the mortar crews breaking out more ammo behind the gun pits. They'd be ready for a new mission in a few minutes. "Ring them bastards down at the FDC and wake 'em up. We got some rounds to get downrange."

LaBella walked toward the field phone, then stopped and pointed at the road leading to their observation post. "Better hang on, Gunny. Somebody's comin' to see us."

Douglas trotted down off the hill, squinting at the dust cloud raised by a jeep approaching at nonregulation speed. He'd have a word or two for the driver when he arrived.

The division sergeant major scrambled out of the vehicle before it came to a full stop and headed for Douglas. "Hey, Tubes. You gettin' any time on target?"

Douglas nodded, wondering what he'd done to merit a

visit from the division's senior enlisted man. "Skipper's down on the line knockin' their dick stiff. What brings you out to the boondocks?"

The sergeant major grabbed Douglas by an elbow and steered him out of the driver's earshot. "Tubes, listen, I got some bad news. The CG is gonna convene a general court for Captain Becker."

Douglas rounded on his visitor and started to laugh. Then he saw the expression that meant dead serious, straight skinny, no bullshit. "He's gonna what? For what?"

"It's that female lieutenant he's been runnin' around with. She's married to some second john out in the Med."

"Hell, the skipper knows that. She's legally separated. They ain't doin' nothin' wrong."

"Depends on who's callin' the shots, Tubes. Officially, the Marine Corps considers her married until they get a certified copy of a final divorce decree. That makes Becker guilty of home-wrecking the way the CG sees it."

"C'mon, Sarn't Major, they don't court-martial people for shit like that—especially not officers!"

"They do when they're tryin' to hang out a corpse for all the other sinners to contemplate." The Sergeant Major shrugged and tapped a temple. "You know the general is batshit about this kind of thing. It's a goddamn crusade with him. He figures to make an example of Captain Becker that'll sew this base up tighter than a popcorn fart. He puts the fear of God into people and no more hanky-panky."

"Jesus H. Christ . . ." Douglas uncovered and scratched at his scalp. "They're really gonna run this railroad?"

"There's an arrest order out as of an hour ago. They're gonna run him up and disk him out, Tubes. I figured you'd want to warn the captain. The way I see it, he gets a good lawyer who ain't beholdin' to the system and he'll probably beat the thing."

Douglas stood stunned as the sergeant major strode toward his jeep. "It's such a crock of shit . . ."

"It ain't the same Marine Corps we joined, Tubes." The sergeant major shook his head sadly and started to add more but Gunnery Sergeant Tubes Douglas was a green blur inside a cloud of dust as he pounded up the hill toward the field phone.

The three men headed his way all wore embroidered armbands over their uniform blouses. As they came closer, Becker stepped out of a gun pit and stared at two enlisted MPs flanking the Officer of the Day. He vaguely recognized the officer as a captain from some section on the battalion staff.

Both MPs saluted smartly as Becker smiled and nodded at them. The OD seemed uneasy. He inclined his head down along the firing line and motioned for the MPs to stand fast. Becker followed him for a few steps. "You gonna let me know at some point what this is all about?"

The OD turned and spoke quietly. "Jesus, Buttplate. I don't know how the hell to do this."

Becker grinned and thumped the man on the shoulder. "Shit, don't make a federal case out of it. You gotta arrest one of my Marines, go ahead. I'll get it squared away later . . ."

"It's not one of your Marines. It's you." The OD turned his clipboard at an angle where Becker could read the arrest and confinement order signed by his battalion commander.

"What kind of shit is this? What are the charges?"

"The CO will tell you the whole sad story. Meantime, I've got to take you back to the rear for confinement to quarters." Becker stared around at his Marines, all standing straight in the mortar pits, staring at the unusual confrontation. He knew there were other eyes watching up on the OP and in the Fire Direction Center. He swallowed hard and stepped toward the OD.

"OK, you got a job to do. I ain't gonna give you a hard time. Just one thing. Send the MPs back to your vehicle. I don't want my men watching me march off under escort like some fuckin' brig rat."

Signaling for the MPs to disappear, the captain waited, pretending to be engaged in trivial conversation with Becker. "If there's anything I can do while you're in hack, just let me know. I don't know what the hell you've done or haven't done, but I respect you as a Marine."

"Thanks, I appreciate it. Now let's go." They strolled casually off the firing line. As they passed the Fire Direction Center, Becker's executive officer ducked out from under the fly-tent canvas holding a field phone receiver.

"Gunny Douglas on the horn for you, Skipper."

Becker nodded but refused to accept the proffered phone. "Just tell him to drop by my quarters tonight, John. You'll be in command until further word . . ." The young first lieutenant cut a glance at the solemn-faced OD and then back to his commanding officer.

"Uh, anything I can do, Skipper?"

"Just continue the march, John. And take care of our Marines. You can reach me in my quarters."

Up on the OP, Gunny Douglas screwed the binoculars into his eyes and saw Captain Becker sitting in the back of the jeep pinioned by two MPs. He tossed the field phone receiver at one of his FOs and headed for the jeep parked at the bottom of the hill.

"You got the conn, LaBella. Tell the XO I had to make an emergency run to mainside."

There was a note on Second Lieutenant Becky Campbell's desk asking her to see Lieutenant Colonel Adelaide Spencer at her earliest convenience. Becky frowned at the note and sipped her morning coffee. Spencer was the senior woman Marine at Camp Lejeune, an administrative officer who was only nominally in her chain of command.

It amounted to an unusual request, but Lt. Col. Spencer had a reputation as an unusual woman. Rumor held that she considered herself the commanding officer for all women on the base, no matter what command they officially called home. The same rumors also had it that many male COs relied on Spencer to help deal with uncomfortable "female problems" within their outfits.

A veteran WM first sergeant once told Becky that Spencer had never recovered from the dissolution of all-female companies at posts and stations throughout the

Corps. The move robbed many aspiring women of the only chance the Corps would offer them to command.

Becky left her office, walked across a parking lot, and entered the main administrative building for Camp Geiger's Infantry Training School. She walked through a reception area and knocked on an office door bearing Lt. Col. Spencer's name and title.

Behind her desk, Spencer sat scribbling on a yellow legal pad. She looked up, pulled a pair of issue reading glasses off her nose, and glared. Becky was not invited to sit. This was clearly not a social call.

"Lieutenant Campbell reporting as ordered, ma'am."

Spencer grunted, replaced her glasses, and picked up a sheet of paper from the desk. "Lieutenant, you are hereby notified that you are under arrest pending court-martial. The charges are conduct unbecoming an officer, illegal cohabitation, and failure to obey a general order. You'll get full details and specifications from SJA, but I suspect you know what all this is about . . ."

"My God, Colonel, it can't be because of my relationship with Captain Becker . . . I . . ."

"You'd be best advised to keep your mouth completely shut at this point, young woman!" Spencer cut her off with a seering glance. Her cheeks were flushed and there were tiny beads of sweat popping out on her upper lip. "It most certainly can be, and is, about your relationship with Captain Becker."

Spencer paused to catch her breath. She didn't need this sort of hatchet-woman duty. It was disgraceful; distasteful and embarrassing for everyone concerned. Women were under enough performance pressure in a male-dominated Marine Corps. She picked up a neatly typed card from the edge of her desk, glared at Becky, and began to read.

"You have the right to remain silent. If you choose to make a statement . . ."

As Becky tuned out Lt. Col. Spencer's sonorous drone, tears began to trickle down her cheeks. Somewhere on the other side of the base, she knew, Becker would be listening to a similar litany. She was facing serious charges with potentially dire consequences threatening to taint the entire remainder of her life. No question about that, but Becky could muster neither righteous indignation nor self-pity as she stood listening to her inalienable rights as an American citizen.

Only one thought protruded beyond the numbing shock of this moment. It hung over her like a ghostly spectre in the stuffy room. She might totally, unmistakably—in her own mind and in the minds of others—be responsible for the death of the last Spartan. While others had tried with shot, shell, and blade in two wars to execute Buttplate Becker, they failed. She managed it with nothing more than self-serving passion. Becky Campbell stood at attention and hoped a human being could die from humiliation.

Spencer made tsking noises between her teeth when she was finished reading the rights of the accused. She glanced up over the rim of her glasses and saw the mascara cascading down Lt. Campbell's cheeks. Shoving a box of Kleenex across her desk, she motioned for Becky to use one.

"This is hardly the time for tears, Lieutenant. You might want to get a grip on your hormones. They seem to have led you astray."

Becky dabbed at her eyes and breathed deeply for a moment or two before she felt capable of rational speech. "I don't wish to make a statement at this time."

Spencer craned back in her swivel chair and crossed her hands over her stomach. "I didn't think so, Lieutenant Campbell. But maybe you can answer a question for me."

Becky nodded as Spencer eyed her up and down, side to side. "You seem like a fairly intelligent person. You look good in uniform. I'd say you had half a chance to make a go of it in the service. How in the hell could you do something like this?"

"Like what, ma'am?"

Spencer snapped forward in her chair and stabbed at the air with a slender finger. "Are you that dense, Lieutenant Campbell? How about disgracing yourself and the rest of the women in the armed forces? Females have enough trouble in the Marine Corps without someone like you putting us on the skyline and making everyone think we're nothing but a bunch of sex-starved man-eaters.''

She drummed her fingers on the desk blotter in a rapid tattoo, breathing angrily through her nose. ''Not to mention the fact that you've very likely helped bring Captain Becker's long and illustrious career to an end . . .''

The words, spoken almost as an afterthought, made Becky wince. She noticed Spencer gathering papers into neat piles. She was about to be dismissed.

''Colonel Spencer, ma'am, can you tell me what you think might happen?''

Spencer lit a cigarette and seemed to relax momentarily. Becky noticed the trace of sweat stains at her armpits and a tremor in the hand that held her lighter.

''There was a time, Lieutenant Campbell, when a thing like this would be dealt with in-house . . . for the good of the Corps. These days we have . . . people in the influential positions . . . who believe . . . well, they get the Marine Corps mixed up with . . . personal morality . . . that kind of thing. It makes it difficult for an officer to lead, uh, anything but the . . . the most conventional of lifestyles . . .''

Spencer exhaled a gout of smoke at the ceiling. ''What it boils down to is this. They don't want you, Lieutenant. They want Captain Becker . . . as an example. You'll be granted immunity and ordered to testify for the prosecution.''

Becky's voice was weak but firm. ''I will not testify against him!''

''You'll do exactly as you're ordered, Lieutenant Campbell. If you refuse, you'll wind up in Leavenworth. They've decided to push this—and your sex won't save you from doing brig time. You don't cooperate and you're nailed. You have a choice of going out standing up or feet first. Either way, you'll be expected to resign once the trial is over.''

''Unless the court-martial board finds us not guilty . . .''

Spencer stubbed out of her cigarette and shook her head.

"Good God, Campbell, this isn't Disneyland! Civilian standards do not apply here. You *are* guilty under the Code. Captain Becker *is* guilty under the Code. Your fellow officers cannot return any other verdict."

When she'd dismissed Becky Campbell to confinement in the BOQ, Lt. Col. Spencer shuffled papers and shifted personnel records from one pile to another. She was disappointed and disgusted at the same time. Busywork at her desk would help ease the anxiety. She'd had her eye on young Campbell for the past few weeks.

Pity about her, Adelaide Spencer thought . . . a pretty woman, in a girlish sort of way . . . really quite attractive. She might have been turned in the right direction given more time. I might have been able to do something for her.

Campbell should have learned what I did years ago, Lt. Col. Spencer mused. Sex is a whole lot better—not to mention safer—when it's kept between us girls.

When the jeep braked outside his battalion headquarters, Captain Becker was whisked directly into the CO's private office. He walked stiffly past the stares of the clerks and heard the muted rumble of whispered conversation build in his wake. The grapevine was vibrating under the weight of ripe fruit. The word would be out everywhere on the base by evening chow.

Becker stood at attention before his commanding officer—a man he'd known and served with for several years—and began to announce his presence. The lieutenant colonel, a long-time infantry officer who felt uncomfortable in formal military settings, waved him to silence and pointed at a chair.

"Buttplate, I don't know what the hell this is all about. Maybe you can tell me. I called the general as soon as I got the arrest order. He damn near hung up on me. Said the charges stand as written. He's already signed the court-martial convening order."

Becker swallowed hard. "What's the nature of the charges, sir?"

The CO reached for a sheaf of papers on his desk and

began to read. "You are charged with the following: Conduct unbecoming an officer, to wit . . ." What followed was a list of instances in which he was accused of consorting with Second Lieutenant Rebecca Campbell, United States Marine Corps, a married female officer, not Captain Becker's spouse.

". . . and wrongful cohabitation with subject officer, to wit . . ." The charge sheet outlined several instances when Becker and Becky had checked into motels together or spent the weekend in his BOQ room.

". . . and failure to obey a general order that it was his duty to carry out, to wit . . ." There it is, Becker suddenly realized. It's General Tobrey and his goddamn morality play. He nodded, nearly smiling, as the battalion commander finished reading him his rights under the Uniform Code of Military Justice. Yes, he understood. He understood all too fucking well.

"Shit, Buttplate. I feel like a jerk doing this. I don't normally have a man who holds the Navy Cross sitting here while I prep him for a fucking court-martial. What the hell is this all about?"

"Truth is . . . I fell in love . . ."

The battalion commander pulled a chair close to Becker's, sat, and stared into his face. Becker looked up from signing acknowledgment of his rights under the UCMJ. He saw sympathy. He saw a concerned man searching for a solution to a distasteful problem.

"Listen to me, Buttplate. There are a lot of people, up and down the Marine Corps, who think a lot of you and admire your record. I happen to be one of those people. I have never seen—and probably never will see—a better leader than you are. The Corps can't afford to lose people like you . . ."

Becker snapped the ballpoint pen closed and handed over the signed documents. "Apparently, General Tobrey disagrees."

"Goddammit, he's not the Marine Corps! You know it and I know it. He lost a daughter to dope, sex, and rock and roll, and he's been crazy on this morality shit ever since. And he's no combat man; he's a post Vietnam aberration."

Becker chewed on that for a moment but it didn't sit well. "I always admired the Corps for tolerating aberrations, but I didn't think they promoted them to general officer."

"The system has flaws . . ."

"I know that, sir. We've spent the past few years down in the ranks weeding out those flaws, trying to make a better Marine Corps. Hell, that's our job."

"Right. I'm a product of the system. You're a product of the system. The system works."

Becker was amazed under the circumstances to feel a grin form on his face. "I don't know, sir. An hour ago, you couldn't have convinced me otherwise. Right now, sitting here, I'm beginning to see another side of it."

The battalion commander grabbed his elbow and shook it. "There's nobody that counts in this green machine that wants you to take a long walk off a short pier. Now give me something I can use to turn this thing off!"

"Like what, sir?"

"You *know* what I mean." The CO's voice was a growl and he increased the pressure on Becker's elbow.

"You want me to make a statement? You want me to say she seduced me? You want me to say she lied to me about a divorce?"

"It would be your word against hers."

Becker pondered his options, searching and sorting; looking for a moral fiber he could grasp and trust. He felt anger, anguish, distrust, disdain, and profound sorrow. Conflicting signals kept him mentally immobilized at each critical crossroad.

"Is Lieutenant Campbell being charged, sir?"

"Yeah. Way I hear it, she's in hack out at the Q. Same charges, but you know they're after you. Senior Marine always fries in a case like this."

Becker rose and adjusted his lean frame into a position of attention. "Seems to me it's the system that's going to trial, sir. I have no statement to make at this time."

Tubes Douglas sprinted into the foyer of the mainside Staff NCO Club and headed for the nearest available phone.

He spilled a year's accumulation of portable crap out of his worn leather wallet and sorted through it with one hand while he dug for change with the other. Scribbled onto a well-creased remnant of a government envelope was a phone number he'd copied earlier in the year after a drunken, disjointed, long-distance reunion.

Despite the East Coast area code he punched into the phone, the voice on the other end conveyed a lilt of the South. "Harrison, Hapgood, and Kramer . . ."

"Lemme talk to Kramer."

"Who may I say is calling, sir?"

"This is Tubes . . . this is Gunnery Sergeant Douglas, Marine Corps, callin' from Camp Lejeune, North Carolina."

"I'm sorry, sir. Mr. Kramer is in conference. May I take a message?"

"Look, lady, me and Kramer were in Vietnam together. You know about Vietnam?"

"Certainly, sir." Some ice melted in the Deep South. "I had a brother and an uncle who served there."

"Right. Bum deal all around. But the guy who brought me and Kramer out alive is in trouble down here. I gotta talk to Kramer about it."

"He really is in conference. I'll be glad to pass him a message for you."

"OK. Tell him Tubes Douglas is calling . . . and Butt-plate is in big trouble. Got that? OK. He'll pick up the phone."

"Do you wish to hold, sir?"

Douglas eyed the small pile of coins strewn on the counter beneath the phone. He grabbed a five spot and waved it at a passing waitress.

"Ma'am, you're talkin' to a Fleet Marine here. I am prepared to hold until hell freezes over."

Leon Kramer glanced at the message pad the receptionist slid toward him across the broad, glossy surface of the conference table. Fortunately, the purple tint of his steel-rimmed glasses hid the startled look in his eyes. At this delicate point in a complex divorce settlement, he couldn't afford to let the opposition think he was rattled or distracted. He cleared his throat and stood, leaning close to the attorney representing the client's soon-to-be ex-wife.

"We're offering enough alimony for your client to lease a fleet of BMWs, Phil. The car is not on the table. I'm going to get coffee. When I return, we can get on to the next item . . ." Kramer breezed out of the room, aware that he'd won a minor point in negotiation and anxious to have the phone message explained.

"Tubes? It's Leon, man. How the hell are you?"

Douglas crammed coins in the phone. While the instrument gulped and beeped, he spewed out the story of Becker's predicament. He didn't know the details but he knew the nature of the charges. And—after sixteen years of kicking around the Marine Corps—he certainly knew bullshit when he smelled it.

"It's a fuckin' railroad, Kramer. We got this CG down here with his head up his ass, man. He's personally gonna turn the Marine Corps into Sunday School."

Kramer opened his leather appointment calendar and began to flip through pages. "Jesus, Tubes, this kind of stuff, it needs a specialist, you know? We're talkin' spirit and principle versus intent and interpretation . . ."

"We're talkin' Buttplate Becker."

"Yeah, I know. He deserves the best. Hell, man, I'm doing divorces and tax-evasion deals up here."

"Buttplate deserves a guy who cares about him in his corner, Leon."

Kramer spun in his chair and spotted the framed snapshot on the credenza behind his desk. The three of them, battered, bloody, and exhausted, ringed around a mortar. Here and there, the bloody hand or foot of a dead NVA trooper who made the ultimate sacrifice trying to silence that tube. That was one tough night. And after that, there could have been a lifetime of tough nights—in prison—but for Becker.

"Tubes, let's get off the phone and get under way here. I got some calls to make and get myself up to speed on the

UCMJ. You get to Buttplate and have him tell the SJA he
has retained me as his defense counsel. Tell him not to say
shit to anyone until I get there. Find me some place to stay.
I'll be there on Sunday.''

Douglas began to feel better. If Kramer was anywhere
near as good as a lawyer as he was a combat Marine,
Becker's odds were vastly improved. ''Hey, Kramer, this is
the marker, man. This is for Vietnam. Remember? You owe
him this one.''

Dial tone droned into Leon Kramer's ear and he gently
replaced the receiver. Yes, no question about that. He did
owe Buttplate Becker *at least* one. He swung to stare at the
picture and then closed his eyes. The debt was incurred in a
game that began in 1967, shortly after they arrived at Quang
Tri.

VI.

Backstep, March . . .

Headquarters of the 1st Marine Regiment at Quang Tri was actually a rambling collection of shot-up concrete buildings that formerly comprised a French Foreign Legion post during Vietnam's colonial days. The American Marines moved in like destitute squatters, covering shell holes with leaky canvas and pitching general purpose tents to escape the chilly, relentless monsoon rains. The air temperature in the area, less than ten miles from the DMZ, hovered somewhere around a comfortable seventy degrees.

But no one was comfortable. There was no way to stay dry and the comparative chill among men who had suffered the seering heat of Vietnam's summer brought colds that teetered constantly on the brink of pneumonia. The main sounds interrupting the steady thrum of rain on canvas were hacking, croupy coughs. Motivated men up and down the chain of command at Quang Tri grew numb under the torrent. Field operations against the enemy sputtered and slowed to a soggy crawl.

Kramer and Douglas developed annoying sniffles by the time their paperwork had been processed one more time and they'd deposited their bags in a leaky hooch in the second battalion area. Before they could find sick bay, the weapons platoon sergeant found them.

Staff Sergeant Calvin Crider was a huge black man with homemade tattoos all over his bulging ebony arms. His dusky, sun-saturated skin kept the amateurish snakes, dragons, and mysterious symbols from sight except under strong artificial light. The Marine Corps had done its best for Calvin Crider over the past fourteen years, but he'd never responded well enough to master more than rudimentary reading and writing skills.

Ignorance made Crider an angry man. He didn't like rain, he didn't like being a platoon sergeant in a chickenshit Headquarters & Service Company, and he didn't like the jive-ass attitude of his black replacements. He hated his platoon leader, he hated hotshots like Becker, and he hated the fact that he couldn't get promoted without coming to Vietnam and laying his sweet black ass on the line.

Unfortunately for Kramer and Douglas, the two newest of a dozen new guys assigned to the mortar platoon of H&S Company, Staff Sergeant Crider owned them—ratchet, satchel, and seabag—for the first week in-country. They were supposed to employ the "admin time" to orient themselves to Vietnam and to a combat command. Staff Sgt. Crider gave that mission low priority in his quest to turn the Quang Tri combat base from a series of hovels into a spit-shined home in which he could take pride.

Douglas and Kramer found Becker in the mess tent and complained about a long list of shit details on which their names were prominently featured. He told them to relax.

"Whatdaya want? Everybody fills sandbags. Everybody burns shitters. Just do it. Crider will get off your back soon as the rain lets up and we start operating again."

It was still raining hard at the beginning of their second week in-country when Crider called a formation of twenty nonrated men and started handing out work assignments. Some went to dig a trench around the regimental chaplain's tent, some went to burn shitters, some went to the armory to clean weapons, some went to help unload a flight of resupply helicopters at the Quang Tri airstrip. When all the details had been parceled out, Kramer and seven other black

Marines stood in the rain wondering what special delight the muscular, soul-brother Staff NCO had in mind for them.

"Ah got some news fer y'all." He paced back and forth in front of them like an angry, wet gorilla searching for shelter in a rain forest. "This tour gonna be tougher on y'all than it will be for them white dudes. And you can lay that shit directly on me. Any y'all think yer gonna get over because yer platoon sarn't is a splib, better change yer mind raht now. Black men in The 'Nam got a few things to prove . . . and a few things to unprove."

Kramer stared straight ahead, wondering which pressure-packed ghetto had squeezed Crider from one sort of bondage into another. Crider answered the question for him.

"Ah come outta West Memphis, Arkansas, fourteen years ago to join the Marine Corps. It took hard work and sweatin', but ah got ree-speck . . . and dig-ni-tee. Ain't nobody gonna fuck that up"—he glowered at them from under a hard ridge of scarred eyebrow—"particularly black Marines in mah own platoon."

Kramer stared back, trying to keep his smooth face open and innocent. Jesus, he thought, the white monkey on this dude's back must be a monster. Still, Crider was a proud man and there was a lot to be said for that.

"Y'all cop an attitude on me and you won't have to worry none about the gooks gettin' yer ass. Ah'll be raht here to take care of that!" Crider turned to point at a four-hole outhouse nestled between a row of GP tents. "Now y'all get hot and start burnin' that shitter."

Kramer caught the conspiratorial grins on the black faces around him as they left formation. He grinned back, starting to feel like a part of the unit. "Yeah . . . right on, dude . . . and thank y'all."

There were a few muted snickers. Kramer was about to run another imitation of Crider's lecture when he was staggered by a painful shot between the shoulder blades. He spun and stared into Crider's menacing face.

"Ah be watchin' yer black ass real close, *Mistah Kramer*. You best be gettin' de fuck wit' de program."

Crider continued to ride the boots in general and Kramer

in particular until Becker finally interceded with the company commander and got both of them released to his mortar squad. The monsoons would blow away south in the next two weeks. They had a lot to learn and not much time for school.

Under Becker's expert hand, they studied the miniature mortar and its ammunition family through constant drills. They learned to break the forty-five pound weapon into three basic man-loads consisting of baseplate, tube, and bipod. They learned how to lay the weapon for indirect fire and they learned to fire it directly onto a target by line of sight in support of advancing infantry squads. They were, Becker told them, the grunts' quick-draw, hip-pocket artillery unit.

Mostly, Kramer and Douglas learned to respect Becker's uncanny ability to hit a target with only the most basic calculation of range and direction to a target. The friendly sergeant was as accurate at mortar gunnery as he was exacting and demanding about the functioning of his crew: *very* accurate . . . and *very* demanding.

"We have to be quick and close. I got no time or use for a mortarman who can't bring it on target in three rounds or less."

They drilled with their weapon in the mud and rain until there was practically no need for Becker to give commands. A hand signal sent Kramer sprawling to slam the bipod into the ground, waiting for Becker to slap down the baseplate and for Douglas to twist the tube into its seat. They could usually get a high-explosive round on the way to any target within two thousand yards in less than two minutes.

After three weeks in The 'Nam, neither Douglas nor Kramer had been on anything more exciting than sentry duty and sandbag-filling details. Kramer caught many more of the latter than the former due primarily to being singled out by Crider. He made it a point to live with the harassment rather than complain to Becker or the platoon leader. The monsoons were breaking up and Kramer felt sure Crider would very shortly have more important things on his mind.

They were practicing on a clear day, trying to put a round

in a fifty-five gallon drum about five hundred meters from the mortar pit where the tube was positioned to provide illumination or defensive fire for the Marine perimeter. Kramer was on the sight, adjusting from the T-shaped aiming stake in front of the pit. He dropped two long and one left.

"It's your eye," Becker explained calmly. "You've got to get better at estimating range. With the 60 in direct fire, you won't have an FO to spot range for you."

Kramer stepped out of the pit and stood eyeing his charges. They were as ready as noncombat exercises could make them. "OK . . . finish up here, clean the mortar, and then start getting your gear squared away. We got a three-day patrol with Foxtrot Company starting tomorrow morning."

"Jesus . . ." Kramer popped the tiny sight out of its receptacle on the mortar bipod. He was ready for anything that took him away from the smell of burning shit. "It's about fuckin' time."

"We're gonna patrol around a ville complex called Nhu Le." Becker squatted and stared at them. "You may wish you were back here burning shitters by the time it's over. The gooks have had a good month to set in booby traps and get the open areas registered for fire. Here's the way we work it.

"We're two men short of T/O, so we hump double weight. We go with six rounds apiece and split the other ammo up among the riflemen in the CP group. We'll need Willy-Pete as well as HE. The Foxtrot skipper likes to prep tree lines and recon by fire. There's plenty of open paddies out there so we got to be ready to fire on targets of opportunity.

"Now, let me tell you what I expect. When we come under fire, you concentrate on getting that tube in action. Don't worry about anything else. Do your job and let the shit fly. The people that get dinged are the ones that freeze with their fingers up their ass. There'll be rifle squads out there screaming for fire support as soon as the first zip pops the first cap on us. When they whistle, we shoot. Any questions?''

Foxtrot had been beating the bush around Nhu Le for two days. They were on a basic cordon-and-search type operation, looking for enemy arms caches or supply dumps. The procedure was to surround and seal off a cluster of thatch huts, corral the villagers in a central area, and send riflemen through to probe and search.

The company commander was frustrated with the lack of results and desultory performance from men who were out of practice. Intelligence indicated a major stash of arms and ammo had been moved in the Nhu Le complex under cover of the rains. The supplies were reportedly destined for delivery to an NVA battalion known to be operating from bases in a hill mass that constituted a barrier between the villages and the South China Sea to the east.

His Marines were moving through the third of six villages in the hamlet and the nearest thing to a weapon they'd found so far was a homemade rice knife. Our luck should change soon, he thought, looking over a fearful clutch of squatting villagers who gabbled and hissed among themselves like a brood of hens. His instincts told him the gooks in this ville had something to hide. He'd expand the search here and snap some of the cobwebs out of his people.

''Sergeant Becker . . .'' The CO shoved by the radioman attached to his side by the handset umbilical cord and walked toward the center of the village where his attached mortar crew had set up their weapon. ''We need to expand the search here. You leave one man on the gun and take some of these CP people through the hedgerow. Shake down the hooches over there and see what you can find.''

Becker nodded and rounded up a spare radioman and several antitank gunners who were humping the bunker-busting light antitank weapons, known as LAWs. As they passed a shaded hooch he saw Crider crapped out and snoring lightly. He grinned, pointed, and shook his head. The other Marines in his search party did not seem amused by the sight.

They moved in single file down a paddy dike toward a tall hedgerow that separated one ville from a mirror image on the other side. The point man had just bulled his way through the brambles when there was a flash and a sharp explosion cracked out over the paddy.

"Booby trap!" Becker screamed and tackled Kramer, pulling him off the dike and into the muddy water. Kramer squatted in the slime, pointing his rifle out over the dike and wondering what to do. There were no targets in sight.

Becker swooped up out of the water and thudded by him at a dead run, headed for the hedgerow and screaming for a corpsman. Kramer stared at the fractured spot in the hedgerow. He could see one man down and twitching on the ground. Leaves and branches, ripped apart by the blast, slowly filtered down like green confetti.

When a corpsman scrambled up the dike, Kramer fell in behind him. He was tense but clearheaded. Not frightened, merely anxious to be with Becker now that his war had started. Most of the other Marines with Becker automatically deployed themselves in a small defensive perimeter around the wounded man. They stood waist-deep in the paddy, pointing M-16s over the dike and staring at the undisturbed terrain through wide white eyes. Kramer ran past them and stepped through the hedgerow right behind the corpsman.

He saw a grisly tableau. The doc was bent over a Marine who lay at an odd angle with his legs twisted up under him. The corpsman unsheathed a razor-sharp knife and tore away at the casualty's web equipment. Unsure of what to do, feeling helpless and sick, Kramer merely knelt and tried to add his eyes to the perimeter watch. But he kept glancing backward, over his shoulder, feeling the spectre of death on the chilly wind.

He'd burned shitters with the mangled man on the ground. His name was Wilson, a thick white guy from Kentucky, who seemed friendly enough when he was whole. Now he was a pitiful sight, but Kramer could not keep from staring.

"What the fuck are you looking at?" The corpsman

motioned at Kramer. "Get a goddamn radioman. Tell him to raise the Six and get an emergency medevac in here. This guy is fucked up bad."

Kramer moved off down the dike looking for a telltale antenna waving in the air over the paddy. Suddenly, he heard the familiar boom of Becker's shotgun and launched himself into the muddy water. Two more shots followed in rapid rhythm. To his right and left, Marines were ducking lower in the water, waiting for some assessment of the threat. It didn't seem right to Kramer. Someone should check; see if Becker needed help.

He scrambled out of the water and pounded up the paddy dike. Becker was kneeling beside a hooch on the other side of the hedgerow, jamming rounds into his shotgun and staring at a patch of jungle that formed the far boundary of the village.

"Little cocksucker got away," he mumbled when Kramer plopped down next to him. "He probably rigged that frag-in-a-can that got Wilson." Kramer wondered what that meant and Becker explained as they walked back toward the corpsman and the casualty.

"Some amateur sonofabitch ate chow out here and left his ration can lying around. The zips pick it up and discover it's just the right size for one of our frags. They put the grenade inside the can, pull the pin, and attach a tripwire. Then they rig the can and wire across a trail or hedgerow and some dipshit bombs into it without checking. The wire pulls the frag out of the can, the spoon pops, and, presto, instant dogmeat."

When they reached the casualty, the doc had him straightened out for field first aid. He was tearing open field dressings with his teeth and monitoring a thready pulse with his bloody hands. "He's torn up like a sieve. Fucking shrapnel opened up his chest and put holes in all the sinus cavities. I don't know if I can keep him breathing long enough for a medevac to get here."

Becker rounded on Kramer. "Tell the radioman to push the medevac. I'm gonna see if I can help here."

Kramer located the radioman back in the paddy and

passed the message. No one seemed anxious to give him another task so he returned to the hedgerow. Becker and the corpsman were sprawled next to Wilson in conference.

"Got to keep his heart going." The corpsman pointed at a loose flap of flesh that rattled as Wilson struggled to keep breathing. "You give him mouth-to-mouth while I try to close the chest."

Becker rose onto his knees over the wounded man. "Jesus, poor fucker's got more holes in his face than I can count." Kramer stared in open fascination. He noticed a peculiar metallic odor wafting up from the casualty. That's the smell of fresh blood, he realized as he watched the corpsman stuff battle dressings into Wilson's violated chest.

Becker arranged the man's head so he could administer resuscitation. He placed his mouth over Wilson's and began to breathe in gusts of air as the corpsman pushed on the man's chest to stimulate heartbeat. Becker gagged and retched, spitting bile onto the muddy ground.

"Can't get any air into him! It keeps blowing out of all these holes." The corpsman bent to place his ear next to Wilson's heaving chest.

"We're losing him, Becker. Where the fuck is the helicopter?" Becker backed away to study the problem from a different angle. Watching from nearby, Kramer wondered how Becker could seem to be studious and aloof next to the gore. The man's nose was almost completely gone and there were rents under each eye where shrapnel from the grenade penetrated. The air Becker breathed in merely whistled out through the sinus cavities.

"Got to play him like a flute . . ." Becker glanced up for the first time and seemed to notice Kramer. "Get over here and help. Stick your fingers here, here, and here."

Becker pointed to gaping holes as Kramer knelt near the wounded man. He moved his hand slowly toward Wilson's distorted face, reluctant to touch the damaged flesh. Becker grabbed his wrist and dragged him into contact. Kramer found the palm of his hand jammed into Wilson's pulpy nasal cavity with two fingers stretched to cover holes in the sinuses beneath the eyes. Becker told him to press hard and then bent over to resume breathing for the injured man.

It seemed to work. Wilson's chest rose and fell regularly and Kramer could feel no air whistling past his fingers. The corpsman shouted as Becker turned his head and puked a stream into the dirt near Wilson's body. "We might just be able to keep him alive long enough . . ." Tension coursed through the three men working on the casualty.

Kramer barely noticed when the company commander stepped through the hedgerow streaming filthy water from his trek through the paddy. "Chopper's airborne. ETA five minutes."

Becker acknowledged the information with a nod, sitting back on his heels. The corpsman poked and prodded for a moment or two and then raised himself to stare at Becker across Wilson's bloody chest. No words were necessary. Kramer felt the shared tension ebb in a flood, leaving Wilson floating in a calm, quiet pool. He stared down at the pitiful face and saw the slack features, undisturbed by internal pressure from pulse or breathing. He was touching death; afraid to move his hand for fear some palpable part of what was once PFC Wilson would escape.

"Change the priority to routine, Skipper." The Doc pulled a sweaty OD towel from around his neck and draped it over Wilson's ravaged features. "He's gone—shock—too cut up to save."

Kramer watched the CO for reaction. There was not much visible. He winced slightly, breathed a long, whistling sigh, and shook his head. "Get someone to help you and wrap him up, Doc. Give the tags to the company gunny. As soon as the chopper gets here, we're moving out."

Becker struggled to his feet, stretching aching muscles. Kramer stood beside him feeling useless, callow, shocky, and confused. What could you say? What should you say? Nice try? No sweat, we'll save the next one? What was the protocol in the face of sudden death?

The company commander approached Becker and stared out over the village with vacant eyes. "That was your scattergun I heard after the blast?"

"Yessir. I spotted a gook running away from the area just after I got through the hedgerow. He was NVA. Green uniform and all. I fired three rounds but he didn't even slow down." Becker indicated a thatch of bush just before the foothills surrounding Nhu Le. "He disappeared into that heavy green over there. I expect he's with his buddies on the high ground now."

The CO nodded. "Probably sent down here to keep an eye on us. We need to get up there, find those dudes, and nail 'em if we're ever gonna secure this area." There was not much else to say. Death in the family or not, he had a company to run and a mission to accomplish. The captain turned, but Becker gently grabbed an elbow.

"Sorry about Wilson, Skipper . . . but he's no boot. He knew better than to go crashing through that fucking hedgerow without checking for tripwires."

"I know." The captain turned his eyes to the mountains and chewed on his lip. "We got to get into night positions. Tell Staff Sergeant Crider to take charge of the body and divide his gear up among the others in the CP group." The company commander moved away, tugging his radio operator like a pull toy and alerting his other platoons that they were moving.

Kramer watched the grim-faced corpsman use his knife to cut Wilson's dogtag out of the lacings of his jungle boot. After a while, nearly everyone takes the tags off their neck and threads them into the laces of their boots. The doc recommended Kramer do the same. Blast effect rips them right off your neck, but they can usually locate at least one boot among the hamburger.

It didn't matter much, Kramer decided. Who cares about identity? When you're dead, you become a lump of cold meat, just like Wilson. He helped to wrap the dead man in a muddy poncho as a CH-46 helicopter shuddered into a nearby rice paddy. The last look he got of Wilson's shattered face reminded Kramer of a picture he'd seen in a sports magazine on the flight to Vietnam. An up-and-coming middleweight had been caught by the ringside photographer just as he took a horrendous knockout blow to the jaw. The staggered fighter had the same bug-eyed, startled look on his face that Wilson wore in death.

The radioman shouted over the clatter of rotor blades. "That's our chopper. Can't stay long. They say get him aboard in a hurry."

Kramer, Becker, the doc, and the radioman grabbed ends of the poncho and began splashing toward the helicopter. A crew chief knelt in the door waving an arm at them to hurry. Medevac choppers were prime targets and this one had no gunship support.

Rotorwash bathed the four of them in slimy paddy water but they managed to muscle the poncho containing Wilson's body aboard the helicopter. It began to stagger and buck, lifting dead weight into the muggy air as the four drenched pallbearers scrambled away from it in the peculiar running crouch infantrymen always seemed to adopt around idling helicopters. There was no chance they could be hit by the whirling rotorblades but they ducked just the same.

Kramer turned around to seek shelter from the blowing spume churned up by the chopper's engines and noticed that most of the rest of the company had their backs turned and their heads tucked into their shoulders. They just turn away when you're dead, he thought. No one cries or makes a fuss. You go from live buddy to dead meat in just a few seconds . . . and everyone turns their back on you.

Kramer was near the CP when the company commander gathered his platoon leaders and passed the word. Wilson's death and the discovery of several more booby traps in the Nhu Le area convinced the battalion commander to explore the high ground. They would begin at first light.

"The plan is to locate the fuckers, bottle them up, and call for reinforcements. Six says he's got two more companies and maybe even enough airlift to reinforce in a hurry if we manage to make contact. We'll set up a patrol base and rotate platoons to sweep the foothills."

The CO folded his plastic-covered map and stared into the eyes of his first platoon commander. "If you run into gooks, hold what you've got and send me some grids. The idea is to locate 'em and then pile on. Choppers are inbound right now to resupply us. Staff Sergeant Crider will be around to pick up people for a working party.''

Kramer tried to hide but he got nailed when Crider came by Becker's gun position looking for hands to help with unloading the helicopters. Becker bitched. He told Crider that Kramer was needed to help improve the gun position and plot illumination for night activities. Crider told him to shut the fuck up and send Kramer down to the LZ.

Kramer spent an exhausting hour splashing through the paddies between the LZ and the company CP, humping rations, water, and ammo. Crider harassed the working party unmercifully. He seemed even angrier than he was in the rear, making constant references to Wilson's death as the result of sheer stupidity. Kramer kept his mouth shut, but every time he passed Crider, he thought he smelled fear.

He dumped the last case of rations unceremoniously at Crider's feet and turned to leave the CP area. Crider snatched at him and spun him around. "Kramer, you beginnin' to piss me off. Pick up them rations and pile 'em over there with the others.''

Kramer shrugged out of Crider's grasp. "What fuckin' difference does it make? You're just gonna break 'em out to issue anyway.'' He was turning to walk away when Crider knocked his helmet off his head with a teeth-rattling slap.

"You don't throw shit at me, nigger.'' Kramer glared at Crider. The epithet was enough to make him fight in other circumstances but he was confused by it here. It was the first time he'd been called nigger by another black man. He was surprised and angry to discover it stung even worse than the few times in his life when it had been sneered at him by a white man. Crider moved closer and growled into Kramer's face.

"Ain't no fuckin' slack out here, boy. Y'all wanna complain, y'all gotta come through me. Now pick up them rations and stack 'em over there with the others.''

Kramer stared at Crider's red-rimmed eyes and decided the man was nuts; insane with prejudice, real or perceived; it didn't matter. Like some shit-heel cracker in a white sheet, Crider picked his target and bored in with all the vengeance of a wronged Crusader. The Marine Crops command structure and the swift and sure discipline of the battlefield suspended any right of appeal and gave Crider the opportunity to swoop down like an avenging angel. For some reason, Kramer stood at Ground Zero.

"Crider, I don't know what the fuck you got against me. You wanna play Marine green lifer and fuck with your own kind, ain't nothin' I can do about it. But I'm only gonna take so much shit . . ."

Crider grinned, showing several gold teeth, and cocked his head to the side. "You gonna take all the shit I want to dish out, Kramer. Ain't no En-Double-Ay-Cee-Pee in mah platoon."

Kramer blinked and stared in Crider's eyes. Black bigots were even more frightening than the white variety. He'd have to deal firmly with Crider or die trying. There was no other way to handle a snarling, racist dog, no matter what color he was. It was all a matter of finding the right time and place.

Foxtrot Company's first platoon set out in predawn darkness, carrying only weapons and ammo into the hills. Packs were left in the Company CP where Becker and his mortar crew were consulting a map and computing a fire plan to support the advancing infantry. Becker sent Douglas for field glasses and watched the platoon as they moved, strung out in a loose left echelon across the face of the hill.

"They'd better take a look around before they cross that clearing." Becker focused the glasses and turned to Kramer. "I make it about a klick and a half. Charge two. Set up to cover that clearing."

The first platoon commander halted his unit at the edge of the open space and moved across in fireteam rushes. While Becker watched from below, the last man cleared the exposed area without incident. It was a perfect spot for an ambush, but the gooks chose not to exploit it. First platoon disappeared into the green vegetation covering the high hillside.

In a clearing near the mortar pit, the company commander paced and listened to the intermittent communication from his bank of radios. It was mostly chatter from the advancing platoon, position reports, and phase-line crossings. Occasionally they reported a cave or spider-hole . . . negative contact.

At noon, the CO reached for a handset. "Fox One . . . Fox Six. Bring it on home. We'll launch Fox Two when we have you in sight, over." He dropped one handset and reached for another to alert his second platoon for a move. Before he could press the transmit switch, a radioman shouted and waved for attention.

"Sir! Contact! First platoon says they're takin' heavy incoming."

Becker scrambled out of the mortar pit and turned his glasses on the hill. There was nothing to see but he heard the distant rattle of rifle fire. At his back, the company commander swung into action like a machine.

"Raise Iron Hand Six and tell them to stand by for a SitRep on the contact. Get me Echo One Actual. ALO, see what's in the air for us . . ."

Two radio operators and the pilot assigned to Foxtrot Company scrambled for their sets. The captain spread his map and tried to compute a location for the contact from the last position report sent by his first platoon. A handset appeared in front of his nose.

"Sir, can't contact the Actual, but I've got his platoon sergeant on the hook." The CO snatched at the handset as Becker moved closer to monitor the developing situation. He motioned for a nearby radioman to switch his set to squelch so they could hear the communication with the unit in contact up on the hill.

The heavy breathing of the first platoon sergeant created an intermittent roar over the snap and crackle of small arms. "Six, this is Two. We walked into a shit sandwich. We started down this little draw and the bastards popped up out of bunkers on either side. The lieutenant is down and we can't get a corpsman up to him. I'm trying to maneuver but there's at least one heavy machine gun on either side of the trail. Can't move at all. Request fire support ASAP, over."

"Roger, understand, Foxtrot One. Just sit tight. I'm working on some air for you. Send me a grid, over."

When the first platoon sergeant sent his best guess, the company commander marked the numbers on his map sheet with a grease pencil and then handed the map to his company gunnery sergeant. He found the grid and placed a finger on the spot where they thought the platoon lay pinned down by machine guns. The CO noted the squads must be in a slight valley between two pieces of high ground. He glanced at the gunny and shook his head.

"Jesus Christ! How many times do I have to tell them to move on the high ground and watch their flanks?"

The air liaison officer moved over to the CO clutching his own handset. "There's a flight of Fox Fours airborne about fifteen minutes from here, Skipper. They've got snake and nape aboard. All I need is a grid on the gooks."

Becker and Kramer watched closely as the CO considered his options. The first platoon had to be extracted from the murderous ambush. Jets with 250-pound general Purpose bombs and napalm would do the trick but they'd have to drop dangerously close to friendlies. The gooks were tucked in tight to avoid just such an option on the part of the Americans. He reached for a handset as various voices around him chattered for attention.

"Skipper, the F-4s are getting low on gas. They want to know if you need them . . ."

"Sir, Iron Hand Six wants more info. He says it's taking too much time to get the airlift organized . . ."

"Captain, Foxtrot Two wants to know if he should move out at this time . . ."

The captain waved a distracted hand in the air. "Tell everyone to wait out. Stay off the net until I can get back in contact with Fox One."

Several tense moments passed before the first platoon sergeant responded to his radio. His voice was strained and cracking. "Skipper, there's more gooks up here than we can count. Looks like we ran into a battalion CP or something.

They're movin' all around us . . . within five-zero meters, over!''

A muscle began to twitch in the captain's lean jaw. "Shit, we gotta move. Tell Fox Two to take off and head for the high ground. ALO, scratch the air . . . danger close."

The company gunny turned from his radio. "Can we shoot some arty in there and take the pressure off so they can withdraw to linkup with Fox Two?"

"Negative, Gunny. He's got gooks crawling up his asshole. Too close for artillery. We'll have to wait for second platoon to get up on the hill and relieve the pressure."

The company gunny caught Becker's glance and raised his eyebrows. It was a solid one thousand meters of thick jungle between second platoon and the ambush site. Without some sort of fire support to keep the enemy from snapping the trap shut, first platoon might not survive to be relieved.

Becker rechecked his own map, swept his eyes across the hillside, and formulated a plan. "Skipper, we can get the 60 mike-mikes onto the gooks. Let me put some rounds out there and they can adjust me on to the machine guns. We can buy enough time for them to withdraw partway down the hill and keep the gooks from chasing them until Fox Two arrives."

"Negative, sergeant Becker. The grid isn't good enough. They can't adjust. It's a Chinese fire drill up there. We'd need an FO somewhere up on high ground to keep from dumping friendly fire on them."

Becker brought his map to the CO and jabbed at a spot with his finger. "See this little finger right here, sir? It overlooks the gook positions. I can get somebody up there to adjust and dump HE right into their fuckin' hip pocket."

The captain looked up toward the spike of rock that Becker spotted. It might work. "OK, we'll give it a shot. Send one of your people up there to spot. You stay on the guns and make sure we don't fire short."

Becker sprinted for the mortars, indicating a general direction of fire and screaming for the ammo-humpers to start breaking rounds out of their canisters. Staff Sergeant Crider began to round up volunteers for the fire control party. He hooked Kramer with a finger and appointed him forward observer.

Becker hopped out from behind the mortar and confronted Crider. "Wait one, Crider. He's a fuckin' new guy. You can't send him up there with just a fireteam. What if they hit gooks along the way."

Crider propelled Kramer toward the small group of volunteers and then rounded on Becker. "CO says he wants somebody who can call fire on a gnat's ass. That would be your boy, right, Becker? You trained him. He's got to get his feet wet sometime."

Becker spun to face Kramer and handed over his binoculars. "Look, man, you get up onto that peak and send me a mission. Let the grunts handle the gooks if you run into any. Hear? Don't stop for anything. I won't have time for spotters. You'll have to adjust HE. We'll bracket that draw and move the rounds from side to side. You just see I don't drop one into first platoon."

Kramer nodded and started to trot after his infantry escort. Becker stared at his back for a moment and then decided there was nothing more to say. Kramer had seen death once today. He had about fifteen minutes to get up on that hill and prevent more.

Located next to Becker's tube was another 60mm mortar. "You fire on me," he told the gunner. "I'll feed you the sight dope and you just keep pumping rounds." They went to work setting their mortars to fire in the general vicinity of the original grid sent by the first platoon sergeant. Becker wished he could call and adjust the larger 81mm mortars back at battalion, but they were well out of range. It was up to the pair of 60s, Kramer's call, and Becker's fine-tuning to keep rounds on a target moving steadily closer to friendlies.

The CO hauled his radio operators over to Becker's mortar position. "Echo One reports he's lost contact with everyone except one squad and the gooks are right on top of him. Second platoon says they're within five hundred meters and they can hear the machine guns."

Becker assimilated the information while he leveled both mortars and prepared them for firing. Douglas was busy pulling powder bags off HE rounds to give them proper propellant to reach the target. It would be close and costly. Becker glanced at his watch, looking for something to do besides wait for word from Kramer.

Finally, the platoon radio crackled causing the tense group around the mortars to start. "Foxtrot Six . . . Fox Whiskey. Fire mission . . ."

The numbers came rapidly. Becker spun the wheel of his portable plotting board and translated them into sight settings. Nothing major was necessary. The first round would land long as calculated. It was accurate corrections that counted and they were all up to Kramer.

"Tell him I'm gonna pop the first one long on the gun-target line . . ." Becker manipulated the deflection and elevation handwheels as he talked to the radio operator keeping him in contact with Kramer.

He turned to Douglas standing by on the other side of the muzzle and nodded. "Charge three. Hang it up there . . ." Douglas slipped the fins of the first round halfway into the mouth of the small tube and waited. Becker whispered a silent prayer for a good lot of ammo and then pulled the sight off the mortar to protect it from recoil damage.

"Fire!"

Douglas let the round drop to the bottom of the tube where it impacted with a hollow thunk. They ducked away from the muzzle as the metallic clang of base charge and burning propellant indicated number one was on the way. Becker straightened, reseated the sight, and leveled the mortar for a second shot as a cracking echo rolled down the hillside. Everyone stared but the fall of the first round was out of view. The radio crackled.

"I got it . . ." Kramer had wisely decided to dispense with radio procedure. Speed was critical. "Drop one hundred . . . right one hundred." Becker bent over the sight, shouting his settings to the second mortar crew as Kramer filled the air with a running commentary.

"I see both machine guns . . . and lots of gooks down

there. Looks like first platoon is spread out along a sort of ditch. Don't see much return fire. Better get another round out in a hurry . . ."

Becker signaled and a second round clanged out of his tube. Douglas whispered, counting the seconds for time of flight and then they heard the echo. Kramer responded immediately.

"Range correct! Fire for effect on the left side of the ditch. Make deflection corrections to spread the sheaf. Gooks are moving! Better tell Fox One to di-di out of there as soon as the rounds start coming in . . ."

The company commander grabbed for a handset as Becker bounded over to the second mortar. "Douglas, you keep pumping them out there. One turn of deflection between each round." Douglas checked the sight and began to feed rounds into the tube. Every spare man in the CP formed a line to pass ready rounds up to the guns.

Becker bent to set up the second mortar tube and shouted at the radio operator. "Tell Kramer I'm gonna range on the right side of the ditch with the second mortar." He squinted through the sight and made rapid calculations, keeping a picture of the impact area in his mind.

He was ready to fire as Douglas dropped the fifth round into the tube. The first round from the second weapon clanged away and Becker took a moment to glance at the company commander. In midsentence, the CO showed him a thumbs-up.

"OK, One . . . we're gonna slam the backdoor now and send Foxtrot Two into the attack. You pull out under the mortar fire . . ." Apparently, the mortar barrage was easing the pressure on the first platoon.

Kramer's correction was late. As the sound of impacting rounds rolled down the hillside, experienced ears picked up small-arms fire from a different direction. The radio rattled. "Six, we got heavy incoming up here. Gooks tryin' to take out the OP."

Becker screamed at the radioman. "Tell him to let the escort handle it. Send me corrections!" Kramer's transmission was jerky but more controlled when he finally responded. He was under fire, ducking and dodging, still trying to keep his eyes on the impact zone and correct the fall of the mortar rounds.

"We got it under control up here . . . first round, second gun . . . was short fifty and left. Add five-zero; right one hundred."

Becker beamed as he spun dials. Kramer was solid under pressure; a good man. He shouted at the assistant gunner over the ear-numbing clang of his own gun. "Hang it up there, half load . . . fire!

Kramer was on the radio with corrections almost immediately. "You're on it. Fire for effect! Same deflection changes as you used on the left side. I'll stand by here to adjust as Fox Two gets closer. I can see them moving up the hill now."

While both assistant gunners worked like well-oiled pistons, dropping rounds into the smoking muzzles, Becker scurried between the two mortar positions making minor deflection and elevation changes to spread the impact of the falling rounds among the enemy positions. He worked with his eyes closed much of the time, scanning an internal picture of the situation up on the disputed hillside.

At least twenty rounds of 60mm high explosive fell among the North Vietnamese Army troops surrounding Foxtrot Company's first platoon on the hill mass. Kramer kept his eyes on the area and reported the enemy troops were being pushed back by rifle and machine-gun fire from the relief platoon.

"I can see them pulling back now . . ." Kramer's voice was ecstatic. "Add five-zero, both guns. Same deflection. Fire for effect." Becker made the corrections while Douglas scrambled to prepare more rounds for firing. He shouted a count over the clang of the smoking mortars.

"We're down to nine rounds of HE. You want me to break out the Willy Pete?"

The company commander responded, "Cease fire, Sgt. Becker. Arty can chase them for a while. We need to save some of that ammo." The artillery forward observer, who had been following the action on his map, had 105mm howitzer rounds falling on the hillside in a few minutes.

Kramer radioed that the second platoon was sweeping through the area, policing up survivors from the first platoon and treating the wounded. The company commander ordered his fire control part down off the observation post with a well-done message. Then he squatted by Becker and slapped him on the shoulder.

"Nice work. You saved some lives. Fox Two says they've got a hefty body count up there. I'll let you know later. In the meantime . . . well, I'm just damn glad to have you aboard. Let me know if there's anything you or your people need."

Becker paused in the middle of breaking down the hot tubes. "Sir, this was the first time out for Kramer. I'd say he did real well. I'd say he did outstanding."

"Roger that, Sgt. Becker. I'll have the gunny write something up when we get back to the rear."

Tyrone Douglas and Leon Kramer stood watching the awards ceremony under a scorching sun that glared up at them in shimmering waves off the macadam surface of Quang Tri's newly constructed airstrip. Becker was front and center, receiving the Silver Star from the commanding officer of 2nd Battalion, First Marines.

The medal citation being read by the adjutant certified him a hero, calm, cool, and collected under pressure and responsible for saving a lot of lives a couple of months ago on a disputed hillside near Nhu Le. Innovative and expert with the 60mm mortar, the citation called Sergeant Becker, indicating at last that he was a man who reflected great credit on himself and on the United States Marine Corps.

Douglas snickered and poked Kramer in the ribs. Becker certainly didn't look like a certified hero, standing out there in raggedy-ass utilities and a pair of scuffed, white jungle boots. They had scrounged the best uniform they could from buddies and the bottom of moldering seabags to get Becker ready for the ceremony. Still, no amount of artistry with needle and thread could hide the fact that this hero was a field Marine who worried more about shrapnel than he did about spit and polish.

As the battalion commander and his sergeant major approached Becker to pin on the medal, Douglas elbowed Kramer again. "Christ, he looks like he just stepped off of a parade deck and Becker looks like he just crawled out from under one."

"Shut the fuck up, Tubes . . ." Kramer hissed at Douglas, staring straight ahead and locking himself into a rigid position of attention despite the irritating rivulets of sweat that tickled cross his rib cage. "He deserves some respect."

"And you don't?"

"Forget about it, man. It don't mean nothin'."

"Uh-huh. Tell that to Buttplate."

Becker had spent most of the previous evening in a rage over news that his was the only decoration to come down from division after the action at Nhu Le. He'd stormed off to see the battalion sergeant major and returned to spend the rest of the night in tight-lipped silence. Kramer tried to shrug it off. "Typical Marine Corps shit," he said. "Senior guy gets the glory. It don't mean . . ."

Becker nailed him before he could finish. "It *does* mean something, goddammit! It means a lot. They don't mind spreading the bullshit; they ought to share the bennies!"

Becker never fully explained himself, but it was clear that he was not about to drop the issue. Douglas and Kramer saw his jaws working as he accepted the medal from the battalion commander.

"Sir, I think you should know there is a Marine who helped save first platoon that day . . . and he's not been recognized in any way. I'd like to know why."

The battalion CO squinted in surprise at Becker's comments. He glanced at his sergeant major who stood at his side holding the plastic box for the medal that now dangled from Becker's utility blouse. "What do you mean, Sgt. Becker?"

"Sir, there's a man in my squad, Lance Corporal Kramer, he adjusted the rounds that we fired to cover what was left of first platoon that day. The platoon sergeant was one of thirteen who survived and he told me personally that if it hadn't been for the FO calling precise shots, they'd never have gotten off the hill at all.''

"Sgt. Becker, yours was the only award recommendation I received regarding that action. I suspect the company commander simply singled out the Marine he felt was most responsible for the success of the—"

"That's not true, Colonel." Becker kept his eyes locked somewhere over the CO's shoulder as he interrupted in a clipped voice. "I saw the company commander last night and he told me he forwarded a Bronze Star recommendation for Kramer. He said it must have been turned down at battalion.''

"Well, I assure you that is not the case. We've got to move on here. I'll have the sergeant major look into the situation. Again, my personal congratulations, Sgt. Becker."

Through most of the following weeks, 2/1 continued to comb the jungle-covered hills near Quang Tri, searching for a decisive fight with the NVA units Recon claimed to see on deep-penetration missions. The Vietnamese winter of 1967 was nearly ended and it did not appear either side would score heavily before the new year dawned. Both the Americans and their Vietnamese enemy punched and counterpunched like wary boxers looking for an opening.

It was sometimes frustrating, more often futile. The elusive enemy seemed to be purposefully avoiding pitched battle as the year drew to a close. Meantime, Buddhists thronged the temples in Quang Tri City, hung bunting, baked pastries, procured fresh piasters, and prepared for Tet, the pivotal season marking the beginning of the Lunar New Year. Even the higher Marine command to the south in Danang seemed to avoid prolonged projects or operations that carried over into the multilateral cease-fire period that had been agreed upon for Tet.

Everyone seemed to be resting, resupplying, reinforcing, or recuperating. Everyone except Sergeant Becker who extended his tour in Vietnam yet another six months. Word was that he would be transferred, possibly to Fifth Marines—the famous "Pogey Rope Fifth"—that was being moved from the Danang perimeter north to Phu Bai as part of an expanded Task Force X-Ray supporting sister elements of the Third Marine Division. Becker told his Marines he was not about to leave Quang Tri until he'd settled the question of Kramer's missing decoration.

Kramer was still having problems with Staff Sergeant Crider and trying hard to keep a low profile. He urged Becker to let the situation rest rather than stir the stick around the weapons platoon sergeant.

"No dice, Kramer. You wanna go to college and law school and all that? Maybe a medal might help. Who knows? Anyway, the system oughtta work equally for everyone. You rate that fuckin' medal and I'm gonna see you get it."

Becker was also having his run-ins with Crider. The senior NCO kept his conduct toward Kramer and a few others he'd singled out teetering on the edge of blatant misconduct or harassment. Still, Kramer found himself stuck on dangerous outposts, riding shotgun on Rough Rider convoys, sweeping mines, and walking point more often than other Marines in Becker's shorthanded squad.

Unfortunately for the case Becker tried to make against Crider with the H&S company commander, there were too many hazardous missions and too few people available to carry them out. Headquarters and Service Company was an available pool of manpower and it was hard to keep shorthanded rifle company commanders from dipping into it at will. The record showed that Becker's Marines—including Kramer—got only their fair share of hairy deals; perhaps a modicum more.

That was because Crider knew where to draw the fine line. He'd been in the Corps long enough to know his detractors would have to prove conclusively that he was doing something more than squaring away a Marine who—in his considered professional opinion—needed it. The fact that both parties to the dispute happened to be black made substantive charges hard to handle and harder to prove in an arbitrary and subjective situation facing an outfit in combat.

Kramer held up remarkably well under most of the pressure. In public, he was stoic; too proud of his mean street origins to admit he suffered under Crider's impact on his life. In private, during long nights in the rear with Douglas and Becker, he let the venom flow from his soul.

"I'm tellin' you, the motherfucker is clearly trying to kill me! I don't know what his problem is, but he don't want me to get out of The 'Nam alive. He keeps sayin' people like me fuck up his Marine Corps. He almost came unglued yesterday when I asked the skipper to write a letter to go with my college application. What the fuck difference does it make to him?"

Douglas had his own considered opinion. "Tell you what, man. Crider is jealous. There it is. That ignorant shit-heel don't want another splib doin' any better than he is. He can't fuckin' stand it."

Kramer cut a look at Becker. "Seems to me the system fucked up makin' Crider anything higher than a goddamn private."

"Hey, the system ain't perfect . . ." Becker jammed his plastic spoon viciously into a can of pear slices. "Guys like Crider can keep a low profile and trade time for power. Works fine until the shooting starts. Then comes a major fucking adjustment . . ."

"Then how come Crider ain't dead?"

"He'll get his . . ."

Staff Sergeant Crider got his from the battalion commander while the unit was preparing for a sweep that was touted as the last major operation before the Tet cease-fire period. The battalion sergeant major, a wiry Irishman with a pug nose scarred by shrapnel from a Chinese hand grenade tossed onto some nameless hill in Korea, dropped by the weapons platoon to see Becker.

"I don't normally feel like Staff NCOs should air their dirty laundry in public, but I wanted to come by and let you know Crider's been relieved of duty. He's packin' his trash right now. Tomorrow he goes to Danang. The Division sergeant major is gonna have his ass.''

Becker wanted to shout for joy but the sergeant major held him firmly by the elbow. ''The reason I'm tellin' you about this is because I figger we owe you an explanation. You remember the day you got the Silver Star and burned the CO's ears about your man Kramer?''

Becker nodded and glanced over to the ammo bunker where Kramer and Douglas were restacking rounds and burning spare powder increments. Kramer would be ecstatic as soon as he could let him in on the news. The system was working.

''Well, it seems you were right. I checked with your CO and he distinctly remembered endorsing a Bronze Star recommendation for Kramer. Meanwhile, we ain't got a record of it up at battalion. I started tracking it and found out from the company clerk that the last man to handle the paperwork was Crider. Anyway, I faced him off about it and he went off the deep end. He wound up admitting he'd shit-canned Kramer's recommendation and two or three others. Battalion commander relieved him on the spot . . .''

Becker felt vindicated, but Kramer was the injured party. ''Does this mean Kramer finally gets his medal?''

''Yeah, he gets the Bronze Star as soon as we can get a chop on a new recommendation.''

''Thanks, Sergeant Major.'' The senior NCO turned to leave but Becker stopped him. ''Hey, Sergeant Major . . . how does a guy like Crider get to be a Staff NCO in the first place?''

''Standards get all jacked around—civilian bullshit—I don't know.'' The sergeant major rubbed his battered nose. It was clearly a troublesome subject he'd considered at some length. ''Seems like a black guy don't have to be a good Marine, you know? He's just gotta be black and the Corps is gonna promote him so they can show there ain't no prejudice. It's OK if the black guy's a good Marine in the first place, but if he's a guy like Crider . . .''

''Well, Kramer will be glad to hear about it. Crider damn near killed him a couple of times.''

The sergeant major shuddered and shrugged. He wasn't going to solve the problem standing inside a tumble-down compound in South Vietnam. There were more pressing matters at hand.

Kramer was glad to hear the news but he was also curious. "What's gonna happen to Crider?"

"Depends on the division sergeant major, I guess." Becker considered what he'd been told. "Knowing Crider, he'll probably scream prejudice and get himself promoted. Don't make any difference. At least he's off our backs."

"Yeah? And if he skates, that sonofabitch will be right back in the bush tryin' to kill his own people. It ain't right, man . . ."

Under the muggy canvas shelter the battalion senior NCO's had erected to serve as an off-duty recreation area, Staff Sergeant Crider was enjoying his last night at Quang Tri, drinking Black Label beer from rusty cans and letting everyone know just what he thought of this chickenshit, racist outfit. He wasn't worried about the future. In fact, he was fairly sure he had the system by the ass. It was a long stretch between indictment and conviction and he'd spent most of the afternoon laboring over a long letter to his congressman back in The World.

Crider was buying but none of the other NCO's wanted much to do with him or his free beer. The word was out. Crider could piss and moan and say what he wanted about being a black man in a white man's Marine Corps, but everyone knew the truth. Crider had fucked over the troops. There were few more mortal sins in senior enlisted circles.

At 2200, Crider sat alone in the tent, mumbling and rambling about mistreatment and injustice. No one was around to hear his tirade. He'd managed to drive even the most dedicated drinkers to their beds. That was fine. He could sit and sulk until the beer ration ran dry.

Kramer felt the firm, plastic bulk of the Claymore mine in his hand as he crept through the dark passage between the shitter and the Staff NCO tents. He was night-blind and there was no moon to help guide him but he'd made a good reconnaissance before sundown and his mental map was working.

There was a fighting hole just off to his left. He'd trigger it from there. No way to trace a Claymore, and if he placed it right, nobody hurt but the intended target. Kramer crawled over the sandbags surrounding the hole and dropped the magneto firing device where he could locate it in the dark. He slithered into the gloom, carrying the mine and keeping an eye on the sliver of yellow light that spilled out of the Staff NCO beer tent.

He stopped about thirty meters from the canvas structure and turned the convex side of the Claymore to face the light. He wiggled it slightly and jammed the device's two wire legs into the ground. Reaching into his blouse he hauled out the blasting cap and wire spool. When he had the cap seated in the well on the top of the mine, Kramer began to crawl back toward the hole, unreeling wire behind him.

Justice is a bullshit concept, he thought as he made the final electrical connection and waited for Crider to leave the tent, just ask any black man in Southeast D.C. Right and wrong don't mean shit. At least in The 'Nam you could rely on a certain process of natural selection to weed out the rotten bastards. When one of them escaped, when combat didn't carve off the rancid meat, well, you had a lot of opportunities to fix things.

Kramer picked up the Claymore firing device and slipped off the safety. When you thought about the stakes involved, when you thought about the lives wasted or the pain inflicted, when you thought about all the killing and maiming that went on in a place like this . . . well, murder was a bullshit concept too.

He held that thought resolutely as the tent flap parted and Crider stood weaving drunkenly in a wash of yellow light. He would have to stagger right over the Claymore to reach his own tent. Kramer watched him lurch forward on wobbly knees and began to count steps. When he reached ten, he squeezed on the Claymore trigger. Nothing.

Kramer squeezed again and again, the snap of the trigger

lever sounding like pistol shots in the night. Still nothing. He glanced over the edge of the hole at Crider's looming shadow and jiggled the electrical connection. He tried again in tearful frustration, despite the fact that Crider had staggered past the mine and out of the killing zone.

Crider began to sing some throaty version of a Charlie Pride tune as he disappeared into the shadows. Kramer heaved the firing device at the bottom of the hole and considered giving chase. He could probably find something hard and heavy enough to crush that thick skull. Halfway out of the hole, he saw another shadow emerge from the line of sagging tents. This one moved toward him.

Sergeant Becker stood outside the hole with a foot propped up on the sandbags. In his left hand was the Claymore mine. The neatly clipped firing wire dangled from his right hand. He stared at Kramer silently for a moment and then slid into the hole dropping the Claymore next to the useless firing device.

"You were really going to kill that fucker, weren't you?"

Kramer supposed there wasn't much use in lying. "I had it planned so well, man. I can't believe he got away."

"You still got time before he leaves tomorrow."

Kramer collapsed in the bottom of the fighting hole and shook his head. It was a long time before he spoke. "No, man. Crider skates by me. I ain't got the guts. Thought I did, but I don't. I'm glad you stopped it."

"You know they'd have caught you eventually. The Corps frowns on shit like this big-time. You'd have shot more holes in yourself than you did in Crider."

Kramer heaved a huge sigh and started to stand. "Fuck it. It's over. Let's hit the rack."

"Nope. Not yet." Becker pulled him down to the bottom of the hole. "You know, Leon, you got me in a trick here, man. I ought to turn you in for this stunt tonight. According to the book, it's my obligation; my duty to do that. I shipped over in the Marine Corps, see? So I guess that makes *me* a lifer . . . and lifers can't go around lettin' snuffies blow away other lifers. That would be fucking up the system, wouldn't it?"

"Listen, Buttplate, you gonna burn me over this shit, go ahead and do it, but don't sit here and preach. The fucking system eats its young and you know it! You hang around this green motherfucker long enough, they're gonna kill you too."

"Shit, man . . . the stakes are real high in this kind of game. You gotta know them stakes before you ante up. I expect I *will* get nailed . . . if not in The 'Nam, then in the next place. It don't matter to me as long as it's honorable. I just don't wanna run, or quit or break . . . or lose any good people needlessly."

"Jesus Christ! You're married to this whole thing, ain't you?"

"Yeah, and I've got to take care of my in-laws. That's why I ain't gonna turn you in." Becker straightened and breathed deeply of the scented night air. "Now police up this trash and hit the rack."

Kramer watched him climb out of the hole and felt a warm flood course through his veins. He knew then that he would survive The 'Nam. He might even make it through college and maybe even law school. Becker was the kind of guy who would die trying to make it happen.

"Hey, Buttplate, thanks, man."

"*Semper Fi,* Leon . . ."

VII.

Platoon, Halt . . .

CONDUCT UNBECOMING
AN OFFICER AND A GENTLEMAN

Any commissioned officer, cadet or midshipman who is convicted of conduct unbecoming an officer and a gentleman shall be punished as a court-martial may direct.

Article 133
Uniform Code of
Military Justice

Discussion: The conduct contemplated may be that of a commissioned officer of either sex or that of a cadet or midshipman. When applied to a female officer the term ''gentleman'' is the equivalent of ''gentlewoman.'' Conduct violative of this article is action or behavior in an official capacity that, in dishonoring or disgracing the individual as an officer, seriously compromises his character as a gentleman, or action or behavior in an unofficial or private capacity that, in dishonoring or disgracing the individual personally, seriously compromises his standing as an officer. There are certain moral attributes common to the ideal officer and the perfect gentleman, a lack of which is indicated by acts of dishonesty or unfair dealing, of indecency or indecorum, or of lawlessness, injustice, or cruelty. Not everyone is or can be expected to meet ideal moral standards, but there is a limit of tolerance below which the individual standards of an officer, cadet, or midshipman cannot fall without seriously compromising his standing as an officer, cadet, or midshipman or his character as a gentleman. This article contemplates conduct by a commissioned officer, cadet, or midshipman that, taking all the circumstances into consideration, is thus compromising.

GENERAL ARTICLE

. . . all disorders and neglects to the prejudice of good order and discipline in the armed forces, all conduct of a nature to bring discredit upon the armed forces, and crimes and offenses not capital, of which persons subject (to the UCMJ) may be guilty, shall be taken cognizance of by a general, special, or summary court-martial, according to the nature and degree of the offense, and shall be punished at the discretion of that court.

Article 134
Uniform Code of
Military Justice

Discussion: Article 134 makes punishable all acts not specifically proscribed in any other article of the Code when they amount to disorders or neglects to the prejudice of good order and discipline in the armed forces or to conduct of a nature to bring discredit upon the armed forces, or constitute non-capital crimes or offenses denounced by enactment of Congress or under authority of Congress.

b. *Disorders and neglects to the prejudice of good order and discipline in the armed forces.* The disorders and neglects punishable under this clause of Article 134 include those acts or omissions to the prejudice of good order and discipline not specifically mentioned in other articles.

c. *Conduct of a nature to bring discredit upon the armed forces.* "Discredit" as here used means "to injure the reputation of." This clause of Article 134 makes punishable conduct that has a tendency to bring the service into disrepute or that tends to lower it in public esteem. Any discreditable conduct not denounced by a specific article of the Code is punishable under this clause.

In a dimly lit, foul-smelling bar a quiet block from the raucous neon tangle of topless joints and pawnshops that littered Jacksonville's notorious Court Street, reporter Jim Payne nursed watery draft beer and waited for the arrival of his secret source. He'd picked this bar primarily because the jukebox was broken and the bartender was willing to run a tab.

Payne sipped, enjoying the silence and examining his background notes compiled from the Jacksonville daily's morgue files. It was your basic love triangle, but nothing to grab headlines across the nation—except for the circumstances and the personalities involved. That made the case something special—and he had the inside track.

The story would work. It was all a matter of angles. This kind of thing was not unheard of in Marine Corps circles. Fewer officers were involved than enlisted Marines, but still a fairly ordinary set of circumstances in an outfit where fully half the married men left their families regularly for extended deployment overseas.

Normally, the Corps dealt with the miscreants quietly and kept their dirty laundry in the dryer rather than flapping on a public line. So, the case was slightly different—both parties are Marine officers rather than a Marine involved with a civilian. So, the illicit sex angle was fairly juicy. From Payne's jaded perspective that made it a good story, but not a headline-grabber.

What kicked the case up onto the front page was the identity of the man involved. The morgue was full of references to Captain Thurmond "Buttplate" Becker, war hero, mustang officer who rose through the ranks, holder of the Navy Cross, a Marine's Marine, the last Spartan. And that guy knelt at the chopping block with a general officer holding the axe. Is this the way the Corps treats its heroes when they err on the end of a stiff dick?

Payne glanced up from his notes and saw Rodney Claiborne enter the bar. He signaled, watching as the lanky lawyer ambled over to slide into the booth. When Claiborne had swept the nearly empty room with his eyes and adjusted his civilian clothes, Payne upended a glass and poured beer.

"I called and got the official line from the Public Affairs Office. Pretty juicy case, given who's involved."

Claiborne drained his glass and held it out for a refill. "It's a dynamite, Jim. Unique all the way around. We'll set precedents in military law."

"You gonna prosecute personally?"

"Got to. The general insists on it."

"Uh-huh. Thing like this can't hurt your career, can it? If you win . . ."

"Can't lose. They're guilty on the face of the evidence."

"Maybe. But there's a hell of a lot more to this story than right or wrong and you know it. Have we got a deal?"

"Yeah. Like I told you, Jim. You got the inside track, exclusive and confidential, provided you steer the national media to me."

Payne extended his hand to seal the bargain. Given his regular beat covering activities on the base, the big-time reporters who picked up on the story would seek him out for background. He could hold up his end of the deal . . . and maybe even follow Claiborne out of the boondocks.

"You know the angle, Rod. The major media boys are gonna interview the Old Corps types and they aren't gonna be happy with a hometown hero going down in flames."

"Hey, these days that'll be seen for what it is—macho chest-beating. Society is changing all around Jacksonville and Camp Lejeune. The Corps can't exist in a vacuum."

"Maybe, but it seems like Buttplate Becker is trying." Payne hauled out copies of old news clippings he'd made before leaving the office. He arrayed them on the table and swept the headlines.

BECKER DECORATED FOR SAVING TRAPPED PLATOON

BECKER AWARDED NAVY CROSS FOR GALLANT STAND

BUTTPLATE BECKER: A PRO IN AN UNPOPULAR PURSUIT

WO BECKER WINS OCS LEADERSHIP HONORS

VIETNAM HERO SERVES WITH MARINES IN BEIRUT

BECKER DECORATED FOR STOPPING ISRAELI INCURSION

Payne motioned for a second pitcher of beer and scratched at his scraggly beard. "Seems to me you guys picked a pretty hard target this time."

"Bullshit . . ." Claiborne leaned across the table. His voice was cold and harsh. "He's not a hero anymore. He's a criminal in the eyes of military law. If he's such a True Believer, how come he's sticking it to another officer's wife? Let's hear the Old Corps cretins answer that. He's guilty, caught in his own trap, and they can take his medals and melt them down to make a tombstone."

The fresh beer arrived as Payne stuffed the clippings into a folder. When the bartender disappeared into the shadows, the reporter fiddled with his pen and stared at Major Rodney Claiborne. Was there more to this than blatant self-interest?

"Tell me something, Rod. How do you feel—as a Marine officer—extinguishing one of the Corps' shining lights?"

Claiborne didn't seem disturbed by the question. He sipped beer and motioned for Payne to shut his notebook.

"This is off the record. OK? Here's how I feel about it. Becker's career is already at an end. He's not smart enough to know it, but it's all over for him. Look at Becker and a few others like him who are still hanging on to the past, they're dinosaurs.

"Yeah, he's a rags-to-riches story on the surface, but where is it going to lead in the modern Marine Corps? You tell me that. He made captain, and he might make major, but that's it. The Corps doesn't allow guys like Becker to advance into significant levels of command. No intellectual capacity beyond the rifle company; no polish to succeed at higher levels."

"And you don't think the dinosaur is gonna kick and claw to survive?"

"Becker will see this for what it is . . ."

"What is this, Rod?"

"Euthanasia."

Jacksonville's tiny airport was typically quiet for a Sunday morning. A few crew-cut Marines grunted and gyrated before a whining, beeping bank of video games and bored, potbellied, former-Marine rent-a-cops prowled the area sucking coffee from paper cups. The day's single Piedmont Airlines flight would be arriving in a few minutes to disgorge a sleepy load of traveling tobacco auctioneers headed for market and some Marines headed for duty at Camp Lejeune.

Gunnery Sergeant Douglas watched the aircraft taxi toward the terminal and tried to relax. Back at Lejeune he had wired in an entire network of senior NCOs to respond to requests for favors. Kramer would need inside information and legwork during the pretrial period and Douglas knew he could count on buddies who thought Becker was getting a bum deal.

The desire of the senior NCOs to quietly muster behind Becker had been the only highlight of the past week. That and the look on Claiborne's face when Douglas handed him the papers indicating a high-priced civilian lawyer from Washington was arriving to represent Becker. They'd never expected him to call out the heavy artillery.

Douglas spotted Kramer at the top of the stairs leading from the aircraft. He looked fine, smiling with the pure joy of seeing his old friend again after all the years since Vietnam. Kramer was maybe a little softer around the middle. The pissed-off tightness around his eyes and mouth had disappeared but he was the same guy. The sleek wardrobe and distinguished grace of his carriage couldn't hide the facts from Douglas.

It was Leon Kramer—former Lance Corporal—the same man who had humped with him and Becker through the jungles of their youth. When he cleared the gate, Kramer dropped two heavy briefcases and threw his arms around Douglas.

"Good to see you, man. Welcome back aboard."

"I can't believe it, Tubes. A fucking lifer . . ."

Douglas picked up the bulky briefcases and staggered toward the baggage claim area.

"Damn, Leon. What the hell have you got in these things?"

"Ammo, man. You ought to be used to humping that. I got copies of case law, opinions and definitions. Everything I could find concerning this kind of situation."

"Well, you and Buttplate are gonna need plenty of ammo. This whole deal is a railroad job. I know it, Becker knows it, and so does everyone else who ain't still shittin' boot-camp chow."

Kramer pointed at a fine leather two-suiter bumping along the baggage carousel. "Now all we've got to do is prove it."

"There it is. What's first?"

"Get me checked into a hotel somewhere near the base. I need to get some background from you. Then I need to see Becker, this Lieutenant Campbell, and my worthy opponents."

Douglas led the way out toward his battered VW van in the parking lot. "Buttplate and the lieutenant are in hack out at the BOQ. That's no sweat. I can get you an appointment with the SJA probably tomorrow. Damn, Leon. I feel a whole lot better now that you're here."

"We'll get this shit thrown out of court or make some kind of deal. Buttplate Becker is not going to go down for the count while I'm around to fight for him. You can bank on that."

"I am banking on it, man. So is Buttplate."

LEJEUNE OFFICER CHARGED
SEXUAL MORALITY AT ISSUE

By Jim Payne

JACKSONVILLE—A well-known, highly decorated Marine officer goes on trial here next week in an unusual case that hinges more on a military jury's perception of acceptable morality than criminal conduct. Captain Thurmond "Buttplate" Becker, holder of the Navy Cross for heroism in Southeast Asia, has been formally charged with conduct unbecoming an officer and gentleman for allegedly having an affair with a female officer, the wife of another Marine who is currently serving with forces on emergency duty in the Indian Ocean.

Also charged in the explosive case, according to a spokesman for Major General Darwin Tobrey, commanding the 2nd Marine Division at Camp Lejeune, is First Lieutenant Rebecca A. Campbell, who was the partner in what Marine sources described as "a torrid, scandalous affair" that has continued over the past six months.

Those same sources, who asked not to be identified, confirmed that charges have been filed, an investigation conducted, and a general court-martial scheduled for Becker. The top legal expert at the base, Major Rodney Carrington Claiborne, Staff Judge Advocate for the 2nd Marine Division, will serve as prosecutor. Becker's defense will be handled by Leon C. Kramer of the law firm Harrison, Hapgood, and Kramer in Washington, D. C.

The base spokesman would make no comment regarding the exact details of the alleged misconduct, citing the need to avoid compromising the opinions of the jury of Becker's peers that will be selected to serve on the court-martial board. What's known at this point is that Becker, a twenty-year Marine veteran who most recently served in combat in Beirut, is accused of carrying on an affair during which he was sexually intimate with Campbell, who is legally separated but not divorced from her husband.

Sources in the North Carolina State Attorney General's office indicated "a situation of this nature would never come to trial" outside the military establishment. Becker's defense is likely to rest on the issue of whether or not a crime has been committed in the eyes of the law. A base spokesman pointed out "Marines are subject to both individual state laws and the Uniform Code of Military Justice. We are pursuing this case as a violation of the latter, not the former."

In other situations of this nature, Marine officials indicated, a public trial by court-martial is rarely conducted. Both parties are normally transferred and admonished or punished by some less-conspicuous means such as a written reprimand in their permanent service records. The publicity and exposure of lurid details is generally something the Marine Corps would rather avoid, according to veteran Marines who commented on the case.

There seems little chance for a low-profile trial in Becker's case. Major wire service reporters and TV network correspondents have already begun contacting the base to make arrangements for covering the courtroom activities.

Both Becker and Campbell have been confined to their quarters on base and meet regularly only with their attorneys or other parties assigned to the case. Neither defendant was available for comment, but a source in the Staff Judge Advocate's office did indicate that Becker is the real target of the court-martial ordered by General Tobrey himself.

Rebecca Campbell is unlikely to have to answer the misconduct charges lodged against her, the sources said. She will be granted immunity and ordered to testify for the prosecution. Under military law, she faces stiff penalties including the possibility of imprisonment if she refuses to testify in the controversial trial.

Reaction among Marines at the base regarding the court-martial is mixed. Several sources, who asked not to be identified, expressed shock and anger that a Marine with Becker's war record and history of outstanding service should be embarrassed by such a trial. Others indicated a conviction would do much to reduce what they described as "a serious moral crisis at Camp Lejeune" involving sexual misconduct among families of deployed Marines.

Veteran observers in and out of uniform agreed that the real issue in the controversial court-martial is not guilt or innocence of the parties involved. "Clearly what's at issue here," said Dr. Rudolph Hester, professor of law at the University of North Carolina, "is the military's definition of acceptable moral conduct for an officer."

Dr. Hester, contacted by telephone at his office, said the precedent-setting legal action may well create waves in military circles that crest well beyond where they were intended. "This sort of thing goes on all the time in our society today," he stated. "We cannot and do not bring it to trial because the issue of acceptable sexual conduct is inexplicit where it concerns consenting adults. What is right and what is wrong is largely a matter of individual beliefs and precepts. Now you have the military saying what's commonplace in the civilian arena among private citizens is not acceptable in the private lives of their officers. A conviction in this case would set a standard. Whether that's right or wrong, it seems to me, is largely a matter of individual conscience."

A friend of Becker's indicated he was speaking for the majority of long-service Marines who don't believe there should be a trial. "A man like the skipper (Becker)," said Gunnery Sergeant Tyrone Douglas who served with Becker in Vietnam and Beirut, "is an inspiration to all Marines, especially the younger enlisted troops. Marines take care of their own and I believe the system will take into consideration what Captain Becker has done over the years."

Major Claiborne rattled the newspaper and set it aside on his desk. Not bad for the opening salvo, he thought. Things were beginning to heat up around Swamp Lagoon. His phone messages included two from network reporters in

New York. The train was on track but there were some dangerous curves ahead. His major task outside the courtroom would be to get everyone involved to maintain their resolve.

He was generally happy with the phone conversations from higher headquarters, even if the icy tone in some senior voices made him shiver. The military lawyers watching the case from on high had warned him clearly. He had no choice but to win now that the press was pumping the story into the public stomach.

He'd also heard from the staff secretary that Tobrey was taking some heat from fellow generals. They didn't much care for the idea of a public trial pitting Marine Corps morality against the civilian version. It wouldn't help recruiting and retention to make the Corps look like a Trappist monastery. A three-star from Norfolk had apparently reminded Tobrey in a secure-line conversation that the Corps had "very little to gain and a whole hell of a lot to lose" in the trial.

Fortunately, the CG was holding his ground. Claiborne knew no officer above the general in the chain of command dared to interfere at this point in the procedure. Doing that would constitute an indictment of a general officer's decision-making capabilities. The senior officers would stand united behind one of their own—right or wrong.

Claiborne hid the newspaper and rummaged for a file folder on Second Lieutenant Rebecca Campbell who was due to knock on his office door in just a few minutes. Reporting seniors called her a strong-willed person on her fitness reports. That likely meant she'd balk and bitch over the grant of immunity and subsequent testimony.

Campbell appeared smart and cagey on the surface but her glands were secreting where Becker was concerned. Claiborne made a note in her file. Perhaps he'd pull back on the security; make some provision for them to get together before or during the trial. Maybe even let them get laid. It might cement Becker's determination to save her from punishment. He felt certain he could rely on Becker to sacrifice himself to save her, but it paid to back your bets, especially when you were facing a civilian shyster with a vested interest in the case.

Kramer had asked for and been granted a midweek audience with Claiborne and General Tobrey. Maybe he had a plea bargain in mind. Claiborne didn't think Tobrey would stand still for a wrist-slap at this point. The train was too far down the track. He snapped the file closed and answered the tentative knock on his office door.

She reported with stiff efficiency, a slight twitch at her eyebrows giving the only indication that she was anything but calm and resolved. Claiborne directed her to have a seat and returned her flat gaze with a cool smirk. She was on his turf and he was in control.

"Lieutenant Campbell, as trial counsel in the government's case against you, I am empowered to make an offer of full immunity from trial on the charges which you face in return for your cooperation as a material witness in the case of the U.S. versus Captain Thurmond Becker. You'll need to examine this pretrial agreement and sign there at the bottom where your name is typed."

Becky sat making wet handprints on the patent-leather military purse in her lap. She stared at Claiborne and did not look at the papers he pushed toward her. "I will not testify against Captain Becker, sir. You can take whatever steps are necessary against me, but I will not testify."

Claiborne leaned back in his swivel chair and steepled his fingers. "Let me present you with some facts in this case, Lieutenant. To save time, we'll be as realistic as possible. If you stand trial on the charges currently lodged against you and are convicted, you face dismissal, forfeiture of all pay and allowances, and confinement at hard labor for up to two years. You'll never get that sort of sentence from a court-martial board. You'll simply be summarily dismissed from the service.

"However, if you fail to testify as ordered in a general court-martial where you are cited as a material witness, I can guarantee you dismissal under dishonorable conditions, forfeiture of all pay and allowances, and as much as a maximum five-year sentence in a federal correctional institution.

"Here's the bottom line, Lieutenant Campbell. Accept immunity and testify and you avoid hard time. Refuse it and you *will* go to jail. Your sex may have gotten you into this mess, but it will not get you out of it."

Her eyes moistened. She blinked to hide it, and assumed a stern expression. "Major, I love Captain Becker. How can you ask me to help ruin his career?"

"It seems to me the ruination of his career is something more properly laid on your plate than on mine, Lieutenant. Be that as it may, you're losing composure when you need it most. Take these papers along to your BOQ and look them over. When you've decided to sign them, give me a call and we'll discuss the nature of your testimony."

Becky rose and wiped at her eyes with a knotted Kleenex. "I wouldn't hold my breath waiting for that call . . ."

Claiborne stared at her and pointed a long finger toward her nose. "Don't compound the trouble you're already in, Lieutenant! Dismissed."

He sat quietly for a few moments after she walked out of his office, ignoring the lights on his phone blinking for attention. Campbell didn't scare easily. But he still had a tactical ace in the hole. Becker would walk barefoot on hot coals to keep his lady love from getting burned. He picked up the phone and ordered the security relaxed out at the BOQ.

Becky had barely composed herself with a dash of cold water on her tear-streaked faced when there was a knock on the door of her BOQ room. She tossed a stack of messages on her desk and whispered a silent prayer of thanks for the interruption. She'd rather speak to anyone other than the press that was beginning to hound her by phone.

She'd never met the tall black man who stood framed in her doorway, but she knew it had to be Leon Kramer. She'd read the papers and seen the pictures. This was the man who held Becker's fate in his hands, an old friend from Vietnam who should be coming after her with a gun.

Kramer pursed his lips for a moment, examining her critically, and then let his face warp into a grin.

"Forgive me for staring, Lieutenant, but I never thought I'd meet the woman who could manage to capture Buttplate Becker's heart. I am duly impressed."

She invited him in and watched as he plopped a bulging briefcase next to the messages on her deck. He found a chair and dropped into it with a sigh. Becky sensed pain, but no anger or nervousness. Leon Kramer, slouched in the spindly desk chair in her BOQ room, exuded confidence and competence. She wanted him for an ally. She wanted him to understand. Becky fought to overcome the flood of emotion that threatened to bring back the tears.

"I guess you know about me," Leon Kramer leaned forward and spoke in soft, serious tones. "I served with Becker back when we both had nothing but war and survival to keep our minds occupied. I don't mind telling you that I owe him a lot. Frankly, I consider him one of the best friends—black or white—that I've ever had. You may also have heard that he saved my life along with several others on more than one occasion in Vietnam."

Kramer stared deeply into her eyes and then reached out to pat her hand. "All that is to put my position in perspective for you, Becky. I'm out to save Becker any way I can." Kramer folded his long fingers in his lap, crossed his legs, and leaned back to examine the most damaging material witness against his client.

She returned his gaze and chewed on her lower lip for a moment. "My position is similar, Mr. Kramer. I love Thurmond Becker with all my heart. We have that in common, I guess. But you're trying to save him and I'm being set up to destroy him. What are we going to do?"

His infectious grin warmed a cold spot down deep in the pit of her stomach. "Why, we're gonna fight, girl. Long and hard as necessary. That's the way Marines do it."

His words broke through the dam of her resolve and the tears flowed. Kramer offered a handkerchief and gripped her hand firmly. "Let's get that out of your system now, Becky. We've got some serious talking to do."

She dried her eyes and poured coffee while Kramer peeled out of his jacket and loosened his tie. He sipped at the brew and then extracted a yellow pad from his briefcase.

"You know it's very important for you to tell me the whole truth here, Becky. Just talk and add anything you think might be important concerning your relationship with Becker."

She started from the beginning with her marriage to John right after graduation from Basic School at Quantico. Kramer was a good listener, prompting her with his eyes or a quiet question when she began to wander from the facts of her courtship and love affair with Buttplate Becker. After an hour, she ended the story saying she'd seen the evidence compiled by the Naval Investigative Service.

Kramer scribbled and made no immediate response. She refilled their cups and sat down on the edge of her bed. "It looks pretty bad, doesn't it?"

Kramer put his notes away and reached for the steaming coffee cup. "Becky, let's get something straight between us here. You and I are on the same side in this case. We both have Becker's best interests at heart. There's no use lying to you or giving you false hopes. They've got him pretty well nailed.

"In the steely, puritan eyes of the U.S. Marine Corps, you are both guilty of misconduct. Look here, the charge—and the definition of the offense in cases like this—is open to a lot of subjective judgment. Having a love affair—sleeping with someone who is not your husband or wife—can be interpreted as misconduct for an officer, despite the fact that people who don't wear a uniform are screwing each other like minks on the other side of the fence. It's *this* side of the fence that we have to concern ourselves with.

"If I tried to formulate a defense based on the fact that you are legally separated from your husband under state law and just waiting for the formality of a divorce, the prosecutor just jumps up and yells 'irrelevant and immaterial.' The fact remains that you and Becker carried on a sexually intimate affair without benefit of marriage. Depending on who's doing the interpreting, that can be construed as conduct unbecoming an officer. In some people's judgment, officers don't engage in sexual relations outside marriage. The fact that one of the officers involved happens to be married only compounds the problem.

"And then there are the related questions of 'conduct prejudicial to good order and discipline' and 'conduct which might reflect discredit on the armed forces.' Becker can be logically accused of engaging in conduct that sets a bad example for others to follow. Forgive my bluntness here, but the question posed will be if Becker can hop into bed with another guy's wife, then why can't the Marines he's responsible for leading do the same thing?

"I presume you've seen the local paper this morning? That bastard Claiborne has obviously got his hooks into the press, so we can't very well claim that your affair won't have some discrediting effect on the image of the Marine Corps. The prosecutor would just introduce a bunch of clippings and videotapes."

Becky began to pace around her small room. Kramer's concise outline of the case against Becker was dissolving all her confidence. "If it's all so open and shut, why do they want me to testify for the prosecution?" Becky grabbed for her purse, plucked the immunity documents out of it, and handed them to Kramer.

He glanced at them briefly. "Standard deal. I hate to phrase it this way. But you're the nail they need to seal his coffin. Regardless of the theoretical arguments I make, you are the one unimpeachable witness who will confirm to the court-martial board that what the government alleges did, in fact, happen."

"I still have the option of telling them to stick this deal where the sun doesn't shine."

"Yeah, you do. But don't kid yourself. They have committed to this trial. Turning it off now would be an embarrassment. If you refuse to testify they will prosecute and see that you get the full load. Women do wind up behind bars these days. I'll do what I can to avoid it, but I'm afraid you'd better plan on appearing on the witness stand."

"At least I can shift some of the blame . . . take some of the heat off Becker."

Kramer shook his head and snapped his briefcase shut. "Remember what I told you. Blame is not the issue. Misconduct is. They know damn well you're a hostile witness. They'll restrict your testimony to a recitation of the facts and I won't be able to get much more on the record in cross-examination."

"Mr. Kramer, please help me decide what to do."

Kramer put his hands on her shoulders and smiled. "Listen, the first thing you do is start calling me Leon . . . and remember we're on the same team. Don't sign anything yet. Let 'em stew for a while. It may not make much difference in the long run anyway. We're not going to try and say your affair didn't happen. They're making this a moral issue, so we'll deal with morality.

"I'm going to hold the morals of America up for critical examination. They say the military is a microcosm of society? Fine. How can we expect people in uniform to behave any differently from their civilian counterparts when it comes to affairs of the heart? If I do my job well enough, there won't be a sinful sonofabitch on that court-martial board who won't be examining his own conscience and voting for dismissal."

She stared into his eyes, looking for confidence and reassurance. Becky saw determination, iron resolve, the same sort of stare Becker exhibited on those occasions when he felt challenged. "Leon, please help us. Please save him. He's so dedicated—and vulnerable . . ."

Kramer chuckled and pulled her into a bear hug. "Buttplate Becker? Vulnerable? That evil bastard chews sheet metal and spits bullets. I've seen it with my own eyes. He'll be fine. You just keep loving him. We'll hope the Big Green Machine also loves him for what he's done over the years."

He released her and reached for his briefcase. The phone messages caught his eyes and he pondered strategy as he walked toward the door. "I'm gonna go see Becker. You might want to answer a few of those phone calls from the press. Tell 'em what's in your heart. I think the American public still likes a good love story."

• • •

Foam spewed onto Kramer's glasses as Douglas popped open cold beers and passed them around to his old friends. They sat around a footlocker in Becker's BOQ room, smiling at one another, unable to say much, feeling the nostalgia of 16 years wash over them like a riptide. Men like Becker, Kramer, Douglas—men who had shared so much adversity and forged such a strong bond—didn't need to talk about it much.

Becker raised a sweaty beer can in toast. "We're all real proud of you, Leon."

"I owe it all to you and the GI Bill."

"If you're talking about that time back in '67 with Staff Sergeant Crider, forget about it. He got his."

"Whatever happened to old Cottonmouth Crider?"

"I heard a tale or two about him right after I got to Fifth Marines. I made staff sergeant about that time and all the senior NCOs were talking about him."

"And . . . ?" Kramer had wiped the vestiges of Crider out of his mind long ago but he suddenly found himself intensely interested in the fate of his old nemesis.

"Well, it seems the division sergeant major tried to give him one more chance to redeem himself. Sent Crider to a quiet little location called Khe Sanh . . ."

"No shit?"

"Yep. When it blew up just before Tet '68, Crider beat feet. Ran like a striped-assed ape. They caught up with him around Phu Bai, court-martialed his ass, and kicked him out. Couple of years later I ran into old Steve Wyatt who was on recruiting duty in L.A. He said Crider got nailed in the Watts Riots. KIA while he was trying to loot a liquor store."

"I'll be goddamned! There is justice after all."

"Except in this case . . ." Douglas handed around fresh beers and passed Kramer's bulging briefcase. The sea stories could wait. It was time for a strategy session. "I ain't never seen a bigger railroad job. Sergeant Major Morey told me yesterday the general is callin' in a military judge from Norfolk . . . guy named Colonel Scales. Turns out Scales was SJA out on Okinawa when Tobrey had command of Camp Butler. The fuckin' fix is in, man.''

Kramer pulled out a yellow legal pad and noted the time and date of their meeting. ''Wish I could prove it. I can challenge the jury members, but there's no provision for challenging the judge.''

''Can't we ask 'em to hold the court somewhere else?''

''Change of venue?'' Kramer shook his head and wiped at his glasses with a soft handkerchief. ''Already tried that. Motion denied for lack of grounds.''

Becker crushed his beer can and rattled it into a waste can across the room. ''So . . . they gonna rip my lungs out or what?''

''Not if I can help it, Buttplate. Although I do wish there was some way we could quietly disappear your lady friend, Lt. Campbell.''

Becker leaned forward with his elbows on his knees and began to rub his hands together. The familiar habit told his friends there was a tension below that belied the surface calm of Becker's demeanor. ''How are they treating her?''

''Not much better than they're treating you. They've got the heat on her to accept immunity and testify. She doesn't want to do it but they're threatening hard time if she doesn't cooperate.''

''Would they really try to lock her up?''

''Buttplate, there's no use in pulling punches here. You know and I know that General Tobrey wants to make you a sad example in his campaign to turn the Corps into a bastion of moral integrity.''

''Where the fuck does he get off . . .'' Douglas was on his feet, ready to express his opinion of the general and his puritan ethic but Kramer waved him to a seat.

''It doesn't matter where he gets off, Tubes. He's the man with the plan. Hell, I don't know. It's probably some kind of knee-jerk reaction to counter the effects of the Peace-Love-Dope generation. Maybe he's born again or trying to prove Marines are moral supermen. Lots of old salts just can't deal with the fact that it's a married Marine Corps these days and that brings with it all the contemporary problems people face on the outside.''

Kramer pulled at his beer. ''It doesn't matter what his motives are. What matters is the fact that he's prepared to go to the wire in this case. He's not gonna take a chance on a sympathetic verdict. He'll force Becky to testify or nail her to the wall. He means business.''

''Then she's got to testify. It's that simple.'' Becker relaxed slightly. He was in a mine field. Nothing to be done about that now . . . except step carefully. ''I'm not gonna let her take the fall for me. Fact of the matter is, I love her.''

Kramer clicked his ballpoint pen and pondered the statement. It was unusual, even shocking to hear the words from a man like Becker, sort of like hearing Jolly Old Saint Nick say ''motherfucker.'' It was also precisely what he expected. A man like Buttplate Becker would never let himself fall into jeopardy with the Marine Corps unless there were intense, unusual emotions involved.

''You'll be happy to hear she shares your feelings. At any rate, there's not much we can—or should—do to avoid her testimony. Denial is hardly the thrust of this case. I figure we might be able to beat them at their own game.''

There was a tense pause while Douglas opened beer and Kramer organized notes. He sipped, looked around at his defense team, and continued.

''I can beat the failure to obey an order charge. That policy letter to all commands from Tobrey hardly constitutes a lawful order. We'll get that one tossed out in pretrial motions. As for wrongful cohabitation under Article 134, I can probably also get them to toss that one. Definition won't hold up to a night or two in a motel and sharing a BOQ room once in a while. Those aren't the real problems.

''What we have to deal with are two basic charges: conduct unbecoming an officer under Article 133 and conduct likely to reflect discredit on the armed forces under Article 134. By definition, I can't beat either charge. Given the circumstances—and given the right jury—I could probably get us out with a letter of reprimand.''

''Wait a minute, Leon . . .'' Douglas wrinkled his brow

and leaned over the footlocker. "That sounds like you're gonna plead the skipper guilty."

"Nope. I'm simply not gonna waste a lot of time in denials. I'm simply gonna say he's not guilty of anything most other red-blooded men and women in our society haven't done at one time or another. He may be guilty of falling in love and then sleeping with a legally married woman. But it was with her full consent and encouragement. In my mind, that takes it out of the context of conduct unbecoming. And anything that has become such common practice in American society can hardly be said to reflect discredit on the armed forces, which are composed of men and women who grew up in that same society. Becker is only wrong if society is wrong. If they want to convict someone, convict American society."

"That's a little deep for an Oklahoma boy." Douglas walked over to Becker's clothing press, rummaged, and pulled out a dress blue uniform blouse. A cascade of clinking medals hung from the left breast in three colorful tiers. "How come you can't just toss these medals on the table, have 'em take a good look at what the skipper's done for his country, and say the man rates a break? How can a guy who wears all these medals for dedication and bravery ever intentionally do anything to discredit his uniform?"

"They won't let me introduce a damn thing about Buttplate's service record into the trial, Tubes. Irrelevant and immaterial to the case at hand. That stuff may help reduce the sentence if we get beat, but it isn't germane to the case. They've got the evidence from the NIS investigation. They've got Becky's testimony. They've got a case, despite Becker's background."

Becker nodded, stood, and walked to the sink where he shaved every morning. He dashed cold water on his face, checked the mirror for a moment, and then turned to stare at his friends.

"Here's the way I see it. Ain't nobody but me got this boat stuck up shit creek and then lost the paddle. I won't give up without a fight, but in the end, I'm gonna trust the system that's supported me all along for the past twenty years. The Marine Corps made me what I am. It educated me, it molded me, it took me out of the pack and turned me from a buck private into a commissioned officer. The system has done good by me. I can't believe they'll ignore all that whether they find me guilty or not.''

Douglas stood and stabbed Becker in the chest with his finger. ''Goddammit, you listen to me! I ain't said anything like this to you since that day back on the hospital ship when you said you was gonna go back to The 'Nam after bein' hit three fuckin' times! You are outta yer mind, Buttplate! The system ain't what it used to be!

''There ain't no professionals left. They was all killed in Korea or 'Nam or Beirut or fucking Grenada, for Christ's sake! The assholes and ticket-punchers are all afraid of guys like you, Buttplate. Can't you see that? Fear makes 'em crazy. They'll kill yer ass and then eat it for lunch!''

Kramer stood and wrapped an arm around Douglas's heaving shoulders. He watched a flash of anger in Becker's eyes fade. The jaw muscles slowly went slack and a smile creased Becker's face. The explosion was off target but Becker was digging in to defend his position.

''We're gonna get out of here and let you sleep.'' Kramer turned Douglas toward the door. ''I've got a pretrial meeting with Claiborne and the general tomorrow morning. I'll come see you right after that.''

Douglas broke free of Kramer's hand, started to say something, and then snatched at Becker in a desperate hug. ''Just let me know what you need, Buttplate. Anything at all, you just let me know.''

When his friends were gone, Becker kicked at a pile of empty beer cans and then shucked off his spit-shined shoes. He stretched out on the blanket and tried to worm some of the tension out of his back and neck muscles. A question kept nagging him away from rest. Were all the professionals gone? Was he the last dinosaur? Surely not. They were out there somewhere. Ally or enemy, staring through the sights, from one end of the rifle or another.

VIII.

Column Left, March . . .

Becker slid a fresh magazine into his M-16 and scanned the bullet-scarred building to his front for enemy movement. He was about to single-handedly sweep the house for holed-up enemy soldiers. It wasn't a very safe or sane thing to do on the north side of Hue City—a city under siege by hordes of North Vietnamese Army regular troops—but Becker had lost the last man in his rifle squad to a sniper this morning and he just didn't know what else to do. His orders said continue the attack toward the walls of the Citadel that lay in massive splendor just two blocks from his present position.

It was either that or give up wasting good men on a bad job. Becker spent some precious time contemplating that the day before, when he was down to just three shit-scared Marines who looked to him for their safe passage through a bloody meat-grinder. He'd decided against giving up, but it was a struggle to make himself continue. For the first time in his military memory, the business of being a Marine in combat seemed frustrating and futile.

The situation in Hue was fairly desperate for both the American Marines in the attack and the NVA infantrymen in defense of the ancient city stronghold. That was clear from the long lines of casualties being carried toward evacuation points along the banks of the Perfume River.

In efforts to reach the Citadel walls, Becker lost eight dead and four wounded since 1st Battalion, Fifth Marines, landed on the north side of the river. He was alone but some other shot-up rifle squad was bound to pass his position soon. Meanwhile, he would drive toward those towering walls. When—and if—he made it, instinct would tell him what to do.

He was exhausted from lack of sleep, nervous tension, and the constant leakage of blood from minor shrapnel wounds. Flying shards of brick, wood, and steel multiplied the killing or wounding effect of every weapon fired in Hue's bloody streets.

Somewhere off to his left a gook was hammering at some poor Marine with an RPD machine gun. Becker identified the popcorn rattle of the weapon and heard the whine of ricochet off stone. He closed his eyes, slid into a sitting position with his back against the cold stone of a wet garden wall, and considered the situation.

The Task Force X-Ray commander at Phu Bai had been expecting a respite for his weary troops during the Tet Lunar New Year celebrations. Fortunately for all concerned, MACV had not let commands in the northern tactical zones stand down for Tet because of the situation at Khe Sanh. At least there were enough troops to react swiftly when the main force VC and NVA swarmed like rats from the sewers in practically every population center of I Corps.

Army advisers and ARVN troops reported the enemy was making an all-out attempt to seize the lovely, French-influenced city of Hue and the task force commander rushed what Marines he could muster to the rescue. Becker, waiting for assignment at the combat base, was caught up in the flood as reinforcing units were rushed toward Hue. Every man who could fire a rifle was needed urgently.

After two weeks of intense combat, fighting house-to-house, the 2nd Battalion, Fifth Marines, managed to push the NVA out of their warrens on the south side of the Perfume River that divided the city. Casualties were extremely heavy and the first battalion of the regiment was thrown into the fray when the assault shifted across the water and focused on the NVA troops holding the ancient Citadel that formed the epicenter of Hue's urban sprawl.

Becker first saw the Citadel from the south banks of the river while he was waiting for a landing craft to take him across at the head of a lashed-up squad of cooks, clerks, and truck drivers. They formed an unlikely bunch that Becker was not particularly anxious to lead, but the orders were clear and unequivocal. All hands into the line; seize the Citadel from the NVA. The South Vietnamese government wanted it and the Americans were expected to make it happen.

As he landed on the north side, Becker lost two men killed and another wounded badly enough to be evacuated. He realized the Citadel was going to be a tough nut to crack. Two- and three-story structures lined the approaches to the gates of the walled city. It was no sure bet that anyone could survive the efforts to clear those buildings, cross the wide moats, and climb the forty-foot walls that surrounded the interior courtyards, gardens, and minipalaces of the royal refuge that had served to protect the ancient emperors from so many other determined attackers.

Certainly, the modern descendants of those mandarin monarchs were not making the task any easier for the Marines. From the highest levels of government in Saigon, word had been passed to the American command. The upstart enemy had to be dislodged but the ancient city was to be saved from the ravages of combat in its streets. That meant only surgical support from heavy weapons. None of the standard massive and unbridled use of naval gunfire, artillery, or air strikes to keep the enemy's head down while the grunts advanced. That meant, as Becker painfully came to understand, an infantryman's nightmare.

Even the air strikes that cleared high command were less than effective. A low, wet cloud cover and intermittent rain that plagued the coastal plains during this time of year kept most aircraft grounded or out of visual contact with events on the ground. In the end, there had been little choice for the

Marines. Weary, bleeding grunts had to smash up against those moss-covered walls like bugs against a windshield until something cracked and they could pour through to rip down the tattered, taunting enemy flag that snapped and fluttered in the wet breeze over the Citadel in Hue.

The entrenched enemy in Hue—mostly dedicated and highly motivated veterans under control of the 6th NVA Regiment—would have to be pried and blasted out of their holes or hides in close-quarters combat. Nothing about that came easy to men who had no special training for urban combat, who spent most of their time thrashing around in rice paddies or cutting through dense jungle in search for an elusive enemy. It was bloody and brutal, mostly a matter decided by bullets and bayonets.

As far as Becker knew, his company had pushed farther than any other. He couldn't be sure. The north side of the city was crawling with refugees, stragglers, survivors, and other lost souls trying to join or avoid the fight. He caught quick glimpses of units—mostly squads or fireteams— moving on his flanks, but this close to the Citadel it was getting hard to find a friendly face that wasn't wearing a death mask.

Becker fumbled for matches, lit his last cigarette, and blew an angry gout of smoke into the muggy air. There were supposed to be ARVN on his right flank, moving steadily parallel to the Marine advance through the homes and offices of Hue's former civilian residents. With a little support from that quarter, he might have saved some of the poor bastards who followed him into the streets.

But the only ARVN Becker saw were lowlifes moving up behind the Marines in trucks, hauling away loot from the cleared buildings and palatial homes near the Citadel. The bastards barely waited until the final shots were fired before they descended like vultures on a block of houses the Marines cleared. He'd emptied a magazine at them once when he caught a clutch of ARVN going through the pockets of a dead Marine. His nominal allies scattered and scurried like cockroaches.

Becker heard firing somewhere behind his position. The

snap and spang of M-16s was clearly audible. Friendlies to the rear. He pulled the charging handle on his rifle and sent a fresh round into the chamber. He'd find a hole inside the building to his front and wait to join up when they swept through the area.

Glancing right and left down the alleyway that led to the vaulted entrance to the building, Becker gathered his remaining strength and prepared to move. He'd be an arcade target for the time it took him to stagger across thirty meters of street and duck inside. He shouldered his rifle, sent a short burst into a likely sniper hide on the second story of the building, and broke cover.

Halfway across the broad alley, he heard the pop of AK fire and felt the sting of cement shards as the rounds smashed into paving stone. There were gooks in the building, but Becker was committed. There was no cover between him and his destination. He'd have to deal with the NVA tenants after he reached their residence.

Becker pounded for the door and ducked inside, chased by another snarling burst of AK fire. He put his back against a clammy wall, caught his breath, and let his eyes adjust to the dark interior. He was in a living room or parlor, one of two large rooms off the long hallway that appeared to divide the house along a central axis. The gook who fired at him would be somewhere upstairs. He glanced at a fancy rosewood staircase and felt for a grenade. He had only one remaining.

As he darted toward the banister railing, the gloom at the head of the stairs was split by muzzle flash. The noise of the burst was deafening as it echoed and clamored off the interior walls of the house. Becker dove for the staircase, rolled, and lay flat on his back, pointing his rifle up at the shadows. When the ringing in his ears receded to a hum, he heard the gook on the second-floor landing snap a fresh magazine into his weapon and rack the bolt. He'd wait, probably prone and sheltered behind a wall or door, for Becker to rush up the stairs.

He laid his rifle across his chest and found the grenade. It was a gamble, but he'd have to expose himself, heave the frag up the stairs, and then follow the blast to be on the gook before he could recover. As he crouched and twisted the pin out of the grenade, it suddenly dawned on Becker that there might be more than one gook waiting for him up there.

He pondered waiting for reinforcements before making his move but discarded the notion. The gook was in a position to cover the approach up the street outside. He'd kill some Marines before they could get inside and give Becker a hand.

The staircase appeared to turn left at the landing. The gook would have his back against the near side, waiting to catch sight of Becker as he tried to loop the grenade upward in a roundhouse lob. He slipped his thumb off the safety lever, swung quickly into the open, and heaved hard. AK fire smacked into the wall near his head as Becker ducked back to grab his rifle. He heard the grenade thud into a wall and then it exploded, showering him with debris and brick dust.

Swinging around to vault up the stairs, Becker triggered three rounds into the haze. He made the turn at the second story and paused to crank two more shots into the smoldering body of an NVA trooper sprawled like a battered rag doll across the landing. The well-placed grenade provided a lethal end to one of his problems.

But Becker had more hostile company on the second floor. A volley of rounds tore into the wall at his rear. He returned the fire, blindly emptying the magazine in his rifle into the gloom of the upstairs hallway. He changed magazines but could not get back into action quickly enough to fire at a green-clad figure who darted across the hallway.

Becker kept his head low, resting about four steps down from the landing, and peered carefully at floor level. The NVA had ducked into the second of four doorways leading off the second-floor hall.

It's one-on-one, unless he's got another buddy up here somewhere. Becker wondered what the gook was thinking. Was he hiding, cringing up there in a corner, saying his prayers? Or was this one of the flinty pros who ignored the smoke and noise, preparing calmly to die for what they believe when the choices are reduced to zero? There was only one way to determine.

He rose carefully and stepped over the bleeding body of the dead NVA. He kept his muzzle trained on the door about fifteen feet ahead and wished with all his might that he had another hand grenade to use as a calling card. Only one man would walk out of that room.

Becker's heart pounded in an erratic rhythm as he neared the door. He breathed deeply and swung his leg back to kick at the latch-plate. When he snapped his boot forward, the door sprung open on well-oiled hinges. He dove for the floor immediately and rolled behind a thickly padded sofa. Two shots cracked by his ear.

There were no windows in the room, Becker discovered as he peered cautiously, letting his eyes follow the muzzle of his rifle around the dark room. Where? He canted his rifle around the edge of the sofa and triggered three rounds into the darkness. There was no return fire as the echo of his shots faded.

And then he heard it. Someone was wrestling with the bolt of a weapon. He could distinguish muffled grunts and the irritating grind of seized metal under pressure. Jam! His fucking weapon is jammed! Becker rose to his knees and fired a burst over the back of the couch in the direction of the sounds. His rounds chewed into a large ornate wardrobe laying on its side along the far wall of the room.

Assuming he had the gook's hiding place spotted, Becker triggered off the remaining rounds in the magazine, dumped it onto the floor, and groped in his trouser pockets for a full replacement. Before he could pull a magazine free of threads on the inside of his cargo pocket, a chilling apparition formed out of the gloom.

Holding his AK-47 diagonally across his short, compact body, the NVA trooper stepped from the shadows onto the edge of the rectangle of dim light that spilled in through the shattered door. Fumbling madly to load his rifle, Becker kept his eyes glued on the target. The gook seemed to be smirking if not actually smiling. He made no move to shoot, hide, or run as Becker aimed his reloaded weapon over the couch and took the slack out of the trigger.

He was a smallish man in a green uniform that showed the rents and repairs of hard campaigning. He looked down at his assault rifle, shrugged slightly, and then dropped the weapon at his sandal-clad feet. Becker eased the pressure on the trigger and stared, wondering what he might do with a POW in Hue.

Standing cautiously, keeping his muzzle pointed toward the center of the NVA's pouter-pigeon chest, Becker tried to remember a Vietnamese phrase for "surrender" or "hands up," anything he might say to make the gook commit himself to something besides staring with a haunted look in his slanted eyes.

The NVA soldier did not move. He muttered something under his breath and brought himself to an exaggerated position of attention as his adversary slowly approached. Becker stared in amazement over the sights of his rifle. The gook seemed to be worrying something over in his mind, searching for words.

When he spoke, his English was poor but there was no strain in his voice. He seemed to presume he'd be understood by the American on the other end of the rifle.

"All soldier . . ." he said, pointing a finger at himself and then at Becker. ". . . we die. Now me. Then you." He stared straight ahead, willing Becker to understand his last earthly thoughts.

And Becker did understand. He cautiously lowered the rifle, wondering if he'd have the guts to do this in similar circumstances. There was dignity here. A fatally jammed weapon, no escape from death, and the man stepped forward to meet his fate; the fate of all fighting men in one way or another. They had a lot in common, Becker decided. This gook and this American Marine, so tired of running, dodging the odds, fighting to do what was expected of them, trying to stay alive just one more day, one more hour.

Becker felt weak and inadequate in the face of such courage. The hard shell of anger that drove him to ruthless measures in combat cracked slightly. Let some other son-ofabitch kill this poor bastard. He rated a break.

"Hey!" Becker motioned toward the open door with the muzzle of his rifle. "Get the fuck out of here. Go on, you sonofabitch. *Di di mau!*"

At the sound of the Vietnamese phrase, the NVA trooper nearly lost his stoic composure. It dawned on him that the American was not going to take his life. He shot a glance at the door and then began to edge cautiously around the barrel of Becker's rifle. His jammed weapon was lying on the floor, frozen solid with a hung cartridge lodged firmly in the chamber.

The gook did not bolt for the door or glance over his shoulder. He walked calmly from the field of honor expressing his gratitude in a clear voice. *"Com ong ngu lam."* And then he was gone.

Becker heard a firefight break out somewhere on the street below the house. He supposed the NVA trooper was dead meat down there. You can play the odds, but you can't beat them. Would the weird face-off have ended differently if the 7.62mm ChiCom round hadn't malfunctioned? Would one of them be dead now if Becker's magazine hadn't hung up on some loose thread in his trouser pocket? Only two things about the close encounter were clear to Becker as he wearily clumped down the stairs and back into battle: the questions would probably nag him for the rest of his life . . . and he would never know the answers.

Rummaging noises on the first floor caused him to hesitate in mid-descent. Someone was down below, looking for something and not finding it from the sound of the cracking wood and breaking glass. Becker decided it was probably Marine grunts scavenging for firewood or searching for booze but logic didn't apply in this seesaw street fight. It could be his NVA soul mate searching for a weapon to finish the business left undone upstairs. He cautiously followed his muzzle down and looked into the living room where he'd initially entered the house.

He saw a fatigue-clad form bending over an ornately-decorated wooden chest. The lid was open and an ARVN was scratching at the contents of the chest like a hungry dog digging for a buried bone. Becker felt a flash of fury lance into his stomach and shoot up his spine. Unresolved tension from the upstairs encounter with the proud little enemy soldier snapped his muscles taut and pulsed through his legs as he stormed down the remaining stairs and into the room where the ARVN was looting with gusto.

"Stop it, you sonofabitch! Get the fuck out of here before I kill you!"

The ARVN jumped and spun to face Becker. He was holding a silver, jewel-encrusted brandy flask and flashing a wide grin that revealed a number of gold teeth. The rank tabs on his collar marked him as an ARVN lieutenant. Probably a staff pogue or supply officer, Becker concluded, noting the pressed uniform and chrome-plated, small-caliber revolver hanging at the man's hip.

Slowly, involuntarily, Becker lifted the rifle into his shoulder and pressed his forehead against the sights. His sight picture was solid on the ARVN officer's upper chest. With his off-eye, he watched the glittering smile melt into a rictus of abject fear. He began to tremble as Becker tightened his grip on the weapon and leaned forward to absorb the recoil.

"No, no, no! GI numbah one! No shoot, no shoot!"

Becker fought rage and revulsion, watching with disdain as the petrified man's trousers turned dark and soggy around the crotch. Unstinting courage and dignity on one floor; abject cowardice and moral decay on the other. Becker felt tired, alone, defeated by an enemy infiltrating his spirit.

He lowered the weapon, shook his head, and turned to leave. He never saw the terrified ARVN officer draw his pistol and he never heard the pop of the shots that drilled into his side.

The surgeon who removed the rounds out on the hospital ship brought him a mangled slug when he made rounds the next day. "Must have been an officer, huh? I've never removed small-caliber pistol rounds before."

Becker didn't want to talk about it. He told the doctor to

keep the slug and unsuccessfully tried to refuse the Purple Heart they passed around several days later.

Leon Kramer scribbled a note on his pad and nervously clicked his ballpoint pen. Tobrey and Claiborne were civil but hardly cooperative. From the moment the meeting in the CG's office began it was clear they were dug in and defending. He'd gotten the list of charges facing Becker reduced to a single count of violating Articles 133 and 134 of the Uniform Code. Now it was time for an end run around the court-martial if he could find a seam in their line.

"Gentlemen, I'd like to broaden the discussion for a moment with your kind permission."

General Tobrey glanced irritably at his watch and let Major Claiborne field the kickoff. "We want the defense to enjoy all possible cooperation, Mr. Kramer."

Tossing his pen on top of his alligator briefcase, Kramer unbuttoned his coat and slouched in the leather chair across from Tobrey's battleship of a desk. "I believe you all know I'm a former Marine . . . and that I served with Captain Becker in Vietnam."

Tobrey nodded his head and offered an icy smile. "We've been briefed on your relationship with the defendant, Mr. Kramer."

"He was Sergeant Becker in those days, and I was Lance Corporal Kramer."

"You've certainly done well for yourself since then." Claiborne seemed to be enjoying the divergence from business at hand. He'd been in a blue funk since Tobrey overruled him about reducing the formal charges.

"Yeah, and you should know from the outset that I owe all that to Thurmond Becker."

"You're too modest, Mr. Kramer. Lots of our black Marines did quite well for themselves after the war."

Kramer glanced at Tobrey and flashed a smile. "Take it from one who knows, General. Not many got to be full partners in a law firm. Most of them wound up hustling out on the streets or in prison. That's sure as hell where I'd be if it hadn't been for Becker. See, he kept me from killing a man over there—a Staff NCO—a black Marine.''

''What has that got to do with the current court-martial proceeding, Mr. Kramer?''

''Nothing directly, gentlemen. It's just to let you know what I'm capable of in a fight, and that I intend to fight to the bitter end if you persist in this matter. It's going to be ugly, very ugly, and I believe I know a better way of doing the job here.''

Claiborne started to object, but General Tobrey motioned for silence. ''If you're trying to make a deal, Mr. Kramer, our meeting is over.''

''I'm trying to appeal to reason and common sense, General. I don't want to hurt the Marine Corps and neither do you. You've seen the series of articles in the local paper. My office informs me the story is being followed by the wire services and the TV people will be arriving here at Camp Lejeune shortly. The Marine Corps is bound to suffer a black eye . . .''

''Sometimes a black eye is the symbol of a valiant stand for what a person believes in.''

''C'mon, General! Where I come from it's the mark of a loser. The loser if this case goes to trial will be the Marine Corps. There is a better way to handle it.''

Claiborne shifted in his seat and struck a thoughtful pose. ''I presume you're suggesting we call off the court-martial and let the commanding officers handle it through nonjudicial punishment?''

''Why not, Major? You've already agreed to reduce the charges. If the goal is to punish the guilty parties. Why not let Becker's CO and Campbell's CO write an official letter of reprimand and get on with life as we know it?''

''We're not being offered much, General. It's hiding the dirty linen rather than hanging it out in the sun, but all that may be moot given the current level of press interest in the case. If we back off now, we could be seen as irresolute in our position; sort of condoning what's happened as not significant enough for serious action.''

Kramer nearly snapped in exasperation. ''Give me a

break, Major Claiborne! We all know *any* sort of disciplinary action in this upwardly mobile outfit is *serious action* against a commissioned officer. Hell, a misplaced modifier on a fitness report can deep-six an officer's career. Look, I can get both parties to plead guilty at a Non-Judicial Punishment proceeding. They'll admit they did something wrong. What more do you want?''

"They may admit to it, Mr. Kramer, but it would not be an admission in public trial. I'm of the opinion that the appropriate message regarding our view of such behavior needs to be transmitted far and wide."

Kramer glanced at both smug faces and nodded his understanding. "Just like boot camp, right? One asshole screws up and the whole platoon has to do push-ups."

General Tobrey ignored the comment and shuffled through some papers on his desk. He propped a pair of half-moon reading glasses on his nose and nailed Kramer with a glare.

"Mr. Kramer, I can't take an official stance in this case for obvious reasons. I have no desire to influence the conduct of this trial one way or another . . ." Tobrey noted the sarcastic expression on Kramer's face and held up his hand. "Kindly let me finish. You came here to talk about issues this morning, so let's do that for a moment."

Tobrey glanced down at the paper in his hand and began to read. "I have here a page from the Manual for Courts-Martial. I quote: 'Article 133, Conduct Unbecoming an Officer and a Gentleman: There are certain moral attributes common to the ideal officer and the perfect gentleman, a lack of which is indicated by acts of indecency or indecorum . . .'''

Kramer couldn't keep silent. He picked up his pen and waved away the words. "That was written for the days of chivalry, for Christ's sake! Using that definition, you'd wind up court-martialing every Marine who ever partied his way through a tour on Okinawa or a Mediterranean cruise!"

Tobrey removed his glasses and folded his hands on top of his desk. His expression was neutral but the lines in his broad forehead deepened with what appeared to be concern for Kramer's understanding of the issues.

"Mr. Kramer, this is the *Marine Corps*—and the rules of conduct and decorum for Marine officers remain the same today as they were in 1775."

As he walked out to the sun-drenched rental car in the parking lot outside the 2nd Marine Division headquarters, Leon Kramer had to admit his case did not look promising. No matter which way he twisted things, he could not seem to squirm out from under the facts. They possessed proof of an active, intimate love affair between Becker and Becky Campbell. His legal training and courtroom experience were flashing warning signals. If it had been any other defendant, Kramer would have recommended throwing themselves on the mercy of the court, but there was clearly no mercy in this court.

He'd have to attack the spirit of the violated regulations and leave the letter of the law alone. He might carry the decision to absolute minimum punishment on such a tack, depending on the rulings he got from the military judge when he began to argue the case, and the selection of just the right court-martial board members. That process, similar to jury selection in a civilian trial, was scheduled to begin on Monday.

He cracked the car windows, cranked the engine, and pulled slowly out of the parking lot. He'd spend the weekend looking for the lowdown on one Colonel Arthur J. Scales, the Military Circuit trial judge who would rule the case from the bench.

As he waited for Colonel Scales to answer the private line in his quarters at the Norfolk Navy Base, Major General Tobrey mulled over his association with the man being called in to preside over Becker's trial. He was using the phone in his private study to keep anyone in the chain of command from knowing about the call. A little research earlier in the day convinced him no one but a few scattered and overburdened investigators would remember a time nearly ten years ago on Okinawa.

General Tobrey ran the sprawling Marine command headquartered at Camp Smedley D. Butler. Scales was an aspiring Judge Advocate at an outlying base on the island; one of the nondescript attorneys who stumbled into uniform when the Corps offered accelerated promotion deals to attract talent and handle a staggering level of disciplinary and human rights cases in the post-war seventies.

He had a reputation as a boozer but Major Scales kept the staggers to a discreet minimum at public functions. None of the professional combat officers expected a lawyer to display much military demeanor and bearing anyway. Tobrey shook his hand once in the course of a year and promptly consigned the man's face and name to the darkest shadows of his concern—except for one incident.

A confidential package from the Criminal Investigation Division of the Base Provost Marshal's Office landed on Tobrey's desk one morning and brought Arthur J. Scales to his immediate attention. Scales, who was petitioning for appointment as a military judge at the time, was the subject of a very sordid report.

According to investigators, alerted by irate Japanese businessmen on the island, a Marine officer was consorting with known prostitutes. Not too much out of the ordinary there, but this particular officer was secretly acting as sponsor for several of the women and skimming a cut of the action for himself. Major Scales had set himself up as a field-grade pimp.

Angry and insulted by the situation, General Tobrey thought long and hard about a course of action. He considered the nature of the crime, the potential for revelation and embarrassment, the rank and station of the officer involved, and any potential victims. In the end, he decided it suited him more strategically to simply end the activity and guard the delicate defense negotiations under way with the Japanese government concerning the massive American presence on Okinawa.

Scales was confronted with the evidence in a private session. Tobrey took a hard line, vowing eternal damnation, public condemnation, and disastrous career consequences if Scales didn't halt his activities immediately.

Scales was a smart enough lawyer to know when a case was not worth arguing. He was also ambitious and by nature a political sort who understood manipulation and power-plays. He would be spared public exposure and roasting over an open flame, but there would be a price. Somewhere down the line, he would have to pay the bill. Scales took advantage of the parachute and bailed out of immediate danger.

That decision nagged at Tobrey's conscience for a long time. It also prodded him into action on the vague, long-range plans he'd been formulating to sweep the Corps clean of Vietnam-era mold and fungus. For such high purposes, even morality could be manipulated—in the best interests of the Corps.

"Art," the general barked when Colonel Scales came on the line. "How are things up in Norfolk?"

The general listened to Scales's guarded response and then got down to business. "Art, it's about this Becker thing. I'm sure you understand that I consider the case to be significant for the entire officer corps. Morality and ethical conduct are very important to the image of Marine officers. Don't you agree?"

Becky's knees ached from pounding along the rutted backwoods trails behind the BOQ, but the pain couldn't compete with the exhilaration she felt at being out in the open, active and free. Kramer had convinced her to take advantage of the relaxed security and stretch her cramped body with vigorous exercise.

His infrequent visits cheered her but she longed for contact with Becker. She longed to tell him how terrible she felt and how much she loved him in spite of everything. More importantly, she longed to hear that he loved her, that his passion was not being dulled by the axe hanging over his head.

Kramer was caught in the middle, trying to concentrate on his case and keep both their heads above emotional water. He carried conciliatory messages, maudlin notes, and bolstering best wishes between them for nearly two weeks.

"Christ, I'm beginning to feel like the head nurse on a terminal ward," he complained when Becky's depression was at a new low. "You're getting on my nerves. Blow some of the cobwebs out of your brain. Get the lead out of your head and your heart."

He was right. It felt good to churn and pump and breathe the crisp, pine-scented fall air. She tried not to think about anything, but the blood pumping past her eardrums was like the endless irritating clock in an empty room. Deadlines were approaching. Jury selection tomorrow. Decision time on the immunity bargain was 1700 tonight.

Kramer told her not to worry about signing the agreement. The defense, as he planned to plead it, would not be prejudiced by her testimony. Still, she had not been able to bring herself to call Claiborne, put pen to paper, and become the live ammo for Becker's firing squad. Somehow, no matter what anyone said, she couldn't believe he would ever forgive her.

Becky broke into a sun-dappled clearing in the tall pines and suddenly discovered why Kramer had been so anxious to have her get out of the BOQ and begin her therapeutic PT today, right now. She stood panting, fighting desperately to keep rein on a flood of emotion that hit her like a painful cramp.

On the other side of the clearing, Buttplate Becker was banging out sit-ups with his toes hooked under a fallen tree limb. He was sweating, looking vigorous and healthy, despite the deep lines etched at the corners of his mouth and eyes.

He caught sight of her in midexercise, his stomach muscles rippling like a washboard as he froze and stared. She could not read his taut expression. She tried a small smile, wondering where to start now that she had the chance to say all the things she'd been composing.

Becker blinked, relaxed onto his shoulder blades, and

breathed deeply. His eyes closed and he seemed peaceful in repose, but Becky could see that none of the surface tension had faded from his muscles. She slowly walked toward him, feeling for the snag of an explosive tripwire. How could he—how *should* he—be expected to act? Part of her wanted him to tenderly take her in his arms. Another part wanted him to jump up and wrap vengeful hands around her throat.

He did neither. Becker kept his eyes closed and wiped casually at the sweat pooling near his navel. His voice was soft, quiet, and unconcerned. "How they been treating you, kid? Got your prison number tattooed on yet?"

"Not yet . . ." She sat quietly on the log by his feet and tried to interpret the question. "They break out the ball and chain at 1700 tonight."

His eyebrows arched slightly and his eyes slowly opened to stare up at her. "How come? Court doesn't convene until 0800 tomorrow."

She shrugged and reached for his hand. "I haven't signed the immunity agreement. Tonight's the deadline."

Becker exploded out of the prone position and pulled Becky to her feet. "You what? What the hell do you mean you haven't signed?"

She stared defiantly into his eyes. "I told Leon Kramer, I told Major Claiborne . . . and I thought you knew. I may have loaded the weapon, but I'm not gonna pull the trigger."

Becker spun on his heel, paced, and turned. The muscles in his jaw were knotted. His eyes were icy-bright and narrowed to slits. "What in the hell are you trying to do? Huh? Are you some kind of lunatic? I don't want this martyr crap from you!"

She stepped forward and shook a finger under his chin. "Well, for once in your life, it's not gonna be what you want. It's gonna be what's right. You can't take the fall for something we both did. I'm not gonna let it happen!"

"So, you're just gonna go ahead, piss 'em off real good, and spend the next couple of years in the women's wing at

Leavenworth? Huh? What the fuck am I gonna do while you do time?''

Becky was shocked into silence. Her anger banked rapidly and she seemed to deflate as the heat dissipated into cold logic. She'd never considered the question.

"You don't get it, do you?" Becker began to pace, his hands clasped at the small of his back. He was every inch the OCS instructor practicing Techniques of Military Instruction. "They're not gonna nail me to the bulkhead on a bullshit rap like this. It's ludicrous and everyone knows that. This whole deal is a showcase, an aberration so General Tobrey can make a point, stage a goddamn morality play. He wants to shrivel some hard-ons around here, make his little corner of the Corps look like something Norman Rockwell painted!

"It's a farce, Becky, but at least it's a trial by my peers—fellow Marine officers—compassionate guys who understand how things happen to people. They'll take the required look at the evidence, listen to Claiborne and Kramer trade horseshit, and we'll all meet at the Club for Happy Hour!''

She stared at him and saw the fervent light of conviction in his eyes. The light spilled inward, sparkling off a facet of Buttplate Becker she'd not glimpsed before, not even in their most open and intimate moments. There was a spot in him—down deep, near the core—where animal instinct, abject devotion, and dangerous naiveté swirled together. Becker was alternately buoyed or drowned in that whirlpool. His values all sprang from that spot. He interpreted the rules of the game from there. Rooted there, she realized, Becker could not understand that the Marine Corps had changed. They kept the uniforms and equipment, but they changed the rules.

"I'm sorry," she said. "I'm so terribly sorry . . ."

He held her tightly then, crushing her to his chest. She could feel his heart beat against her breast. He was trying to inject her with his strength. She nuzzled his naked chest and let the tears mix with his sweat.

"Now, you sign that immunity paper. You go ahead and

testify. Don't worry about anything. Kramer is an ace, believe me. We'll get over this. We'll be together. We'll do whatever civilians do when they're in love. Just don't let them send you to prison. Don't leave me alone after all we've been through.''

Gunnery Sergeant Tubes Douglas held the handsome leather-covered flask to his ear and shook it. A satisfying slosh indicated there was still a dose of restorative available to help chase the weariness from his body. He glanced at the bubbling coffeepot in a corner of Leon Kramer's motel room/office and weighed the potential effect of an alternate beverage on his jet lag. The whiskey won in a walk and he poured a generous dollop for himself as Kramer emerged from the shower with a soggy towel wrapped around his middle.

"OK, Tubes—road trip—readeeeee, report!"

Douglas wiped Jack Daniel's dribble from his chin and grabbed at a notebook full of scribbles. "I feel like I been shot with a shit pistol. I seen more civilians in the past four days than I have in the past four years."

"Any of 'em give you a hard time?"

"Nah, they all got your phone messages and most of 'em have seen something about it in the papers or on TV. So here's yer lineup. Dr. Markos from Northwestern University thinks he can add something to it all by talking about the military being what he calls 'a microcosm of society.' He's waiting for your call.

"I seen this Dr. Linfield from L.A. and he says he'll help any way he can too. Seems he spent a lot of time counseling people who get themselves into similar situations. He's writing a book on infidelity and how to deal with it. Also says the biggest problem is people consider it a crime when it's really just a social and psychological problem. Same deal. He'll fly down when you give the word.

"Last stop was D.C. where I managed to see Major General Stokey, Buttplate's old CO from The 'Nam. He's eatin' ingots and shittin' nails over this whole deal. Can't bring any pressure to bear officially, but he'll testify any way you want him to.''

Kramer slipped on clean underwear and a sweat suit. He slid into the chair opposite Douglas and picked up his own notes. ''What about Mrs. Beaman? Did you reach her?''

''Yeah, we talked on the phone while you were in the shower. She's been doing family counseling for Navy Relief the past twenty years. Regular fuckin' lifer. She's a little shaky about testifying at a court-martial, but I convinced her she could help.''

''OK, Tubes. Nice work.'' Kramer smiled at his old friend and stretched. It was bound to be a long night with trial procedures beginning early in the morning. ''Now send 'em all a telegram with travel details, get motel rooms, and start making notes on these dudes.''

Douglas sipped whiskey and ran his eyes down a list of ten Marine officers, complete with rank and current unit. ''This the fuckin' firing squad?''

''Yep . . . or at least somewhere from five to seven of them will likely wind up on the court-martial board. I want to know what kind of targets I'm shooting at in voir dire tomorrow morning.''

''What the hell is that?''

''Same thing as jury selection in a civilian trial. We get to examine the background and opinions of the officers eligible to serve on the board. Idea is to eliminate ringers. If we get warning lights, we challenge. If the trial judge buys the argument, that guy is excused. If all else fails, both the prosecution and the defense have what they call a single peremptory challenge where we can kick somebody off the board just because we don't like the way he picks his nose. It's an important part of the trial, Tubes. We can't let 'em load us up with Jesus Freaks or people who just happen to hate Buttplate Becker for one reason or another.''

Douglas retrieved a water glass from the counter near the bathroom and poured Kramer a healthy shot from the flask. The light from the desk lamp glinted on the silver surface and gave a rosy glow to the burnished leather.

"That's a hell of a canteen you got there, Tubes."

"Yeah. Buttplate give it to me for Christmas when we was in Beirut. My God, Leon, you shoulda seen him in command over there. He was at the top of the mark—even for a guy like Becker . . ."

IX.

Right Oblique, March . . .

Buttplate Becker ambled through the cloying red mud-flats between the helicopter landing zone and his weapons company command post. In that eerie, tense period of silence following yet another deadly dose of incoming fire, Marines were slowly, cautiously crawling back into the sunlight, sniffing the air for danger like nervous prairie dogs. He nodded and grinned at a few of the familiar faces emerging into the dusty wind and pale sunlight of winter in the Middle East. The return smiles were strained. Beneath the shadow of steel helmets, squinty eyes darted and probed, sweeping up to the foothills of the Chouf, searching for the telltale flash of round or rocket leaving a Moslem tube headed for a high-explosive landing in their battered midst.

Duncan, the Georgia preacher's boy turned Dragon anti-tank gunner, blew on a steaming canteen cup of coffee and waved at his company commander. Becker fought hard against the anger coursing through his veins and paused by the perimeter bunker sited to cover a road access to Beirut International Airport.

"How they hangin', Duncan?"

"'Bout half a bubble off plumb, Skipper. How you doin'?"

"Just seen the colonel. Told him I ain't gonna ship over until he starts lettin' us shoot back."

Duncan snorted into his coffee and some of the tension faded from his face. "Well, that oughtta do it. You want us to lock and load?"

Becker caught a flash of color down by the dun-colored mound that marked his CP bunker. "Don't let's be hasty, Duncan. Gunny's givin' 'em another Maggie's Drawers."

They turned to watch as Gunnery Sergeant Tubes Douglas crawled up on the command bunker and began to wave a large red flag at Walid Jumblat's Druze gunners. It was the traditional taunt for a Marine who completely misses his target on the rifle range. A ragged cheer broke out along the airport perimeter. Duncan whistled and waved a dirty middle digit at the invisible men watching through binoculars from the Moslem neighborhoods of the Chouf.

"Them Ragheads couldn't hit a bull in the ass with a bass fiddle."

Becker forced a laugh and continued to walk. The anger returned and pooled painfully in the pit of his stomach. Despite the morale-building gags, the bloody facts were getting hard to hide in Beirut. The Ragheads up in the foothills of the Anti-Lebanon Mountains and their Shiite brethren in the battered village of Hay-es-Sallom on the other side of the airport perimeter wire were accurate and unsettling with their Soviet 120mm mortar and 130mm artillery fire. Even worse were the random salvos of Katyusha rockets that roared into the perimeter like big flying shit cans full of high explosive and heavy shrapnel.

It was a rocket that got the three Marines Becker sent on a working party that morning. Caught in the open filling sandbags, they were hotfooting for a nearby bunker when the Katyusha landed. Huge chunks of tailfin, motor, and rocket body fanned out from the explosion like whining buzz saws. Dodging a second salvo, Becker scrambled to the impact area with a corpsman and supervised the evacuation.

A dark, darting cloud scudded in from somewhere over the azure-blue Mediterranean horizon and rain began to fall in slanting sheets. Captain Becker squinted up and saw a CH-46 helicopter driving nose-down through the dirty sky, rushing his wounded Marines to the sanctuary of Navy ships offshore. Pondering names and faces, anxious eyes seeking reassurance, the pleading grip of bloody hands, Becker let the shower wash over him.

There was nothing more he could do for the men dripping their life's blood into the rain and rotorwash. Becker consigned those phantoms to a secret part of his mind from which the ghosts of so many other Marines—massacred or mauled at his side in one part of the world or another—based periodic hauntings.

In the distance, Becker spotted Gunny Douglas approaching with his poncho. Ever-vigilant, always guarding the man who introduced him to combat, who presided over his rite of passage into the brotherhood of warriors, Douglas committed extortion and blatant blackmail at Camp Lejeune to insure he went along to Beirut as Becker's senior field NCO. He was the rock-solid, shrapnel-deflecting, bullet-proof and bombproof wall that Becker leaned on when the frustrations of expeditionary service in Beirut threatened his judgment and self-control.

Douglas offered the rain garment, a wry grin, and a soggy cigarette. They sat on a pile of sandbags and critiqued the weather like veteran infantrymen.

"Mud oughtta hold down the shrapnel fan . . ."

"Better get some more sandbags down to the east side of the perimeter . . ."

"Make sure the squad leaders have their people put on dry socks . . ."

"If it gets much worse, they'll probably ground the helicopters . . ."

"You get the casualties out OK, Skipper?"

"Uh-huh . . ."

"How'd they look?"

"Christ, I don't know, Tubes. You can't tell with those fucking shrapnel wounds. I'd say Gerheim will go all the way to the States; Ault and Bernston will probably come back to

us if they don't develop complications and . . . this shit
pisses me off!''

Douglas quietly put a hand on Becker's elbow and
squeezed. So many men counting on this one man for so
much. Becker was the glue, the mustang who'd seen it all
before, if he fell apart . . .

"Seems like it pisses Colonel Stokes off too. He was
down at the CP lookin' for you . . ."

"Yeah, I saw him over at the LZ."

"And?"

Becker spit smoke into the rain and shook his head. "And
we are denied permission for counterbattery fire up into the
Chouf. The battery can't take 'em on with the 155s, the
tanks can't cut loose, and we can't fire anything but
illumination rounds from our 81s."

"He give you any idea why the fuck not?"

"You know the colonel. Hard to understand anything
around the profanity when he's pissed, but it's basically the
same old shit."

Douglas nodded and recited the irritating litany passed to
them through the American Embassy in Beirut. "Too great a
possibility of civilian casualties . . . not our job . . . let the
Leb Army do it . . . don't take sides . . . don't make
waves . . . bleed and die on command . . . bullshit . . .
bullshit . . . bullshit."

Becker swept his eyes across the Druze Moslem enclave
in the Chouf foothills. Dirty grey smoke roiled over a
backyard firefight. The Christian Phalange was making
another effort to rezone a Moslem neighborhood. As the
rattle of small-arms fire rolled down into the basin containing the American contingent of the multi-national peace-
keeping force, Becker chuckled, remembering an old
antiwar wheeze from the sixties. Fighting for peace is like
fucking for virginity.

Douglas followed his gaze and read his mind. "You
know, I believe you've seen some shit like this before."

"Yep. Vietnam, 1965 . . ."

Becker remembered those confused, chaotic days following the first large-scale commitment of U.S. forces to Vietnam.

Up in I Corps, they labored under a ludicrous set of rules designed to convince everyone—except the Vietnamese—that America was only involved in a limited police action. You can't return fire unless you have a clear target; the target has to have clearly fired on you first with intent to kill; and you must see a weapon in his hands. A lot of good Marines died trying to live by those rules. Marines were still dying eighteen years later in Beirut where the rules of engagement remained both ludicrous and fatal.

In other ways, Beirut was worse than the early American experience in Vietnam. Field commanders in Southeast Asia at least had some latitude in tactics driven by situation and terrain. In Beirut, the man commanding the 24th Marine Amphibious Unit was hamstrung. He was forced by political considerations to burn the book and do everything wrong. The Marine dispositions in Moslem West Beirut could be used as a primer for flunking out of OCS.

They held only the low ground at Beirut International Airport rather than occupying the high ground surrounding the cantonment. They had to stuff some six hundred men including armor and artillery into a perimeter that could easily be defended by a reinforced rifle company. Existing structures were overcrowded with no room to spread out under constant harassment by rockets and artillery. They were not allowed to probe and patrol beyond fixed limits that provided a sanctuary for hostile elements and a haven for indirect fire weapons. They were squeezed by limited liaison with friendly elements, notably the Israelis who operated on their flanks with violent authority and little regard for lines of communication. They were not allowed to take charge of their own physical security and forced to rely on shaky, sometimes mutinous elements of the Lebanese Army as a buffer around vulnerable positions at BIA. And God forbid they should ever shut down airport operations. That would send all the wrong signals about the stability of the duly-elected Lebanese Government, according to the pundits at the State Department.

Arguments, outraged demands, and brain-numbing rhetoric flew back and forth between the grunts on the disputed ground and the analysts in a great wall of ivory towers. Meanwhile, Marines were dying and Becker's battle-hardened heart was breaking. He stood and blinked away the rain, staring up at the Chouf. Somewhere up there, tucked snugly into alleys, garages, carports, and gazebos, were the weapons killing and wounding Marines. He could sit down here crying the poor-ass at the mercy of the bastards and the bureaucrats . . . or he could do something about it.

"Tubes . . ." Becker turned to smile at his old friend. "As an expert on the subject, what should a good Marine say when his superiors piss him off to the max?"

"Fuck 'em—all but nine—six for pallbearers, two for road guards, and one to count cadence."

"And what should that good Marine do about the situation?"

"Whatever seems appropriate at the time . . ."

"Roger. You get the jeep and pick up Captain Dyer at the MAU CP. Draw some beer and then bring him down to my tent."

The electronically amplified call to Moslem prayers barked, growled, and whined over Beirut, disrupting the evening stillness like a lonely hound howling away his solitude. Becker rolled over on his rack and squinted at his watch. Almost time.

"Up yours, Allah." He jammed his feet into soggy boots and lit a series of candles spotted around the tent. He just had time to splash water on his face when he heard jeep tires squishing in the mud outside.

Captain Denton Dyer, Public Affairs Officer for the Marines in Beirut, ducked inside the tent, grinned at Becker, and tossed a sweaty beer can in his direction. "Greetings, sahib. The Beirut Press Corps clamors for your attention."

Becker motioned him to a seat and waited for Douglas to enter. The weapons company gunny was carrying a case of cold beer when he managed to struggle through the tent-flap. He dumped the beer on the muddy ammo pallets that served as Becker's deck and slumped onto a spare cot.

"Just like old times, ain't it?"

Becker smiled and raised his beer in a silent toast. They had spent many long nights in similar circumstances in Vietnam. Kramer was usually around back then, when they were all enlisted men. Dyer was a regular companion as a Marine combat correspondent attached to the battalion and a frequent volunteer for straight combat assignments when spare grunts were more important than publicity.

He often said he owed his success in the Corps to writing outlandish stories about Becker and peddling them to the civilian press. In fact, it was Dyer's stirring, straightforward account of their stand on Hill 513 in the Hai Lang Forest—snatched and spun into worldwide publication by the civilian media who missed the action—that bolstered Becker's Navy Cross recommendation.

His reputation for guts, candor, and talent grew as Dyer went with Marines into various postwar hot-spots, insuring they got the attention and credit they deserved. It also fostered for him an unusually candid and solid rapport with the elite of American's foreign correspondents. Most of the media veterans in Beirut knew and respected Dyer from previous engagements around the world.

The trust he enjoyed on both sides of the fence gave Captain Dyer free run of the downtown Commodore Hotel, the Beirut command post for the Western press. That access was foremost in Becker's mind as he smiled at his old friend.

"What's the party line today, Denny?"

"Same old shit, Buttplate." Denton cupped a hand at an ear and spoke into a beer-can microphone. "Marine casualties are the result of stray rounds meant for other targets as internecine fighting continues in the strife-torn city of Beirut . . ." Dyer made a face and barked up a hollow belch.

"That's what the embassy says and as long as they stick to their guns, we don't have to answer too many questions from the homefront about why we don't shoot back. It's bullshit and the press knows it's bullshit. So what's new with you?"

"Not a goddamned thing . . . but we're gonna fix that. Does our Lebanese buddy still own the souvenir shop across from the Commodore?"

"Wafic? Sure, he's a fucking fixture . . . not to mention an unusually reliable source for the press."

"OK, it's good to go. You arrange the trip for us to visit the press. Cover our ass over at the hotel while I talk to Wafic."

Douglas passed cold beers and stared at the two officers. Something here remained unsaid. "Christ, if you want to buy some teapots or worry beads, you can sure as hell beat that Dune Coon's prices."

"Has to be Wafic, Tubes . . . and it has to be a secret."

"What's so fucking secret about buying souvenirs?"

"We ain't buying souvenirs. Wafic's gonna set up a little excursion for us . . . up into the Chouf."

"Wafic's got more contacts than a hydroelectric plant. He can get us up into the Druze area and out again." Denton grinned around a mouthful of cold beer. "We hit a couple of those rocket launchers and maybe the bastards will think twice before they punch the button next time."

Douglas began to pace, tapping his beercan with a grimy fingernail. "So the whole Commodore routine just sets up an alibi?"

"There it is. Denny's got some unimpeachable sources who will swear we spent the night in question being interviewed by them."

"Shit, Skipper . . . we get caught and we get fucking killed . . . either by the Ragheads or the Marine Corps. And even if we make it up into the Chouf, how you gonna find them Katyusha launchers? They mount the goddamn things on trucks and change locations all the time."

"Wafic will know where they're parked . . . or knows somebody who knows."

"And he's just gonna tell you all about it for free?"

Dyer stood and began passing out helmets and flak jackets. "Listen, Tubes, my sources gave me the word on Wafic. He may be a thieving, gun-running, drug-smuggling, money-grubbing sonofabitch . . . but he's also a patriot."

* * *

They sat cross-legged at a low table sipping the strong, syrupy Turkish coffee served by Wafic's wife. The inane pleasantries were long past and it was time to lay it all on the line or leave. Becker offered his host an American cigarette to buy time and stared at the portly, olive-skinned man burnishing an ancient Moslem *masbaha* in the nicotine-stained fingers of his right hand. The rhythmic click of the prayer beads sounded like a cheap clock in the strained silence.

Becker had first met Wafic Chihab through a former-Marine buddy who was bureau chief for the Associated Press in Beirut. Shortly after his unit arrived in Lebanon, Becker read a particularly insightful analysis of the debilitating differences in the nation's coalition government. He queried his reporter friend and discovered that one of the primary, unnamed sources of insight was the garrulous proprietor of a run-down souvenir shop located across from the Commodore Hotel. Becker frequented the shop in the halcyon days before the MNF became a solidifying target for sectional disputes and often sought Wafic's opinion. They were candid, friendly, and only slightly distrustful of each other.

Chihab and several other descendants of Lebanon's Phoenician merchant class formed a cadre of "veteran observers" who the Western press regularly cited in their analyses of the ever-changing political and military climate in the Middle East. These men were fluent in the Esperanto of trade and finance that forged the only common link between the area's diverse special interest groups. They dabbled in gold, silver, and other commodities, but their real stock in trade was information and influence.

Like many of his cohorts, Chihab was a moderate Sunni Moslem with a large family spotted in strategic locations around Beirut in Shiite, Druze, and even Christian neighborhoods. His family formed a network of sources, servants, syncophants, shysters, and other shady characters that allowed patrician Wafic to successfully ply his trade.

Wafic's only true fear was foreigners. He could be struck

impotent by the influence of Syrian, Iranian, Israeli, French, or American outsiders on the status quo in Lebanon. Becker banked on that fear and made his pitch.

"Wafic, what I say to you now must remain secret. If it does not . . . well, there may be serious consequences."

"What can bring threats between friends, Captain?" Chihab shifted onto another haunch and pocketed his worry-beads symbolically. "I give my opinion to many but rarely share a confidence. We will talk in the strictest of confidence. Your ears, mine . . . and Allah's."

"Fine, my friend. I wish to get into the Chouf, destroy some rocket launchers that have been hurting my men, and get out again without being discovered."

Wafic frowned, crushed out the American cigarette, and popped one of his own foul-smelling Galloise between his lips. He pumped smoke at the ceiling and then turned his dark eyes on his American visitor. "Why take such a chance? The offending guns can be knocked out easily by your ships or planes."

"No. There would be too many innocent civilians killed. We must hit them with precision. I want to take out two launchers. No more."

"There are many launchers, guns, and mortars in the Chouf. Why just two?"

Becker smiled and sipped at the fresh coffee delivered by Wafic's eldest daughter. "An old Bedouin tactic, Wafic. You slip into an enemy's camp and cut the throat of one sentry while the other sleeps. In the morning, you have one dead man and a hundred unable to sleep the next night. I want Jumblat and the Druze gunners to realize they are vulnerable to attack at any time."

The gap-toothed smile revealed Wafic's approval of the concept. The frown that followed showed he still had reservations. "This is a very dangerous thing you propose. Why should I become involved?"

"Because you are Lebanese, Wafic. And this is your city. This is Beirut, not Damascus, Tehran, Tel Aviv, Paris, or Washington. You want it to stay that way and I want it to stay that way . . ." Wafic's head nodded slowly and Becker plunged ahead with passion.

"Look at the situation in Lebanon, my friend. Everyone wants a piece of your country. The Israelis are poised on the outskirts of Beirut, the Syrians are swarming all over the other side of the mountains, the Iranians are flooding into the Bekaa Valley. What's keeping them at bay? The Americans, French, and Italians sitting in the middle of it all. If we leave now, Lebanon ceases to exist except as a battlefield."

"And you are preparing to leave?"

"Wafic, my country is tired of losing soldiers in other country's causes. If the shelling continues, if more Marines die, we will leave . . . and Lebanon will fall."

"But the Druze . . ." Wafic shrugged and waved a hand over the table, shooing a fat fly and dismissing the threat posed by a small Moslem minority. ". . . surely you have more important problems."

"But not more pressing ones, Wafic. The Druze are killing my men right now, today. Will you help?"

Wafic signaled for more coffee and then considered quietly as he peeled a tangerine. Half the fruit was in his stomach before he spoke. "I have a cousin, Nasir, who married a Druze woman. They live in the Chouf. He says the rocket launchers are mounted on trucks. They are driven to firing points and then taken to different garages for rearming."

"That's why I need a guide, Wafic. I want to know where and when two of the launchers are parked close together on a specific night."

"To reach these places in the Chouf, you must pass through an Israeli checkpoint on the mountain road then then make it through one or more Druze or Shiite checkpoints."

"A small strike team can do that, Wafic . . . with your help."

"I would look upon it as helping my country and my family, Captain. Consider this proposal. On a night of my selection, you meet me along the coast road at a place between the Israeli checkpoint and the seaside gate to the airport. I will be driving a truck with my cousin Nasir. We will take you through the checkpoints and into the Chouf. The buildings containing the launchers will be marked. From that point, you are on your own."

Becker pondered the plan. If they were caught or killed trying to get back down out of the Chouf, the Moslems would have a major propaganda coup. Even if they were returned alive to friendly hands, they'd wish for death by the time the shit storm blew over. The risk seemed acceptable given the alternatives, but Becker was in the market for insurance.

"Your plan sounds good, but I'm worried about escaping at night without a guide. If there was a way to get us through the confusion and out of the Chouf quickly and quietly after we have done what we came to do . . ."

Wafic crossed his hands, arched his back, and stared at the rattan fan slowly revolving overhead. "There is a man," he said, "a Druze with family in America. He might be convinced to help . . . for a price."

It was the bottom line Becker had been expecting. He reached into a pocket, withdrew his wallet from a plastic bag, and laid ten crisp American one-hundred-dollar bills next to the fruit bowl. Wafic did not look at the cash. He rose stiffly and extended his hand to Becker. The meeting was ended.

"Prepare yourself, Captain. Watch the coast road beginning Sunday. When you see a red flare, we will be ready. Meet me on the road the next night at eleven P.M."

"Thank you, Wafic. I'll see you soon."

"*Inshallah,* Captain. If God wills it."

Over the next three days, Becker kept Douglas and Dyer busy while he tended to command chores and continued carping at the battalion commander for permission to fire up into the Chouf. It was always denied.

Captain Dyer used his contacts in the press corps to locate a reliable, out-of-the-way dry-cleaning establishment where three sets of standard Marine Corps utility uniforms were quietly dyed jet-black. Gunny Douglas made a series of clandestine jeep trips to Wafic Chihab's contact points where he plunked down large amounts of their pooled cash to purchase a folding stock Soviet AKM assault rifle, an old Winchester twelve-gauge trench gun, and a Russian 9mm Makarov pistol. Meanwhile, Becker flimflammed a careless combat engineer and walked away from the MAU Service Support Group with twice the standard allotment of C-4 plastic explosive needed for a simple demolition job. The clothing, weapons, ammo, and explosives were wrapped in ponchos and buried under one of the pallets in Becker's tent.

At 2215 on a blustery Thursday evening, four days after Becker held the meeting across from the Commodore Hotel, the inky sky over the westernmost quadrant of BIA was pierced by a pencil-thin shaft of red light. A red-star cluster blossomed low over the Mediterranean surf line, hung for several seconds like a sputtering star, and then disappeared.

Marines on perimeter watch passed the word to take cover. The unusual light in the sky might be a registration mark or signal for Druze gunners. The Americans at BIA lost sleep but no lives. The rocket launchers were stowed safely in nondescript garages for the night. Wafic Chihab and his cousin Nasir knew exactly where.

The next night, just after dark, Becker and Douglas employed Denton Dyer's good offices to let the command know they would be downtown meeting with the press. Dyer had taken the precaution of submitting a falsified formal request for the interview earlier. A PAO driver took them to the Commodore where he was dismissed with assurances they would be returned to the compound by a driver for one of the TV networks.

They trooped into the Commodore lobby carrying a large, but otherwise inconspicuous satchel. Denton and Becker sauntered into the bar where they were sure to be seen by several of the correspondents and then slid out the back by failing to return from a piss-call. Douglas was waiting beside a dusty cab. After a brief haggle over the fare, they climbed into the Mercedes and ordered the driver to take them south toward the airport using the coast road.

Traffic was light along the highway which paralleled Beirut's sparkling Mediterranean seacoast. They paid the driver and dismissed him at a point about a half mile from the well-guarded seaside entrance to the airport. Dodging into the dense brush between the BIA perimeter and the black ribbon of highway, the team walked about a mile to a covered position that placed them between the Marine perimeter gate and the Israeli checkpoint that guarded the road winding up into the foothills.

"This is it," Becker whispered, dropping the satchel among the weeds. "Let's get changed." They dug a hole and buried their standard uniforms and equipment.

Douglas produced three tubes of camouflage paint and they darkened all exposed skin, checking each other to insure a patch of pale flesh didn't give them away in the misty moonlight. All forms of identification had been removed and left behind. Chihab was due in less than fifteen minutes by Dyer's watch.

Douglas and Becker used the time to cut lengths of fuse from a roll and crimp them to nonelectric blasting caps. They measured sufficient lengths to burn for four minutes, allowing adequate time for clearing the blast area. The C-4 plastic explosive was molded into football-shaped charges of a half pound each. Weapons were checked and magazines loaded.

As they worked by feel in the dark, Becker whispered a review of the plan. Dyer would carry the AK and serve as out-guard for the team somewhere between the two target sites. He would have to find and recognize their Druze escape guide using directions and a description provided by Chihab.

Douglas would carry the shotgun and rig one of the target launchers for demolition. Becker, wearing the Makarov at his hip, would rig the charge on the second launcher. Once the fuses were lit and burning, the two demo men would join up with Dyer and head for the escape guide. Each man had a pocketful of American dollars and Lebanese pounds in case a bribe proved necessary. Each also had a small compass taped to the underside of a shirt-pocket flap. If the whole plan went into the crapper, they would split up, head north, and meet back by the place where their uniforms were buried.

At 2200, they were dressed and ready, crouched in a wooded copse beside the coastal highway, waiting for their ride into the Chouf. Dyer nudged Becker at 2203 and pointed wordlessly at the lights of a truck swinging off the road. When the dome light went on and the driver jumped out, Becker recognized Wafic. He ambled to the front of the beat-up truck, opened the hood, and spoke briefly to a short, dark man they presumed to be cousin Nasir. It looked like engine trouble, a common sight along Lebanon's serpentine highway system.

While Nasir fiddled with a healthy engine, Wafic strolled casually along the tree line at the side of the road like a man looking for a place to piss. When he heard a whisper from the shadows, Wafic glanced at the empty road and then ducked into the trees. Becker emerged slightly from the shadows and offered his hand. They squatted, listening intently as Wafic outlined the plan.

"The ride will not be pleasant. Tonight we are plumbers on a late call. The truck is filthy and full of equipment. You will ride under a canvas. It is so dirty, the average soldier will not want to touch it. If Allah gives us only average soldiers at the checkpoints, you will be safe.

"I have selected two targets within a half a block of each other. The first is most dangerous—an open carport beneath a two-story building. Two trucks loaded with rockets are parked there. No lights but you could be seen by someone passing on the street. There is a wide alley west of this building. Head north up the alley and you will find the second target.

"It is an enclosed garage containing one rocket launcher and a storage area for spare rockets. This area is guarded. I do not know how many sentries. Each building is marked with a small white triangle near the ground on the side that faces the street. Tonight, the streetlights are not working. We have arranged this.''

The raid team concentrated hard on Wafic's words. There could be no reconnaissance or rehearsal. It would be a matter of trust, memory, and instinct once they reached the Chouf.

''Nasir and I will park the truck momentarily in the alley. We must leave quickly to avoid the Druze patrols. When you have done your work, continue north up the wide alley. You will find a shop with a lamb carcass hanging in front of it. Go to the rear of the shop and knock three times on the door. A man will come out carrying a rifle with three silver bands on the stock. Tell him *'Allah Akhbar'* . . . God is great. He speaks no English, but you must follow him. He will lead you out of the village. Now, we must go.''

They followed Wafic out of the tree line and crawled into the back of the truck. Nasir mounted after them and gingerly lifted the corner of a greasy tarp. The smell of rancid petroleum products was stifling. By the dim glow of a flashlight, they snuggled into a large cardboard box and sat silently as Nasir arranged the filthy tarp over their heads.

As the truck jolted into a turn and swung back onto the highway, Becker struggled to breathe in the cloying atmosphere and whisper final instructions.

''Denny, find an OP somewhere in that alley. Stay out of sight but be ready to distract any patrols that stop. If we don't show up two minutes after the first charge goes, split. Find the guide and get out. Tubes, you got the garage. Try to avoid the sentries, but if you have to take one out, do it quickly and quietly.

''Weapons are last resort only, guys. Don't let yourself get panicked into a firefight. If a sentry pops you or you run into a patrol, just take off running. Either go for the guide or lead 'em away from the area and head north toward Beirut. If you get your backs up against a bulkhead, then do what you have to do to make it out. Any questions?''

There were none. Each man was lost in his own thoughts. Becker slowed his breathing and tried to relax. It would all be over—one way or the other—in less than six hours depending on delays at the checkpoints.

Wafic Chihab slowed the truck and pulled into a line of four cars waiting for clearance at the Israeli checkpoint. The IDF detachment manning the area had pulled two M-113 Armored Personnel Carriers across the road to halt the free flow of traffic. Drivers were stopped and checked between the two vehicles and had to weave around to regain the road if they were passed by the soldiers.

An Arabic-speaking Israeli corporal approached their truck bearing a flashlight and wearing a Galil assault rifle slung across his chest. The man's eyes twitched nervously in the shadow cast by a round paratrooper helmet covered with camouflage netting. He asked for papers and both Wafic and Nasir handed theirs over along with the required merchant's permit for the truck.

The soldier scrutinized both sets of documents, shining his flashlight into the Lebanese faces briefly to match their appearance with the pictures on the papers. He seemed satisfied but did not return their IDs. "Where are you headed this night?"

Wafic smiled and shrugged from behind the steering wheel. "Tabiyat, a village up in the hills. A cousin who is too cheap to pay for local service has called us to do some repairs on his water supply. We work in the city by day. Family matters must be attended at night."

The soldier nodded but did not smile. "Down, both of you. Let's look in the back of the truck."

The Israeli corporal waved another soldier to his side and walked toward the rear of the truck. Wafic and Nasir dismounted, followed, and manipulated the latch to swing open the cargo bay. This was the critical time. Wafic whispered a silent prayer that the soldiers had bathed or changed uniforms recently.

As the choking smell of oil and grease wafted over them, the soldiers played their flashlights around the interior of the truck. They seemed to be contemplating a more thorough search but the old parts, tools, and lubricants jumbled

around in the cargo bay made the task repugnant. And it was
late, almost time for shift change.

The Israeli corporal snapped off his flashlight and handed
back the identity documents. Nasir closed the cargo doors
and followed Wafic slowly toward the cab of the truck.
Grinding noisily on the gearbox, Wafic got them under way
with a wave at the sentries and steered the truck around the
second APC. They were silent until the muted lights of the
checkpoint disappeared from the rearview mirrors. Nasir
breathed loudly through his long nose.

"It will not be so easy at the Druze checkpoint near
Tabiyat . . ." Wafic merely grunted and downshifted for
the winding climb into the Chouf.

It took thirty minutes to reach the outskirts of the village
selected for the American mission. Wafic slowed the truck
at a sandbagged position blocking the road and rolled down
his window. The solider who approached was wearing a
heavy green sweater and fatigue trousers. A well-oiled
AK-47 was slung casually around his neck.

"This is a controlled area. What is your business here?"

Wafic did not recognize the man. He would be Druze
militia from one of the organized flying squads that roamed
the area. "A better question, brother. What are *you* doing
here? This is the neighborhood of my family."

The soldier bristled slightly but did not reach for his
weapon. He snatched the proffered identity documents and
hit them with a small penlight. The false address listed was
a street on the other side of Tabiyat. "Why are you so late
returning from Beirut?"

Wafic shrugged and lit a cigarette. "There is no schedule
for leaky pipes, brother. We come home when the job is
done."

The Druze militiaman motioned them out of the truck
with the barrel of his weapon. Wafic climbed down and
noticed the sentry sported a pair of expensive French shoes.
He began to feel better about their chances. Standing next to
Nasir at the back of the truck, Wafic feigned fatigue and
irritability.

"There is nothing back here but tools and equipment. Why can't we go peacefully to our beds?"

"My duty is to protect you, brother." The soldier reached for the latch on the cargo doors. "Who knows what we might find back here?"

When the doors swung open, the militiaman flashed his light around the interior. The filthy conditions did not seem to bother him as he climbed up and began to poke around with the barrel of his rifle. Nasir climbed up beside him.

"Let me help so we can be on our way . . ." Nasir grabbed an overflowing oil can and managed to slop thick black oil over the militiaman's shiny shoes. The soldier began to dance around the truck bed, kicking furiously, trying to shake the substance from his feet. He jumped to the ground, stomped his soggy feet, and began to curse.

"You clumsy bastard! You have ruined my shoes."

Nasir jumped to the ground and shrugged. "An accident, brother. We are tired. My apologies."

The sentry tossed their papers on the ground without a second glance and began to scuff his shoes against a rear tire. "Get your filthy truck out of my sight!"

Wafic and Nasir drove away slowly in low gear. As they turned off the highway onto the winding streets of Tabiyat, Wafic switched off the headlamps and strained to navigate by the dull glow of the parking lights. Three blocks from the highway turnoff Nasir nudged his elbow and motioned for a right turn. They swung slowly into a wide cobblestone alley and switched off the engine.

While Wafic watched the street, Nasir popped open the cargo door and climbed inside the truck. He wrestled the tarp and recoiled as the black muzzle of a shotgun nudged his nose. "Quickly! This is the area. We must hurry!"

The raid team scrambled silently from under the tarp and dropped to the ground at the rear of the truck. It was pitch-black but their eyes were long since adapted to the gloom. Nasir grabbed Becker by the hand, led the team to the mouth of the alley, and waved an arm toward the right. "The garage is up there. Count six houses and cross the road. The sentry is on the left side of the building."

Nasir faced in the other direction and pointed. "The other trucks are parked just to the rear of that building. Now, we must go. God be with you."

They hugged the wall until Wafic and Nasir disappeared into the gloom with their truck. Dyer jumped when a dog began to bark at the night somewhere up the block. Becker put a hand on his shoulder and shoved him down into a crouch. "Relax. Find a place around here and set up your watch. If a patrol spots you, just distract them. Don't worry about us. And remember—two minutes after the charges go, you split. The guide should be somewhere up at the other end of this alley."

As Becker and Douglas sprinted away into the dark, Denton Dyer tightened his muscles and fought a violent urge to piss. He pulled back the sleeve of his uniform, turned his wrist, and checked the time. 2340. He reckoned by midnight Becker and Douglas should have the charges rigged and the fuses burning. Detonations should be somewhere around 0004. Dyer decided to ignore Becker's instructions. He'd wait until 0010. If it all went as planned, they should be on the way out of Tabiyat by 0020 or so. And the Druze assholes would be minus three rocket launchers, scratching their ass and wondering what the hell happened.

Gunnery Sergeant Tubes Douglas was crouched below an open window outside the stone garage when he spotted the sentry. The man was stretching and yawning. He wore a checked *keffiyeh* on his head and carried an AK-47 slung muzzle-down across his back. Douglas smiled tightly. The bastard would never reach the weapon before he died.

The sentry moved casually to a clump of bushes about twenty meters from where Douglas crouched clutching the pump shotgun. When he began digging at his crotch, Douglas saw his opportunity. He heard the splash of urine, leaned the shotgun against the wall, and made his move.

Breath whistled through the man's thick mustache as Douglas lunged to snake a muscular arm around his neck. Locking his hands together and squeezing hard, Douglas leaned back at a radical angle, pulling the sentry off balance.

The Druze struggled briefly but ineffectually. Douglas increased the pressure to insure the man could neither scream nor breathe and violently bent the sentry down across his knee.

Twisting violently, wrenching the sentry's head to the rear, Douglas felt the spine snap and the sentry sagged like a soggy pillow. Lowering him silently to the ground, Douglas shoved the sentry through a puddle of piss and out of sight under the bushes.

First blood went smoothly, but there was no way of telling when the dead sentry was supposed to be relieved or whether he was supposed to report regularly. If either was the case, Douglas might have serious problems. Pulling a red-lensed map light from his pocket, he fought the raging stream of adrenaline and tried to relax.

When the night remained silent and tranquil for two long minutes, Douglas retrieved the shotgun and levered himself through an open window on the side of the garage. He put his back against a wall and cautiously flashed a small cone of red light around the garage.

Stacked in a corner off to his right were eight of the long 122mm Katyusha rockets. In the middle of the dank garage was a nondescript pickup truck. His light revealed the skeleton shape of the launcher racks bolted to its bed.

Crawling toward the truck, Douglas reached into the demo bag at his side and retrieved two one-pound blocks of C-4 plastic explosive. His hand felt for and found the steel upright of the launcher mechanism. With detonating cord from his kit, Douglas wrapped two charges around the main braces of the Katyusha launcher. The high-speed det cord would triple the destructive power of the explosive. He shook nervous sweat from his eyes and carefully poked two of the prepared fuse combinations into the explosive charges.

Working by feel, he twisted the bitter ends of the fuses into an M-1 fuse lighter and tightened the retaining cap. To arm the charges, he merely had to pull the pin on the fuse lighter. He flashed his light briefly to get bearings and moved toward the pile of spare rockets. He rigged similar charges and paused briefly to mentally critique his work.

"Give me four minutes from the time I pull the pins," he muttered, "and you can kiss all this shit good-bye."

Captain Buttplate Becker cautiously pulled himself out from under the first of the rocket-launcher trucks and peered into the gloom. It was tough work under the low-slung vehicle but he'd rigged charges on the chassis to stay hidden while he worked in the open space of the carport. The past ten minutes had been dicey—sweating on his back, trying to keep dirt, rust, and road grit out of his eyes, while two roving patrol vehicles full of heavily armed Druze militia cruised the area. A searchlight washed briefly over the truck on one pass and Becker felt the old, familiar "plus four pucker-factor" as he reached cautiously for the cocked-and-locked Makarov pistol at his hip. But the Druze patrol passed, chatting amiably into the dark. Now it was time for the second target parked eight feet away in the next bay.

He grabbed the demo bag containing the remaining C-4 and wriggled like a frightened garter snake. As he broke cover, he pulled the fuse lighter behind him into a position where he could reach it without having to crawl back under the truck. Worried that Douglas might be ahead of him, he checked his watch. 2350.

Under the second launcher truck, Becker strained and blinked road dirt out of his eyes. Each time he packed plastic into the cross-members of the frame, accumulated crud cascaded into his face. He got the second charge rigged, wrapped in det cord and fixed with a four-minute fuse, and then wriggled out from under the truck.

Becker pulled the pins on both fuse lighters, crouching in the dark shadows of the carport. He was gratified to hear the snap and hiss of two burning fuses. In four minutes, the shit would hit the fan in Tabiyat.

Tubes Douglas was crawling out the window of the garage, listening to the hiss of two burning fuses at his rear when he heard the voice. He didn't understand the Arabic but he recognized the tone of a corporal of the guard. He scrambled to the ground and wedged himself against the damp wall of the garage. There was a slug in the chamber of the Winchester followed by a round of buckshot and another slug. He slid the safety off and waited.

The Druze sentry poked his head around the corner of the garage and called a name. When he got no response, he snapped on a flashlight and began to probe the darkness. Just before the cone of light landed on the dead sentry's boots, he died.

Douglas shouldered the scattergun and swung the muzzle toward the man's chest. The senior sentry was fumbling frantically for his AK when Douglas pulled the trigger. The zero-range shot blew the militiaman completely off his feet but Douglas barely noticed. The sound of the shotgun was deafening as it echoed off the stone walls of the garage. Douglas vaulted the bleeding body and ran hard for the alley to his left. At his rear he could hear the angry shouts of a reaction force.

He spun and fired blindly at the noise, hoping to put the Druze on his tail and keep them away from the fuses burning under the rocket-launcher trucks. It would take them a while to get organized and give chase. But would it take them three or four minutes? Douglas decided it was well out of his hands and pounded toward the rendezvous with Dyer and Becker.

Captain Denton Dyer flinched and nearly bit through his lower lip when he heard the boom of the shotgun. It was followed by screams in Arabic and the wild rattle of AK fire. Douglas had to pop someone. It was clear from the sounds. It was unclear whether any of the answering shots might have left Douglas dead or dying over near the garage.

As he was tightening the grip on his nerves, Dyer caught a flash of movement on the street side of the alley. He brought the AK to his shoulder and stared over the sights as Becker emerged from the gloom breathing hard. Dyer flagged him down and ducked reflexively as the muzzle of the Makarov swung in his direction.

"Looks like Tubes got popped . . ." Becker struggled to catch his breath as he knelt at Dyer's side in the shadows. "About two minutes until my charges go. We'll wait that long and see if he shows."

Dyer had counted to one hundred fifteen when they heard footsteps and a long leather skid as someone in boots negotiated a turn toward the alley. They raised weapons simultaneously, steadying on the entrance to the alley just as the first explosion split the night.

Tubes Douglas was propelled into them by the force of the blast and they tumbled in a tangle of arms and legs a few feet down the dark corridor. They could barely hear his voice for the ringing in their ears.

"Jesus H. Christ! I had to grease one of the motherfuckers! Let's get the hell outta here!"

They were halfway down the alley when the detonation of Becker's charges added to the chaotic din building over Tabiyat. They heard the grind and roar of car and truck engines as Druze reaction forces scrambled. In the flickering firelight of the infernos on either side of the alley, they caught stroboscopic glimpses of panicky militiamen scurrying for muster points.

Dyer was leading as they puffed nervously up the dark alley. He raised a hand to halt them and pointed at a lighted storefront. A bloody carcass, covered in a black blanket of flies, hung from a hook screwed into one of the roof joists. The insects milled around sedately on the meat, clearly the only things in Tabiyat unaffected by the post-explosion chaos.

Dyer led the team into a muddy side alley running alongside the shop and motioned them into the shadows. He cautiously approached a shuttered wooden door and, keeping one hand on the pistol grip of his AK, knocked loudly three times. Stepping aside gingerly, he ducked into the shadows and covered the door with his muzzle. At his side, Becker and Douglas were aiming at the same point.

A long minute passed. He considered knocking again when the door swung slowly open to reveal a bearded Lebanese wearing a Turbanlike hat of the devout Druze.

The man glared into the shadows but gave no sign of recognition. When he stepped into the alley, they saw the ancient bolt-action rifle at his side. Against the worn ebony of the stock, three silver bands were clearly visible. Without a word, he hitched the weapon onto his shoulder and turned to walk off into the darkness.

With an uneasy shrug, Becker led the team in his wake. They kept a steady separation of twenty meters from the guide who looked neither right nor left as he stomped through the back alleys of Tabiyat. Becker was disoriented but his compass told him they were pressing north as they walked through the twisting, turning streets, too narrow at most points for vehicles.

The guide—if that's what he was—seemed smart to avoid areas regularly cruised by Druze militia patrols. He was only slightly reassured by the decreasing level of sound at their backs. If nothing else, they seemed to be moving at a steady pace away from the smoking holes in central Tabiyat that were once rocket-launcher sites.

Dyer slid up beside Becker and whispered, never letting the guide out of his sight. "What do you think? Is that fucker leading us out of here . . . or into a Druze patrol?"

"Hard to say. Something about it doesn't feel right. Sonofabitch looks too much like the Ayatollah for my comfort. You push on with Tubes. I'm gonna move out onto the flank a bit."

It was nearly 0200 by Becker's watch. The strike team and their silent guide were a half hour out of Tabiyat, into rolling sand dunes and scrub brush. At his back, Becker could see the entire skyline of the Chouf village spiked by tongues of flame and glowing in the gloom.

Abruptly their guide stopped and motioned with quick hand motions. He still did not turn to face them. Dyer and Douglas closed the distance and stared into the gloom where the man was pointing. They stood on a slight rise. Below, a black snake of macadam highway slithered around a bend. Off to the left they could just make out the glow of Beirut skyline.

"Sonofabitch," Dyer breathed a sigh and slung his AK over a shoulder. "Looks like we made it."

They were looking around for Becker when they heard the snick of a well-oiled bolt. Their guide was kneeling in the dirt with his weapon pointed at their bellies. His grin sparkled in the pale moonlight. They watched him slowly bring the old rifle to his shoulder like a stalking hunter.

"Allah Akhbar," he whispered, lowering his bearded chin to the stock. Those were his last words.

They heard two shots and slammed themselves into the ground in an adrenaline-fueled reaction to the noise. In slow-motion, the turncoat guide lowered his weapon and turned. He was jolted by another impact and crumpled to the ground. In the muzzle flash, Dyer saw a red stain spreading across the man's chest.

Becker stepped out of the shadows, holding the Makarov in both hands, pointing it directly at the dying Druze on the ground. He walked toward the bleeding man and nudged him with the toe of his boot. No reaction. The last round had hit him in the neck and severed an artery.

"Fucking ringer. I'd have dropped him earlier but he seemed to be leading us in the right direction."

Dyer picked up the man's weapon and shook his head. "Wonder why he didn't just grease us back in the ville or walk us into a patrol."

"Hard telling. Weird set of rules. Probably thought he'd earned his money once he had us out of Tabiyat. From that point, he could freelance. Who knows?"

Douglas stared back at the blazing skyline. Suddenly, he was crushed by internal pressure. He nearly pissed himself getting his trousers unbuttoned. "Christ, what a rush! You think it didn't scare the piss right outta me? Let's get the fuck outta here."

Becker knew they were exhausted after a rapid-paced ten-mile trek down the road. The adrenaline rush had long since worn off, replaced by a debilitating weariness. Tired men make fatal mistakes, so he halted the team a safe hundred meters from the IDF checkpoint. He moved forward to a slight knoll on the beach side of the road and lay prone to check activity.

What he saw was a honking, steaming line of cars and angry drivers that stretched back beyond the Marine perimeter gate. The Israelis were halting all traffic headed south because of the situation up in the Chouf. It still looked and sounded like a pitched battle up there.

He picked up his team and led them on a circuitous route around the IDF sentries. All ten of the soldiers they passed were busy brandishing their weapons at the frustrated Lebanese motorists who were returning to the Chouf from night work or play in Beirut. With a near riot on their hands, the Israelis paid no attention to their flanks and the assault team slipped by without a hitch.

At the roadside area where they buried their uniforms, Douglas found the entrenching tool and began to dig. The weapons and black uniforms went into the hole as the regulation equipment was pulled out. In just under five minutes, they emerged from the woods as slightly disheveled Marines headed home after a night in the Commodore Hotel bar.

Becker and Dyer pulled Douglas through the sentry position at the perimeter gate like concerned officers escorting a reluctant drunk. The young PFC on guard at the gate bid them good night and returned to staring at the commotion out on the coast road. Fucking officers always managed to get liberty while he was stuck watching the Yids harass the Lebs and missing a night of much-needed sleep.

The sun was just beginning to peek through a pall of smoke hanging over the Chouf when they ducked into Becker's tent. Douglas went directly to an upturned steel helmet where he'd planted three beers in a bed of ice before leaving on the strike. He passed the cans and proposed a toast.

"Fuck a bunch of incoming!"

They drank, shook hands silently, and dropped off into a deep sleep.

Colonel Stokes, the MAU commander, was in an expansive mood as he addressed his assembled officers and Staff

NCOs after Church Call on Sunday. "We don't know who it was," he crowed, pacing up and down with his hands on his hips. "And we don't give a shit!"

There was a chorus of guttural shouts from the senior Marines. They had something to celebrate at last. The MAU Intelligence officer's morning report said three Katyusha launchers had been destroyed by unknown causes during the night. More importantly, the Lebanese were reporting a mass exodus of artillery and rocket vehicles out of the Chouf. The Druze were heading for different ground and everyone knew that would mean a sharp decrease in incoming fire for a while.

At a signal from the colonel, Captain Denton Dyer, freshly shaved and looking like a sedate staff officer, stood and read from his notebook. "I have here a clipping from the *Jerusalem Post* . . ." He giggled and the crowd laughed along with him, sensing a joke to follow.

"Apparently, Walid Jumblat is claiming a strike team of American Marines did the deed up in the Chouf!" The hoots and caustic comments echoed around the MAU CP. Becker and Douglas feigned disbelief and then collapsed in laughter, shaking their heads at the sheer insanity of the concept. Colonel Stokes was nearly in tears when he stood and waved everyone to silence.

"Can you believe that shit? Huh? They think *we* sent someone up there to take 'em on in their own backyard! Christ, I wish . . ."

X.

Column Left, March . . .

Becker trudged slowly beside Kramer up the hot cement walkway leading to Camp Lejeune's Law Center. He could not remember a time when he had more difficulty holding his head high and maintaining a correct military posture. Images from old Jimmy Cagney movies kept unreeling in his mind. The governor didn't call. The condemned man takes his last walk.

He frowned at the painful knot that had formed in the pit of his belly and slowed his step even more. The hot concrete seemed to stick to his dress shoes like glue. Leon Kramer put a reassuring hand on the small of his back.

"Relax. This is just jury selection. You remember what I told you to say?"

Becker swallowed a lump and nodded slowly. He stepped through the heavy door Kramer held for him and tried to steady his gait as they turned left heading for the courtroom area of the Law Center. Farther down the empty corridor Kramer grabbed at polished brass handles and pulled open a pair of polished oak doors. Becker stood frozen, gazing at the battlefield.

The courtroom glowed with the dull sheen of well-polished wood. The luster was the fruit of labor carried out over the years by brig rats and other Marines performing penance for some transgression. Becker was reminded of old *Perry Mason* reruns as he swept his gaze across the spectator's gallery and a low railing fronted by a set of hinged gates.

A long table stood beyond the railing to the right. There were seven severe wooden chairs aligned behind the table. In front of each someone had placed a pristine yellow legal pad. Well-sharpened pencils lay across each pad at a perfect forty-five-degree angle. By the numbers, that's the Marine Corps way. Everything by the numbers.

Two shorter tables were aligned parallel with the railing on either side of the gates. Two chairs stood behind each. There was a smaller table just in front of the judge's bench. A corporal with a tight white-wall haircut sat fiddling with a recording machine. As the court reporter, he would parrot every word spoken into a megaphone-shaped mask that contained a microphone.

It all registered as Becker followed Kramer toward the front of the courtroom. When they were seated at the left-hand table, Becker stared up at the empty judge's bench that dominated the room. The place smelled mostly of furniture polish, but Becker could detect another scent. He breathed deeply and recognized the door. It was fear. Men had sweated in abject terror in this room. He felt his armpits dampen under the uniform blouse as he became one of them.

Colonel Arthur J. Scales cleared his throat and tugged nervously at his tie. He flipped down his trial guide and tried to ignore the rainbow blaze of ribbons stacked over Becker's left chest. Facing the symbolism of long and heroic service, he felt cheap and inadequate. His recently rekindled anger over the dagger General Tobrey was holding at his throat surged briefly and he fought for control of his voice. It was all such a long time ago . . . and almost as much bullshit as the case currently before his court.

"Captain Becker, I want to explain your right to be tried by a court with members and your right to request trial by judge alone. You have the absolute right to be tried by a court consisting of not less than five officers. Do you understand this?''

"Yessir." Becker's response was a throaty croak.

"The Uniform Code of Military Justice provides that a court-martial with members votes by secret written ballot. Two thirds of the members must concur in any finding of guilty. If you are found guilty of any offense, the court again votes by secret written ballot to determine the sentence, and two thirds of the members must concur in the sentence. Do you understand this?''

"Yessir."

"You also have the right to request trial by judge alone. If you are tried by judge alone, then I will decide if you are guilty or not guilty. If I find you guilty of any offense, then I will sentence you. Do you understand this?''

"Yessir." Kramer had ruled out the solo trial. He was suspicious of the information Tubes Douglas surfaced indicating a vague prior connection between Tobrey and Scales. He wanted a collective conscience at work in this trial.

"Have you discussed this with your counsel?''

"Yessir."

"I do not have a request in writing for trial before judge alone. Does the accused desire to request trial by me alone?''

"Nossir, we do not." Kramer responded without looking up from the notes he was arranging on the table.

Scales ordered everyone to be seated. Kramer finished with his notes and glanced across the aisle at the trial counsel. Major Rodney Claiborne looked fresh and combat-ready.

"Does either counsel have other matters to bring up before the members are summoned?''

They did not and Scales signaled for a staff sergeant bailiff to bring in the proposed members of Becker's court-martial board. Ten Marine officers filed in through a rear door. Becker counted a male colonel; a male lieutenant colonel; four majors, three male and one female; and four captains, two men and two women. He recognized about half of them and was about to mention it to Kramer when the trial judge began to issue initial instructions.

"Ladies and gentlemen, I'm Colonel Arthur J. Scales, the trial judge detailed to preside in this case. Major Rodney Claiborne is the assigned trial counsel. Mr. Leon Kramer is the assigned defense counsel. The accused is Captain Thurmond Becker and he is seated with his counsel.

"This court has been convened by Major General David E. Tobrey, Commanding General, 2nd Marine Division. A copy of the charges in this case have been provided for each of you.

"Earlier, the accused pled not guilty to the charges and specifications. Every accused at a court-martial has the statutory right to have the findings and his punishment determined by an unbiased, impartial court. To sit as a member of a court-martial, you have to meet certain qualifications.

"You may be disqualified if, for example, you investigated any of the incidents alleged in the charges and specifications, or if you have formed or expressed an opinion as to the guilt or innocence of the accused or the sentence to be awarded in this case.

"If any of you know anything about this case or if you have any preconceived opinions that you cannot set aside and that might affect the outcome of this case, you may be disqualified to sit as a member."

There were no questions or voluntary disqualifications. Kramer had expected it. Everyone wanted to be in on the spectacular trial. Hell, there might be a book or even movie rights to consider.

Scales stared at the officers over his black, half-moon reading glasses and went back to reading.

"Both the government and the accused may challenge any member who they believe to be unqualified. If I agree with counsel, I'll excuse the member. Each side also has the right to challenge one member peremptorily, that is, without any reason whatsoever. Since counsel may have many reasons for challenging a member, no one who is excused should consider that as a personal reflection upon him or herself.''

Closing his trial guide with a sharp snap, Colonel Scales asked the bailiff to escort the prospective members of Becker's court-martial board from the courtroom. Both Kramer and Claiborne sat furiously scratching notes. When the court was clear, Scales turned to Claiborne.

''Does the prosecution wish to question any of the members further?''

Claiborne rose and consulted his notes. ''Sir, we wish to call Major Eldon Wright and Captain Tracy Hawthorne for further examination.''

The bailiff ducked out and returned leading a balding Marine officer with a respectable stack of ribbons over his left breast pocket of his uniform. Kramer winced when he spotted the maroon and blue Good Conduct Medal given only to enlisted Marines.

Major Wright climbed into the witness chair and settled comfortably. Claiborne nodded and smiled.

''Major, do you know the accused, Captain Thurmond Becker?''

''I do not know Captain Becker personally, sir, although I have heard of him over the years.''

''Over the years? How many years would that be?''

''Well, let's see . . . I've been a Marine for twenty-four years now.''

''Did you serve any of those years as an enlisted man, Major Wright?''

''Yessir. I spent my first twelve years in the Corps as an enlisted Marine.''

''So you'd consider yourself a mustang, Major?''

''Yessir. I believe I fit the definition.''

''Have you read any of the publicity concerning this case?''

''Yessir, I've read the papers. Although I've made an honest effort not to form an opinion without hearing both sides of the issue.''

''What part of that publicity impressed you most, Major?''

''Well, as I say, I've tried to keep an open mind. I guess

what struck me was Captain Becker's record as an enlisted man. He's got quite a combat record. That's of interest to all Marines.''

"Thank you, Major Wright. The prosecution has no further questions for this member.''

Kramer glanced at Becker and shook his head. ''No questions for this member, Your Honor.'' While the bailiff escorted Major Wright out and returned with another member, Kramer whispered an explanation.

"No sense fighting for a mustang. He'll never sit on the board.''

A petite woman Marine took the stand. She said her name was Captain Tracy Hawthorne. Caliborne consulted his notes for a long moment and then glanced up with a friendly smile on his face.

"Captain Hawthorne, do you know Second Lieutenant Rebecca Campbell?''

"I believe I may have met her at some social function, but I can't say I know her.''

"Have you read any of the publicity concerning this case?''

"Yessir, I read the daily papers.''

"Captain Hawthorne, where did you go to college?''

She looked slightly puzzled but regained her composure quickly with a glance at the trial judge. "I went to the University of Southern California in Los Angeles.''

"While you were in college did you belong to the National Organization of Women and did you actively campaign for the Equal Rights Amendment?''

"Yessir, I did.''

"What is your opinion of extramarital sex, Captain?''

She turned to stare at Colonel Scales and tugged at her uniform skirt. "What does that have to do with my qualifications to sit on a court-martial board?''

Scales did not look up from his own notes. "Answer the question, Captain.''

"I believe a woman should have freedom of choice in her sex life the same as a man. What's good for the goose is good for the gander . . . if that helps answer your question.''

Claiborne did not seem inclined to pursue the evasive response. He turned to nod at Kramer. ''Nothing further for this member.''

Kramer rose and scratched at his chin for a moment. His courtroom manner was looser, more relaxed than Claiborne's rigid approach. ''Your response to counsel's question intrigues me, Captain. Does it mean you would expect a female to be punished the same as a male if sexual misconduct were an issue in a case?''

''It does. However, I don't think misconduct is an issue where love is concerned.''

Kramer nodded and scratched her name from his list of potential members. ''No further questions for this member, Your Honor.''

Scales glanced up as Captain Hawthorne cleared the room and asked Kramer if there were any members he wished to question. Kramer consulted the background notes compiled for him by Tubes Douglas. Three names were highlighted.

''Yessir. We'd like to question Captain Foreman, Major Glover, and Lieutenant Colonel Simmons.'' As the bailiff went after the first person named, Kramer slid Douglas's notes across the table for Becker to scan. Foreman was a born-again Christian, Glover was married to a woman Marine officer, and Simmons had once fought strenuously when Becker charged one of his Marines with misconduct.

Both sides bored in, searching for chinks in the armor.

Kramer: Captain Foreman, what's your opinion of marriage in our society today?

Foreman: The Bible tells us it's a holy bonding that no man should set asunder.

Claiborne: Captain, are you the kind of man who lets religion influence his performance of duty?

Foreman: I don't try to convert anyone to my way of thinking if that's what you mean. I've never had a compatibility problem between my religion and my career.

Kramer: Captain Glover, what is your opinion of woman Marines?

Glover: They have a lot of unique problems, sir. On the whole I think a lot of them. I married one.

Claiborne: Hypothetically speaking, Captain. If you or your wife were ever unfaithful, would you consider that a personal problem or a professional problem?

Glover: It's obviously both, sir. I believe the professional questions would have to be settled first and foremost.

Kramer: Colonel Simmons, on or about 12 July of last year did you engage in an argument with Captain Becker?

Simmons: Yessir. It got quite heated. The captain wrote a charge sheet on one of my Marines that I believed was unwarranted. He disagreed.

Claiborne: Sir, do you consider it professional to carry a grudge?

Simmons: Certainly not. We all have disputes. Win, lose, or draw, they have to be put behind us while we get on with the mission.

Scales listened attentively with his chin cupped in a hand. When the last questions had been asked, he scribbled a note and addressed both lawyers. "Does the prosecution have any challenges for cause?"

Claiborne stood and tugged at his uniform blouse. "The prosecution challenges Major Wright and Captain Hawthorne."

Scales consulted his own notes and then slipped the glasses off his nose. "The trial judge agrees with both challenges for cause. Those members will be excused."

Kramer nodded and whispered to Becker. "Just what I figured. Now we get a chance to even things out." He stood when Scales called.

"Your honor, defense challenges Lieutenant Colonel Simmons, Major Glover, and Captain Foreman."

Scales slipped his glasses back on and scanned his notes. He flipped a few pages, pursed his lips, then removed the glasses. His expression was a study in dispassion.

"The trial judge does not agree with challenges in any of those cases, Mr. Kramer. I can find no pertinent reason to disqualify any of the members you've named based on testimony here today."

Becker stared up and caught the look of surprise on Kramer's dark face just before it warped back into composure. "Sir, I submit that each of the members I have challenged for cause bears either a preconceived notion of the rights and wrongs in this case, or has personal or moral convictions that would not allow them to render a fair and impartial hearing. I think that's been made clear."

"Obviously, Mr. Kramer, I do not agree. Your challenges for cause are denied. The members will sit."

Kramer scooped a handful of notes and thumped them into a neat stack while he fought to control his temper. "Your honor, I request a brief recess to consult with my client."

Scales consulted his watch with obvious displeasure. "Very well, Mr. Kramer. You have fifteen minutes. This court is recessed."

In the corridor outside the courtroom, Kramer steered Becker to a chair and gulped water from a sweating fountain. "That sonofabitch knows damn well none of those members should sit! There's something wrong here, Buttplate."

Becker lit a smoke and hung his head between his knees. He felt like he'd just boxed five hard rounds with a hard-hitting heavyweight. "Sure ain't what I expected. Anything we can do about it?"

"Not right now . . . but I've damn sure got some solid grounds building for overturn on appeal. Meanwhile, we've gotta take the best shot with peremptory challenge. What do you think?"

Becker dragged on his smoke until the ash threatened to burn his fingers. "Shit, I dunno. Seems to me the guy married to the WM might change his mind. Colonel Simmons is basically a good officer. He was just trying to stick up for one of his Marines. I say we challenge the Holy Roller."

Scales didn't care for the peremptory challenge when Kramer announced their decision, but he allowed the defense to disqualify Captain Foreman. When the bailiff brought in the seven remaining members of Becker's court-martial board, he picked up a Bible, raised his right hand, and asked the approved jury to do the same.

"Do you, and each of you, swear that you will faithfully perform all the duties incumbent on you as a member of this court; that you will faithfully and impartially try, according to the evidence, your conscience, and the laws applicable to trials by courts-martial, the case of the accused now before this court; and that you will not disclose or discover the vote or opinion of any particular member of the court upon the finding or sentence unless required to do so in the due course of law, so help you God?"

The ragged chorus of "I do"s sounded like a funeral dirge to Becker. He stood beside Kramer feeling numb as Scales rapped his gavel sharply. The sound echoed through the courtroom like a pistol shot.

"This court is now assembled."

XI.

Fix Bayonets . . .

"Trial Counsel, do you wish to make an opening statement?"

Major Rodney Claiborne rose to his full height and turned to address the court-martial board. He smoothed the front of his uniform blouse, cleared his throat, and began in a rich baritone.

"Ladies and gentlemen, the United States intends to accomplish a relatively simple, straightforward task in this court-martial action. We intend to prove—using the testimony of not only a witness but a participant in this offense—that Captain Becker did conduct himself in a manner unbecoming an officer and a gentleman in his affair with Second Lieutenant Rebecca Campbell. We intend to show beyond a reasonable doubt that his conduct in this affair was prejudicial to good order and discipline in the military service and reflected discredit on the Marine Corps.

"As the person charged with representing the United States Government in this case, I will use only a few items of evidence to prove Captain Becker is guilty of the offenses with which he is charged. I do not intend to engage in high-flown rhetoric or to depart in any way from the issue at hand. That issue, ladies and gentlemen, is whether or not

Captain Becker actually did what he is being accused of here. I underscore that point because I suspect other, irrelevant issues will be brought up during this trial.

"In summary, I can only echo the instructions you have heard from the trial judge and urge you to concentrate on the heart of this case. Did Captain Becker—or did he not—carry on an illicit affair with Lieutenant Campbell? Did their affair constitute or create a situation in which good order and discipline were prejudiced? And, finally, did the public knowledge of their affair besmirch the image of the service? We believe our evidence will clearly show that the answer to all these questions is yes.

"Finally, ladies and gentlemen, allow me to express the confidence that the government has in the fairness and professional acumen of this board of Captain Becker's peers. We believe that Marine officers who are themselves subject to the same strict code of moral and ethical conduct as the accused will arrive at a fair and just conclusion. Thank you."

"Mr. Kramer, opening remarks?"

"Ladies and gentlemen, you just heard counsel refer to a trial by Captain Becker's peers. He was, of course, talking about each of you on the board here today. You are all Marine officers and Captain Becker is a Marine officer. That should make you peers, but I submit that it does not. We have no one on this board who rose through the ranks from private to master sergeant, to warrant officer to a regular commission. We have no one on this board who holds a Navy Cross and a Silver Star for gallantry in combat . . ."

"Objection, Your Honor! The accused's service record has no relevance to the issues at hand and should not be disclosed for fear of prejudicing the board."

"Sustained. The board is instructed to disregard defense counsel's remarks concerning decorations or service history."

"Your Honor, Captain Becker's distinguished career has every relevance when he stands accused of conduct unbecoming a Marine officer!"

"The objection is sustained, Mr. Kramer. Proceed in a different direction or waive your opening statement."

"Ladies and gentlemen of the board, you will see evidence during this trial of only one thing regarding the relationship between Captain Becker and Lieutenant Campbell. You will see evidence that they fell in love. Now, the Marine Corps has come a long way from the days when individuals were only allowed to consider wives or lovers as if those persons were issue items found in the seabag at boot camp. The Corps today recognizes love and romance as a very real part of each human being's life. In fact, the Corps has built a significant support establishment at most of its bases that does nothing more for national defense than cater to members of Marine families or counsel those individuals whose love life creates problems with duty performance. That's a significant attitudinal consideration that I urge you to bear in mind as the evidence in this proceeding unfolds.

"You will see evidence in this court that Captain Becker and Lieutenant Campbell engaged in the natural expression of their love. What you *will not* see is evidence that this relationship in any way, shape, or form caused Captain Becker to do anything that could be construed as conduct unbecoming an officer or a gentleman.

"You will hear evidence that our society does not consider falling in love to be a crime, nor should the Marine Corps, which is after all merely a reflection of the society it serves. We will make the point that society's attitude toward love and marriage has changed. And we will demonstrate that Marines—men and women who spring from American society—should not be subjected to an arbitrary code that denies them the rights enjoyed by all other American citizens.

"The defense in this case is as simple as the prosecution claims the government's case to be. The question you should be asking yourselves is this: Can we condemn a man—a human being with all the attendant frailties of the species—for falling in love and seeking happiness with the person he loves?

"The defense also trusts in the professional judgement of

this court-martial board. But we more resolutely trust in the humanity that underlies each of your professional military exteriors. Perhaps the most confident man in this courtroom today is Captain Becker himself, who has consistently told me of his belief in what he calls 'the system.' He assures me at every turn that our process of military justice is humane and fair. He trusts that each of you—in your own good conscience and knowledge of human nature—will find nothing in his behavior that is wrong . . . or that reflects discredit on the service he loves. Captain Becker believes that, ladies and gentlemen, and so do I.''

XII.

Aaaaaattack!

Scales: Trial Counsel, you may call your first witness.

Claiborne: The government calls Second Lieutenant Rebecca Campbell.

Bailiff: Do you swear that the evidence you shall give in the case now in hearing will be the truth, the whole truth, and nothing but the truth, so help you God?

Campbell: I do.

Claiborne: State your full name and unit, please.

Campbell: Second Lieutenant Rebecca A. Campbell, Headquarters Battalion, Marine Corps Base, Camp Lejeune.

Claiborne: On or about 1845 on 15 August, did you and the accused Captain Becker engage in sexual relations on the shore of a public lake in the area of Norfolk, Virginia?

Campbell: I—I don't remember exactly.

Claiborne: Then perhaps these photographs will help refresh your failing memory, Lieutenant.

Kramer: Objection to this evidence, Your Honor!

Scales: Nothing has been formally introduced or shown to the board as yet, Mr. Kramer.

Kramer: Then make him stop shoving that picture in her face!

Claiborne: Your Honor, kindly instruct the witness to answer my questions.

Scales: May we continue, Lieutenant Campbell?

Campbell: Yes. Let's get it over with.

Claiborne: We'll move on to another time, Lieutenant. On or about 2030 on 26 August, did you check into the Fairwinds Motel in Norfolk, Virginia, with the defendant?

Campbell: Yes.

Claiborne: And while staying with the defendant in that motel did you engage in sexual relations with him?

Campbell: Yes.

Claiborne: On or about 1945 on the evening of 28 August did you and the defendant . . . (list of twenty-nine instances during which Campbell and the accused engaged in sexual relations)

Campbell: Yes . . . yes . . . yes . . .

Claiborne: Did Captain Becker know of your marital status when you began seeing him regularly?

Campbell: Yes.

Claiborne: Did Captain Becker know your husband was a fellow Marine officer?

Campbell: Yes.

Claiborne: How did he find out about that?

Campbell: I told him.

Claiborne: So he had full knowledge that you were a legally married woman and that your legal husband was deployed overseas, yet he chose to proceed with a romantic relationship, to engage in sexual relations with you?

Campbell: It was a mutual thing—a mutual attraction—we . . .

Claiborne: Thank you, Lieutenant. No more questions for this witness, Your Honor.

Scales: Cross-examine, Mr. Kramer?

Kramer: Lieutenant Campbell, exactly what was your relationship with your husband at the time when you met Captain Becker.

Campbell: There was no relationship. We were legally separated but he was headed overseas so the divorce could not proceed until he returned. I begged him to waive his rights and let me go ahead with the final divorce, but he wouldn't allow it.

Kramer: Was that because he was still in love with you or he wanted to preserve the sancity of your marriage or what?

Campbell: None of these things, sir. He flatly told me he did not love me. The reason he wouldn't let the divorce proceed was because he thought it might be a blemish on his career record.

Claiborne: Objection, Your Honor. The witness cannot speak for her husband.

Scales: Sustained. Where are we headed here, Mr. Kramer?

Kramer: Simply establishing some emotional background, Your Honor.

Scales: Proceed, but keep it relevant.

Kramer: How did you feel during this time?

Campbell: I felt trapped.

Kramer: And while you were feeling trapped by this marriage in name only, you met and fell in love with Captain Becker.

Campbell: Yessir. I finally discovered what love really should be . . .

Claiborne: Objection. Irrelevant, Your Honor. Counsel is leading the witness down a primrose path.

Scales: Sustained. Ladies and gentlemen of the board, the last question asked by the defense counsel and the answer given by the witness are improper. I have directed that it be stricken from the record. You are instructed that you must completely disregard the statement and no inference whatever may be drawn from it. This means that you must not consider it for any purposes whatsoever; you must cast it out of your minds just as if it had never been said.

Kramer: I have no further questions for this witness, Your Honor.

Scales: Anything further, Trial Counsel?

Claiborne: Your Honor, I have here a complete transcript of a report of surveillance, including photographs, of the defendant's activities relating to his association with the witness. Also contained in this evidence is the report of the Marine Corps investigating officer who examined the original report and made a finding of fact that prompted the charges now standing against the defendant. We would like to introduce it as evidence and have it marked Government Exhibit A.

Kramer: Objection to the evidence, Your Honor. This surveillance was conducted illegally with no probable cause.

Claiborne: Your Honor, probable cause was a report of suspected illegal activity made by a Marine officer to the Naval Investigative Service as provided for under current regulations.

Kramer: The evidence was illegally obtained.

Scales: Mr. Kramer, this is not a civilian court. The Marine Corps has every right, indeed every obligation, to investigate reports of alleged misconduct by its officers. I will accept the evidence. Ladies and gentlemen of the board, I am giving you Government Exhibit A. I'd like you to take it into the member's room and examine it. You can make notes if you want to, but don't talk about this exhibit and don't talk about the case. Let the bailiff know when you've finished and we'll continue with the trial.

Kramer: Shit.

During the recess, reporter Jim Payne stood beside a pack of other reporters jostling for control of three pay phones and dialed his editor's number. He was angry and upset when he finally got through to the editorial desk.

"This is Payne out at Camp Lejeune. They're in recess while the jury reads a transcript of the investigation. Yeah, they got the pictures and all. He ain't got a whore's chance in hell, if you ask me.

"Uh-huh. There's some strings being pulled somewhere. Kramer is getting buffaloed all the way down the line. I'm gonna leave and make a few calls. Block me out some space on the OpEd page."

XIII.

Thrust . . . Parry . . . Thrust . . .

Major Claiborne rested the government's case against Captain Becker in a subtle, succinct speech that marked him as a champion of the Corps' most basic tenets and traditions. As defender of the faith, he alternated his tone and vocabulary between reverence for the greater good and righteous indignation. When he had ticked off his last element of proof, narrowed the focus, and driven home his final point, he made a courtly gesture toward Kramer and folded into his seat.

Colonel Scales seemed decidedly uncomfortable with the rhetoric, frequently gazing out a courtroom window or up at the acoustic ceiling. It was over for quite some time before he finally picked up a pencil and pointed at Kramer.

Becker's attorney stepped out from behind the defense table and spent a moment pacing, deep in thought. It was a studied display of gravity and passion designed to contrast with Claiborne's style.

Reporters—bored with stiff, mincing court-martial procedures and searching for color—had described the different courtroom demeanors in a steady stream of features and updates on the controversial trial pouring out of Camp Lejeune. Claiborne rarely moved out from behind the trial counsel table, standing at a modified position of attention and using his rich voice to punctuate, underplay, or emphasize. He came off in depictions as self-assured, aloof, tough-minded, even arrogant, depending on the reporter's perspective. Kramer was described as committed, bombastic, emotional, manipulative, charming, or—most often—as a man grasping at emotional straws to keep his client afloat.

The case continued to garner space in daily papers and time on radio and television around the nation. Much to Claiborne's dismay, Becky Campbell held a press conference following her testimony. Much to the delight of the reporters, she got on the record all the things about her relationship with Becker that Claiborne would not allow her to say during the court-martial. Across America, the case of Don Quixote Becker versus The Unfeeling Thugs became instant soap opera.

Tobrey was outraged. Kramer was delighted. Claiborne was confident since the board members were kept media blind and deaf. Becker was merely confused. Meanwhile, Becky was transferred to temporary duty at a remote logistics base in rural Georgia.

By the third day of the trial, press pool odds on an acquittal for Becker were long and dwindling. With a confident smile for the board members and a covert wink for his stoic client, Leon Kramer counterattacked.

"Defense calls Mrs. Wanda Beaman."

An elderly, distinguished woman in a simple business suit rose from her seat in the crowded courtroom and moved slowly to the witness stand. Claiborne administered the oath, then took his seat looking slightly amused.

"Will you identify yourself for us and tell us where you work?"

"My name is Wanda Beaman. I live here in Jacksonville and I work at the Camp Lejeune Family Services Center."

"What sort of work do you do at the Family Services Center?"

"I'm a counselor. I try to help young military men and women who are having trouble with their family lives or with domestic situations."

"And what qualifies you for that sort of work, Mrs. Beaman?"

"Well, I have been a Navy wife for more than thirty years. My husband is a retired Navy captain. When he left active duty, I thought I could put my experience with young military families to work and try to help them solve some of the problems they encounter these days."

"Do you have any other qualifications for your job?"

"Over the years I've managed to complete an undergraduate degree in psychology and I have a master's degree in counseling."

"What would you say is the most common family problem you see in your work here at Camp Lejeune, Mrs. Beaman?"

"Well, you have to understand that the Navy and Marine Corps are somewhat unique as regards family life. They spend so much time at sea or deployed away from their families that the problem of loneliness—and all the attendant problems—is the major issue, I guess."

"What sort of 'attendant problems,' Mrs. Beaman?"

She squirmed in the hard wooden witness chair and cut a nervous glance at the trial judge. "Well . . . it's the problem of seeking companionship and understanding, I suppose . . . on the part of both partners. When the husband is away from home so much, a young wife frequently falls into a relationship with another man. Or the husband becomes involved with another woman someplace away from home. It causes real tensions that threaten to break up a marriage."

"Do many military marriages break up over that sort of problem?"

"Unfortunately, yes. I'm sorry to say we don't have a very good track record with keeping people together in situations like that."

"And what do you attribute that to, Mrs. Beaman?"

"Divorce is so easy to get nowadays. The young people get angry or disenchanted and run to some lawyer for a cheapie court action that ends their marriage."

"You seem rather negative concerning divorce. Is it always a bad thing?"

"It's always a traumatic thing, but there are as many good divorces as there are bad marriages. Sometimes a man and a woman really do have irreconcilable differences and they *should* leave each other. If they don't, it's likely they'll never be happy."

"Would you say, Mrs. Beaman, that the situation you described earlier—that of a married, military man or woman falling in love with someone else—is common here at Camp Lejeune?"

"Well, it's clearly the most common problem we encounter at the Family Services Center. And I think we only see it at all because commanding officers or other supervisors send their people who are having trouble to us. If they didn't do that, or if we weren't there, most people would just run to a lawyer."

"Based on your experience as a psychologist and a counselor, would you say the rate of people involved in extramarital affairs here is uncommonly high?"

"I can't contrast it to every place in the country, but the rate of people I see who have become involved in that way is certainly high."

"Thank you, Mrs. Beaman. No further questions from defense."

Major Claiborne rose and leaned forward to rest his weight on the table. From Kramer's perspective across the aisle, the trial counsel looked like a bird dog on point—or a shark.

"Mrs. Beaman, you mentioned earlier that you had been married to a naval officer for more than thirty years. Is that correct?"

"Yes, Major. My husband and I were married in the chapel at the Naval Academy the week after he graduated in 1952."

"There's been a lot of water under the bridge since that time . . ."

"My goodness, yes. We've been around the world a time or two with the Navy."

"Were there ever times when you considered divorcing your husband or that he considered leaving you?"

"Well, yes. I suppose all couples contemplate divorce at one time or another, especially when there's pressure or they find themselves not getting along for one reason for another."

"Tell us why neither of you ever carried through and got a divorce."

"Well . . . I, uh . . . I suppose it's because things like that just weren't done in Naval service families back in our turbulent days."

"Why not?"

"Well, Major, it was a different time. Society was not quite so liberal about such things back then."

"Is that the only reason you never proceeded toward divorce when you weren't getting along with your husband?"

"No, I suppose you could say the cohesiveness of the Navy family had some influence on the situation."

"Would you elaborate on that, please?"

"Well, there is some pressure that's put on families like ours to stand by each other when times get tough. I guess the service simply expects us all to do our duty. That is, to stand by each other even when we'd rather not."

"Thank you, Mrs. Beaman. No further questions, Your Honor."

With a grunt of grudging respect for Claiborne, Kramer stood to call his next witness. "Defense calls Dr. Wayne Markos, Your Honor."

A short, wiry-haired man sporting oversize spectacles mounted the witness stand and raised his right hand for swearing. When he was seated, Kramer bored into the attack.

"State your name and address for us please."

"I'm Dr. Wayne Markos and I live in Chicago, Illinois."

"What is your profession, sir?"

"I'm a sociologist. Also a Ph.D. and Professor Emeritus at Northwestern University where I lecture in several disciplines. I am also occasionally employed by the government to do research.''

"What is your connection with or special knowledge of America's military forces?''

"The sociology of the standing military has always been a special interest of mine. I did my doctoral dissertation on the American enlisted man. During the period when the Pentagon was considering abolishing the draft and going to an all-volunteer service, I led the research team that reported to the President.''

"Have you ever heard of a thing called the Microcosm Theory, Dr. Markos?''

"Yes. In fact, I believe I may have coined the term during the research for the Department of Defense.''

"Would you explain it in terms we laymen can understand?''

"Well, sir, it's really not very complicated. My theory was—and is—that the social definition of America's military forces mirrors that of the society from which they spring. In other words, I believe what social phenomena you can spot in American society, you will also, inevitably, spot in the ranks of the American military.''

"And what was the significance of your theory to the planners in the Department of Defense?''

"I think my contention—and all the research we did tending to confirm it—ran contrary to long-standing notions on the part of professional military people.''

Scales arched his eyebrows at Claiborne and then turned his attention to Kramer. "I presume there is some point to all this, Mr. Kramer?''

"Yes, Your Honor. I intend to deal here with the elements of the offense. I'm aiming for a definition of unbecoming or unacceptable conduct.''

"That definition is presumably clear in the Uniform Code of Military Justice, Mr. Kramer. I will allow you to proceed only if you are brief with this witness.''

"Thank you, Your Honor. Now, Dr. Markos, I was asking you to expand on the theories held by professional military men that run counter to your own.''

"For many years, at least since World War II, the American military establishment—that is, professional officers, NCOs, and the like—were of the opinion that they constituted a separate breed or strain of person within the fabric of American society. This belief manifested itself in a sort of perverse elitism that led professional military people to believe the laws, codes, ethics, and morality commonly accepted in American society did not apply within the armed forces. They believed they were operating by a different code."

"And your research did not bear that out?"

"No, it did not. I maintain that in the eighteen to twenty years the average military recruit spends in civilian society before he dons a uniform, he has firmly socialized and internalized the ethics, morals, and basic philosophies of his society. And that was the sticking point, you see. The military—in particular the Marine Corps—believes that through some magical, mystical training experience, they can force young men and women to internalize an entirely different—frequently alien—code of social behavior."

"And have events since you developed your theory and made your report tended to bear you out, Doctor?"

"I believe they have, quite clearly. Statistics speak for themselves. Take the drug abuse problem or racial prejudice, for example. The services go through all sorts of machinations to prevent these problems and consistently fail. Why? Because the society in which these soldiers and sailors grew up—the society in which they formed their most strongly held beliefs—does not always teach that such things are very wrong."

Major Claiborne rose and addressed the bench. His voice was dry and bored. "Your Honor, I fail to see where all this is leading. It seems to me most of what this witness has testified to is irrelevant to the case at hand."

Scales removed the prop from under his chin and folded his hands. "With all due respect to the witness, Major, I tend to agree with you. Mr. Kramer, either make a relevant point or I will excuse the witness."

"Yessir. Dr. Markos, what is your opinion of the current

military standard of appropriate moral conduct as it relates to officers and gentlemen?''

"Objection, Your Honor! Subjective opinion of the witness is not germane.''

"Sustained. Both counsel approach the bench.''

Scales seemed uneasy staring at the lawyers. He fidgeted momentarily and then leaned forward. "This is taking us nowhere, gentlemen. Mr. Kramer, I have been patient but you keep dancing around the pertinent issues here. I'm going to excuse the witness.''

"Your Honor, I can't defend my client without some latitude to establish frame of reference. The UCMJ is not the only standard here.''

"It most assuredly is, Your Honor.'' Claiborne bristled and raised his voice above a drone for the first time in the trial.

Kramer matched his tone. "Your Honor, defense objects strongly to these artificial restrictions.''

"That's enough, gentlemen. Mr. Kramer, you are arguing extenuation here. I will not allow you to put the Marine Corps on trial. Now, proceed or rest your case.''

"Defense calls Dr. Curtis Linfield.''

A tall, well-dressed individual with a bronze tan glowing from distinguished features entered the courtroom trailing the bailiff. He took the stand and repeated the oath after Claiborne. They sounded like two Shakespearean actors practicing lines.

"Please state your name and address.''

"I'm Dr. Curtis Linfield of Los Angeles, California.''

"Are you a medical doctor, sir?''

"Yes, I'm a clinical psychiatrist by training and I currently have a private practice in the Los Angeles area.''

"Dr. Linfield, what is your special connection with or knowledge of the military?''

"Well, I served four years in the Marine Corps during the Korean War and for the past four years or so I have specialized in studying marital problems among military people.''

"What led a person with access to a wide range of patients to focus on the military?"

"I mentioned my service in the Corps. Even back in the days when I was in, there was what I considered to be an inordinate number of marital problems and domestic difficulties among married Marines. Now, through my training and practice as a psychiatrist, I got interested in the problems attendant to infidelity. I eventually decided to make a study of it. That required a measurable, controllable test base. I remembered the Marine Corps experience and decided to study Marine families to see if I could draw some conclusions that could be projected onto society at large."

"And did you reach any such conclusions, Doctor?"

"Yes, I did. In fact, I eventually wrote a book about the problems of infidelity in America and much of the writing that went into that book was drawn from my work among military families."

"Can you state your major conclusion for us?"

"Certainly. I concluded that the problem of infidelity in American marriages is rampant. You can lay that on a number of doorsteps: more liberal attitudes toward sex between consenting adults, the general decline of the American family as an inviolate institution, the unwillingness of modern women to suffer needless oppression . . . as I say, a number of reasons.

"The point, I think, is that this vast increase in marital infidelity clashes head-on with conventional morality as passed along by age-old societal standards. The result is guilt. In short, many people, married or otherwise committed to another person, engage in extramarital affairs and suffer enormously from guilt when, in fact, they should not feel guilty. They should simply accept that fact of their life and make some move to resolve the guilt-producing circumstances."

"Let me see if I understand all that, Dr. Linfield. You conclude that guilt in a person who has been involved in an extramarital affair is caused because that person perceives the infidelity to be a sin or moral wrong—a crime—when it is not perceived that way by other members of our society."

"That's an oversimplified version. What I'm actually

saying is that society has become so accustomed to the activity that people don't perceive it as wrong. They simply perceive it as a fact of life, so there is no reason for the modern person to suffer from guilt and the related psychological problems.''

Claiborne did not bother to rise. ''Objection, Your Honor. Society at large, regardless of attitudes or opinions held within it, is not germane to this case.''

Scales scrubbed his face and cocked his head at the witness. ''We'll hear a little more, Counsel . . . as a matter of general interest. Please summarize, Mr. Kramer.''

''Dr. Linfield, how did you conclude that society no longer considers marital infidelity or sexual indiscretion to be a great crime?''

''Simple really. Merely a matter of auditing police and court records. Over the past ten years or so, the instance of arrest, prosecution, lawsuits, et cetera over marital infidelity has declined dramatically. You need only ask the police or attorneys why that is. It's because there is virtually no chance of winning an indictment or a major lawsuit based on such charges. Follow that reasoning and you'll find that not very many people can be relied on to judge such activity as criminal or even culpable.''

''And these conclusions were first suggested to you during your study of Marine Corps families?''

''That's correct. I found that the Marine Corps—and I suspect the other services too—tended to accept such activity as an inevitable part of the life-style. Indiscretion, yes . . . maybe. Criminal behavior, no. They were most reluctant to pursue or prosecute such cases.''

''Can you sum it all up for us, Dr. Linfield? What about society and the attitude toward extramarital affairs?''

''I'd say that our society no longer considers it a crime to become involved with a person who is not one's spouse. They may look on it as distasteful or sacrilegious, but they have accepted certain patterns of modern human behavior to such an extent that they will not brand the people involved as offensive.''

''Thank you, Doctor. No further questions.''

"Cross-examine, Major?"

"Dr. Linfield, you mentioned that you served several years in the Marine Corps. Is that correct?"

"Yessir, it is. I served in Korea with the 1st Marine Division at Inchon and the subsequent push to the Yalu River."

"And did you serve as an officer?"

"Yes, I did. I was a second lieutenant at Inchon and finished my tour as a captain commanding a rifle company at the Chosin Reservoir."

"So you were trained and indoctrinated in the code of honor, ethics, and moral behavior that is required of an officer by the Marine Corps?"

"Yes, I went through Officer Candidate School at Quantico. I think I see where you're going here but . . ."

"There's no need to characterize your answer, Doctor. I merely asked if you'd been trained in or exposed to the code of conduct required of a Marine officer. A simple yes or no will suffice."

"Objection, Your Honor! Trial counsel is not providing an opportunity for the witness to explain himself."

"Overruled, Mr. Kramer. You had your turn. Proceed, Major Claiborne."

"Now, Dr. Linfield, you stated that you were subjected to training concerning the expected code of conduct for a Marine officer. Is that correct?"

"I was."

"And to the best of your understanding, what was the purpose of that code?"

"I imagine it was to set a standard of behavior that would allow an officer to retain the respect of his men and cause him to behave in a certain prescribed manner."

"What manner is that?"

"The Corps sets an arbitrary pattern of behavior. They want the sort of officer who will not sully the reputation of the officer corps in front of the men, I suppose. I was never given a reason for it all."

"So, you were taught this was simply the way things were done. Never mind the reason?"

"We were told the purpose of maintaining an image was so that we would inspire unquestioned respect and obedience in combat."

"And did it work that way in Korea?"

"For some it did, yes."

"Given what you've testified here, Doctor, is it your opinion that a highly moral code of conduct for Marine officers is right or wrong?"

"Objection, Your Honor. That calls for a subjective opinion the witness is not qualified to give."

"His opinion was hardly immaterial when you were asking the questions, Mr. Kramer. Your objection is overruled. The witness will answer."

Kramer exploded toward the bench. "Your Honor, this travesty has gone far enough. Move for mistrial!"

"On what grounds, Mr. Kramer?"

"I believe you know what grounds, sir. If nòt, the transcript of proceedings from voir dire onward should provide the answers. I am prepared to submit a full brief citing specific irregularities in the morning."

"Mr. Kramer, this court has been more than patient with you. I must remind you again—strongly and publically—that this is neither a circus sideshow nor a soap opera. I will take your motion under advisement when cross-examination of this witness is complete. Until then, sit down and remain silent or I will have you removed from the courtroom."

There was a rumble from the audience and a muted hiss from the press gallery. Several reporters scrambled for phones in the corridor. Scales banged his gavel and ordered silence as Kramer collapsed into his chair and glanced at Becker. He seemed to have shriveled inside his form-fitting uniform. There was a weary hunch to his broad shoulders. His blue eyes were moist and clear but the skin around them was pale and sagging.

Kramer understood the feeling. As the cross-examination continued, he began to mentally review the procedures for redress through the Court of Military Appeals.

"Dr. Linfield, I asked your opinion concerning the code of moral conduct for Marine officers. Given your own experience in combat, do you believe it's right or wrong?''

"I suppose it's correct in some instances.''

"Thank you, Doctor. No further questions, Your Honor.''

"The witness is excused. Do you still wish to move for mistrial, Mr. Kramer.''

"I most assuredly do, Your Honor.''

"I will consider the motion. Court is in recess. Bailiff, escort the members out. Mr. Kramer, I'll see you in my chambers in fifteen minutes.''

On his way to see Colonel Scales, Kramer folded the morning newspaper to feature the editorial page and looked around the deserted corridor for his client. Becker was slouched on a bench behind the water fountain.

"Why don't you go on over to the BOQ? I'll be by in a couple of hours with some cold beer.''

"I'll wait here for a while, Leon.'' Becker smiled but his eyes were sad. The old Buttplate Becker was still gamely facing the enemy, but he was fighting a retrograde action, giving ground and taking hits. "I don't want to deal with that mob of reporters outside.''

"Speaking of which . . .'' Kramer handed him the paper and crouched to stare into his eyes. "Read this—and for Christ's sake, don't fall apart on me. We've still got some rounds left to fire. I've gotta go see the judge. I'll be by your place around seven.''

OUR OPINION
An editorial comment
by Jim Payne, *Daily News* Staff Writer

The train hauling Captain Thurmond "Buttplate'' Becker to the end of a long, distinguished career as a United States Marine is on track and running fast.

The metaphor fits given the petty, possibly illegal activity of the men who now hold Becker's future in their hands. Under the ideal situation—and we realize military justice is far from an ideal system—no one person should hold sway over the outcome of a trial. And, indeed, there are seven officers appointed to the court-martial board in this case who should be weighing the evidence to determine whether or not Becker is guilty as charged of conduct unbecoming an officer in his relationship with a married woman. But a jury can only make competent judgments if it is allowed to hear and evaluate all the evidence. When it is manipulated, when its objectivity is compromised by high-handed legal maneuverings, no just verdict can ever be reached.

In a case like that, the military judge is supposed to intervene in the interest of the accused to get things back on an even keel. When that does not happen, the trial becomes a travesty. It becomes, in fact, a nonstop express railroad to a predetermined verdict.

There is little doubt about the verdict in this case. The question on the minds of most Marines here at Camp Lejeune is why it ever came to trial in the first place. Where this general court-martial is being discussed on the base—and that's practically everywhere—you hear comments about the Marine Corps' attempts to "legislate morality." You hear senior Marines wondering aloud why the command is singling out Captain Becker and prosecuting him when so many others are guilty of the same "crimes."

And you hear, over and over again, the one comment that is most telling in the consistent argument that the trial should never have reached a courtroom: "There, but for the grace of God, go I."

Still the Marine Corps insists on considering its members some sort of superhumans, subject to a different code of behavior in their private lives than other citizens of the society the Corps helps defend. Perhaps it is that mentality bringing the spectre of command influence to bear on Captain Becker's trial. Or, perhaps, it is some more sinister vendetta, as some sources at Camp Lejeune suggest. If that's true, the highest authorities in the Defense Department need to take a hand in this case and see that justice is done.

After what he's done for our country, Captain Buttplate Becker deserves no less.

XIV.

Buttstroke . . . Slash . . . Jab, Jab, Jab . . .

Leon Kramer was not invited to sit and he was damned if he'd stand at attention, so he crossed his arms and glared down at Colonel Arthur Scales. The trial judge glared back from under bushy eyebrows and then pushed back in his swivel chair and laced his fingers behind his head.

"This is not a two-way communication, Mr. Kramer. I'll do the talking and you'll do the listening. We all know the charges and the nature of the required evidence here. If you intend to continue bringing in these so-called expert witnesses, stop being obtuse. Make your point and get on with it.

"I will not tolerate a stall or an attempt at misdirection. We will move this trial through to conclusion in an expeditious manner. I will not grant your motion for mistrial. Is all that crystal clear to you, Mr. Kramer?"

"What's crystal clear to me, Colonel Scales, is that we're dealing with a self-fulfilling prophecy here. The command wants Captain Becker found guilty—and that's the way it's gonna be."

Scales swiveled with an angry squeal of springs and stared out the window of his office. From a flagpole in the distance the American flag hung in limp folds, unruffled by wind on a still day, unaffected by the controversy that swirled among its most ardent defenders. He shook his head, ran a hand through his thinning hair, and turned to face Kramer. His gaze was clear and steady, but Kramer saw pain behind the eyes.

"Colonel, I know you're in a tough spot. Can we talk off the record?"

Scales loosened his tie and pointed at a chair. When Kramer pulled it close to the desk and sat, Scales held up a hand for silence. He reached into a desk drawer and came out with a bottle of scotch whiskey. He found two glasses in another drawer and poured for both of them.

"It's been a tough week, Leon. Let's bank the fires."

"Thank you, Colonel. I've been waiting for an opportunity like this." Kramer drank and welcomed the warm glow that spread through his chest and settled his nervous stomach.

"Get it off your chest, Leon."

"Sir, you are deliberately not allowing me to make my case."

"What case? You've been arguing extenuation and mitigation since the trial began. The points you're trying to make have nothing to do with whether or not Becker is guilty as charged. You're arguing that the UCMJ is wrong so Becker should be found not guilty by default."

"What else have I got, Colonel? I've got to pull out all the stops. I owe Becker a hell of a lot."

Scales sipped his whiskey in silence for a moment and then burned a look into Kramer's eyes. He spoke clearly and distinctly.

"I know all about debts and obligations, Leon. More than I care to know, in fact."

Kramer frowned over his whiskey glass, staring at the intense expression on Scales's face. He sensed an unspoken message in the comment. The trial judge was trying to communicate something more than he was saying.

"Colonel Scales, a smart lawyer can do a lot with a little evidence of prejudice. I believe it's called command influence in the military . . ."

"That's what it's called, Leon, and it's an insidious thing wherever it's found. Consider the officers on the board. They're career people, each and every one of them. They want to survive, succeed, and enjoy a pleasant retirement—just like I do. If they cross the line, if they declare themselves against the accepted code of conduct for Marine officers, they'll never make it."

"The decision of the board is no reflection on you, Colonel. Why are you making it so tough on me and so easy for Claiborne?"

Scales smirked and poured himself another shot of scotch. He contemplated the amber liquid for a moment and then downed it. "Leon, I'm a good lawyer. I'm an experienced trial judge. I don't make many mistakes."

"Then what the hell is happening out in that courtroom, Colonel? The transcript is gonna be full of procedural holes and irregularities."

"And what does a good defense attorney do when he finds irregularities?"

"He appeals in a heartbeat and . . ."

Kramer watched the furtive smile spread across Colonel Scales's face and was nearly blinded by the light.

"Give it a rest, Leon. Win your case on appeal."

With studied care, Buttplate Becker capped the whiskey bottle and spread a pristine white towel on the lid of his footlocker. He began to field-strip his old M1911A1 .45-caliber pistol in the precise manner he'd been taught and had practiced for twenty years. It was comforting, like brushing the coat of a friendly old dog.

He depressed the magazine catch on the left side of the pistol and glanced briefly at the five bull-nosed rounds of ball ammunition. He placed the ammo carefully at the upper-left corner of the towel and proceeded with the mindless chore. In a neat line from left to right he laid out the recoil spring plug, barrel bushing, slide stop, receiver group, recoil spring, recoil spring guide, and barrel. The familiar orderliness of it all brought a smile to his face.

He reached for a rag and a bottle of small-arms lubricant

and began to lovingly massage each part, working the oil into a micro-thin sheen on the worn metal. And then he began to reassemble the parts in reverse order. Nothing was forced or jammed as his hands moved economically around the weapon.

The slide snicked smoothly to the rear against the tension of the recoil spring. He closed his eyes and let the slide fly forward, feeling the jolt of the empty weapon as it went into battery. He sighted on his shaving mirror and squeezed the trigger. The hammer fell unexpectedly with a sharp snap. Smooth pull, no creep or catch . . . just as he'd designed and modified it over the years.

The loaded magazine slipped into the pistol with a fluid rasp and he gave it a tap with the heel of his hand as he'd been taught in training. The slide moved smoothly to the rear on freshly oiled channels and snapped forward to push a round of .45 ACP into the shining chamber. He slowly rotated the weapon and stared with fascination into the dark cavern of the muzzle.

Leon Kramer rattled the doorknob of his BOQ room and then burst inside carrying a sweaty six-pack. "Jesus, Buttplate, why don't you answer the door? I thought you went over the hill on me."

Becker eased the hammer home on his pistol, jammed it into a salty old leather holster, and pointed at the cleaning equipment spread on his locker. "Sorry, force of habit. Got lost in my thoughts."

"Well, I hope those thoughts are pleasant. I just came from a very interesting meeting with Colonel Scales, our trial judge."

"Listen, Leon. I'm tired of dancing. Never was any good at it. We're losing this thing by the fucking numbers, aren't we?"

Kramer tossed his coat on Becker's bed and passed a beer can. He leaned against the wall and contemplated the question. "OK, here it is, high and hard. They're not letting me make the case I planned on making. It keeps coming back to the issues I've been trying to avoid. I think they're gonna find you guilty, but . . ."

"But what, Leon? But that's OK? But I can continue the march?"

"Yeah! This ain't Corregidor. You don't have to surrender to the bastards."

"They could vote to boot my ass out. That's what Tobrey wants and so far he's had it all his way."

"Bullshit! After I get General Stokey on the stand as a character witness, they'll whack you lightly on the pee-pee and forget all about it."

"So what? Remember how I used to tell you and Tubes to trust the system? How am I gonna face troops again and preach that sermon? I'm gonna make a statement, Leon."

"Awwww, Christ, Buttplate, we've been over this a hundred times! That's not smart. You don't want to piss 'em off before they vote on a sentence . . ."

Becker sipped at his beer and then began to rub a cloth absentmindedly over the shiny surface of his dress shoes. "I talked to Becky on the phone yesterday . . ."

"Yeah? What's she say?"

"She says to give 'em hell, Leon. That's what I'm gonna do. I've got a right to make an unsworn statement after they deliver the verdict and that's what I want to do."

"Listen to me, goddammit! Let me tell you what Scales had to say tonight. He damn near admitted this thing is a setup; command influence all the way. He's been making sure there are irregularities on the trial record. See? The fucking judge is on our side! We'll get the whole thing tossed out on appeal. No harm, no foul."

"Appeal means begging, doesn't it, Leon?"

Buttplate Becker stood gasping and blowing on top of the sixty-foot wooden tower at the end of the gut-busting Confidence Course. He checked the luminous dial of his watch as a gentle breeze dried the sweat on his heaving chest. 4:12. Not bad for a roller-coaster series of sprints, swings, shinnies, twists, turns, climbs, and vaults that was rated at five minutes on a good day.

He growled at a pale moon hanging over the pines, enjoying the husky rumble in his chest as the sound rattled off into the dark. That special feeling still coursed in his veins—that old Marine Corps feeling. He still had it. They could kill him, cut his fucking heart out, bash his balls in a Browning breech-block . . . no matter. It was still there, down deep inside him, impregnable, untouchable; a classic fortified position guarded by interlocking fields of fire.

The Corps was camped below his perch. On the right, clerks cramming and jamming over service record books, the paper machine grinding along behind the firing line. Cooks greasing the grills and flinging the occasional string of snot into the chow; mutiny battles monotony. Label-lickers and box-kickers, hoarding the good stuff and craving war to reduce their inventory. All of them secretly hoping with all their hearts that the day comes when they can bitch about being drafted into the grunts.

On the left—on one end or the other of the red tracers lancing the dark—the black-hearted infantry. Fuck peace, pray for war. Stand by to land the landing force. If I die in a combat zone, box me up and ship me home. Hey-diddle-diddle, right up the middle. And when this bloody cruise is over . . . tell the skipper for me he's got only twenty-three . . . he can roll up the ladder, *Semper Fi* . . . and I love you. With all my heart and soul, I love you.

"AAAAAAAAAA-OOOOOOOOO-RAAAHHHHH!!!"

Buttplate Becker grinned and barked into the dark over Camp Lejeune.

XV.

Stack Arms . . .

WAR HERO DECLARED GUILTY
IN CONTROVERSIAL TRIAL
by Jim Payne

JACKSONVILLE—a seven-member general court-martial board returned a verdict of guilty today ending the stormy trial of Captain Thurmond "Buttplate" Becker, a highly decorated Marine war hero. Becker, 42, a colorful figure in Corps ranks, could be facing dismissal from the service depending on the sentence decreed by the same board that found him guilty of "conduct prejudicial to good order and discipline" while declaring him innocent of a second charge of "conduct unbecoming an officer and a gentleman."

Becker refused to grant interviews after the announcement of a verdict in the case that was delivered after a weekend of deliberation by the court-martial board, composed of Marine officers all equal or senior to Becker in rank. His attorney, Leon C. Kramer, spoke briefly with reporters outside the Camp Lejeune courtroom and indicated his plans for an immediate appeal to the next higher authority.

"We are happy the board saw fit to find Captain Becker not guilty of conduct unbecoming an officer," Kramer stated, "but we cannot and will not accept a verdict that holds a man like him guilty of behavior that reflects discredit on the Marine Corps."

Kramer's comments were refuted by the government's attorney, Major Rodney Carrington Claiborne, who told reporters that "justice has been done in this case."

"Despite defense efforts to obfuscate the issue," Claiborne continued, "we kept the focus where it belonged throughout the trial. The board merely had to separate the wheat from the chaff."

Claiborne's comments referred to efforts on the part of Becker's defense to indict the military's Uniform Code of Military Justice that leaves the definition of proper conduct open to "liberal interpretation," according to Kramer. The defense argued that Becker did nothing wrong in his six-month love affair with Second Lieutenant Rebecca Campbell, then the legal spouse of Second Lieutenant John Stewart, also of Camp Lejeune, who remained deployed with his unit overseas during both the affair and the subsequent trial.

Defense arguments apparently had some impact on the court-martial board that refused to convict Becker on the most serious of the two counts lodged against him by the government. Following testimony by character witnesses and arguments for clemency scheduled for this week, the court-martial board will again be sequestered to consider possible punishments.

Becker faces a maximum penalty of dismissal from the service without pay or related benefits, but informed sources expect him to get only an official censure in view of his previous exemplary record in combat and in peacetime service. In a surprise development, sources close to the defense revealed on Sunday that Becker—who was not called to testify and has remained silent throughout the trial—will make a statement in his own behalf before the court-martial board meets to decide on a verdict in the controversial case.

Major General Darwin Tobrey gently pinched his wife's elbow and escorted her from their reserved seats in a front pew of the base chapel when Sunday services were concluded. Sensing his distraction, she'd held his hand tightly throughout the proceedings and tried to convey her empathy with a squeeze when he bowed his buzz-cut head in fervent prayer.

The general and his lady smiled and nodded their way through a throng of acquaintances and well-wishers as they headed for the rear of the chapel. When they passed the Protestant chaplain and his wife, Tobrey motioned for his aide to assume escort position. Mrs. Tobrey had a post-service social to attend and he had a phone call to make.

It was no coincidence that the Commandant of the Marine Corps called him at home shortly after the court-martial verdict was announced, just as it was no real surprise to hear he was being transferred to another command. What caught Darwin Tobrey off-guard was the tense tone and curt manner of the Commandant's call. They'd known each other for twenty years on and off the battlefield.

Still, there was no mistaking the resentment in the hoarse voice that brought him the bad news. The overt message was simple: Pack your bags, Darwin, we want you to take over the Supply Center at Barstow, California. The covert message was obvious: Sorry, Darwin, but you will not be considered for a third star.

When his driver dropped him off at 2nd Marine Division headquarters, General Tobrey slowly climbed the stairs, paced the empty corridors, and entered his office. He spent some time reviewing his career, staring at the framed photographs that lined the walls, fondling the statues and souvenirs collected over a lifetime of service to Corps and country.

And then he dug around in his desk for the home number of the defense contractor who offered him a job anytime, anywhere, when and if he should decide to retire.

• • •

Gunnery Sergeant Tubes Douglas scrawled his signature on the bottom of the Administrative Action form with a flourish that nearly tore the carbon paper. He thumbed the ballpoint back into recess and handed the pen to the division sergeant major.

"Tubes, you need to reconsider this. Promotion board meets in two months."

"Tell 'em to look for my record book over in the ree-tired section, Sarn't Major. By my count, I got 22 days and a seabag drag."

"It ain't over, you know. General Stokey testifies tomorrow and Captain Becker ain't had his say yet. Could be he walks with nothin' but a bullshit letter in his official file. That don't mean nothin' to a man like him."

"You got it all wrong, Sarn't Major. The skipper don't stay where he ain't wanted. Never has and never will. Neither do I."

"We need good Staff NCOs like you, Tubes. Now more than ever."

"Naw, Sarn't Major. Marines like me and you . . . we're dumb as stumps, you know? Just like them fuckin' mules on my granddad's farm in Okalahoma. You can't push 'em. You got to lead 'em. And we ain't got enough leaders left to keep me in harness."

XVI.

About Face . . .

Leon Kramer ambushed Buttplate Becker in the corridor just outside the rear entrance to the courtroom on the final day of the general court-martial. Blocking entry with his body, he fired for effect.

"Buttplate, don't do this, man. Please. Let me get General Stokey on the record and it's over. You'll walk with a punitive letter and we'll get the whole thing tossed into the crapper on appeal."

Kramer held Becker by the shoulders and stared directly into his eyes. He was transfixed—a little frightened—by the gleam he saw, the flash of passion and fire. It was the old Becker born again, bursting with energy; ready to do battle.

"I'm proud of you, Leon. I was proud of you in Vietnam and I'm even prouder now. Thanks for all you've done. You always were a damn fine Marine. And no Marine should ever be ashamed of losing—especially when he's outnumbered, outgunned, and overwhelmed. The important thing is to fight well—and you did that, my friend."

Becker pushed by his attorney and entered the courtroom. The effect on the noisy crowd was instantaneous. Following his client, Kramer was frozen in midstride by the sudden hush. It was as if someone had suddenly pulled the plug on a TV set hissing with irritating white noise. Every eye in the silent chamber was locked on Buttplate Becker.

He walked slowly toward his seat, stiff-necked in the high-collared tunic of his Marine Dress Blue uniform. The rattle of his medals was clearly audible in the hush. He stood for a moment beside his chair, eyeing the crowd, examining them as critically as they examined him in all his martial splendor.

Becker's uniform glittered, twinkled and glowed with every decoration and medal he'd ever won. At the top of a colorful waterfall that cascaded from his left breast, the Maltese cruciform of the Navy Cross hung from a muted blue and white ribbon. Snuggled next to it was the Silver Star, the Bronze Star and all variety of commendation medals, each emblazoned with the ''V'' device for valor in combat. His Purple Heart medal bore four gold stars for separate war wounds. Below the blaze of glory hung three tiers of campaign medals followed by a rack of foreign decorations including the gaudy sunburst of the Vietnamese Medal of Honor, held by fewer than a handful of living American veterans. A gleaming set of gold Navy and Marine Corps Parachutist's wings were forced nearly to the epaulet over his left shoulder. Above the right breast pocket of his uniform were three rows of unit commendations and the Combat Action Ribbon for battle action in two wars.

Becker executed a precise about face, glanced briefly at the empty bench and lowered himself into a seat beside Kramer. He was on his feet a moment later when Colonel Scales entered and called the court to order.

''Good morning, ladies and gentlemen. Trial Counsel, publish the data concerning the accused.''

Claiborne stood and glanced at Becker. It was a long moment before he could pull his eyes away from the medals and focus on his notes.

''Ladies and gentleman, the accused is an active duty captain in the United States Marine Corps and is forty-two years old. His current term of service began on January 4, 1962, and is for an indefinite period. He has fourteen years of service as an enlisted Marine during which he reached the rank of first sergeant. He was appointed a warrant officer in 1976 and commissioned a regular officer in 1978. He has been under restriction in lieu of formal arrest at Camp Lejeune pending this trial.''

"Thank you, Major. Ladies and gentlemen, the maximum punishment that may be imposed in this case is dismissal from the service. Trial Counsel, do you have any matters in aggravation to present?"

Claiborne turned to study Becker. He shrugged, closed the lid of his briefcase, and snapped the locks. "The government has nothing to add, Your Honor."

"The defense may proceed with extenuation and mitigation."

Kramer shuffled the notes prepared for him in a cramped longhand by Tubes Douglas. He read from them for the next ten minutes, calmly reciting a complete list of Becker's medals, decorations, honors, and awards as a United States Marine. When he finished, he put down the papers and called the only character witness he hoped his friend would need.

Major General Mike Stokey charged at the witness stand like an angry bull. He rattled through the oath and sat with a smile and a wink at Becker. Kramer stayed behind his table to keep from blocking the board's view of the general's decorations and rank insignia.

"General, will you identify yourself please?"

"Major General Michael W. Stokey, U.S. Marine Corps, currently serving as assistant chief of staff for Personnel, Headquarters, Marine Corps."

"And do you know the accused in this case?"

"Most assuredly. He's Captain Thurmond Becker, one of the finest Marines to ever wear the uniform."

"How did you first become acquainted with Captain Becker?"

"He was Sergeant Becker in my outfit in Vietnam, and he was an extraordinarily fine NCO. He had the ability to think on his feet and lead men in stressful situations. I personally recommended him for that Navy Cross he wears after he withstood a massive enemy assault on a hill occupied by the squad he was leading in 1967. General Doan, the Vietnamese commander in I Corps, personally presented him with the Vietnamese Medal of Honor.''

''General, based on your experience with Captain Becker, are you of the opinion that he would intentionally do something to disgrace his uniform or bring discredit on the service?''

''Let me tell you something, mister. That's nonsense. It's just not in the man to do something like that. I know Captain Becker very well and I know he is a man of principle both in and out of combat. While a lot of officers and NCOs scramble around trying to add a few dollars to their next paycheck or sucking up all the benefits, Captain Becker takes care of his Marines and honors the Corps.

''He is not now—nor was he ever—some kind of sunshine soldier or part-time patriot. You are looking here at a man who believes so deeply in what we are all supposed to represent that he has dedicated his entire life to it. In short, you are looking at a genuine United States Marine. He may be the last of a dying breed, and by God, all the world will mourn his passing.''

When he was excused, General Stokey stormed off the stand and stomped out of the courtroom, pausing only briefly to give Becker's shoulder a reassuring squeeze. Kramer took his seat in the general's wake and whispered to his client.

''We're on a roll. Please reconsider . . .''

Becker glanced over at Claiborne and then up at Colonel Scales. He shook his head and motioned for Kramer to proceed.

''Your Honor, my client wishes to make an unsworn statement at this time.''

Scales nodded, flipped open his trial guide, and addressed the jury. ''Ladies and gentlemen, the accused is going to present an unsworn statement to you. This statement is one way that an accused has to bring certain information to your attention. Neither an accused nor his counsel can be cross-examined on an unsworn statement, nor can they be asked any questions about it. An unsworn statement is not given under oath. Nevertheless, it must be given appropriate consideration by you. Like all other matters in this trial, the weight and significance to be attached to an unsworn statement rests within your sole discretion.''

Buttplate Becker rose stiffly to his feet, slowly unfolding into splendor like a night flower under a full moon. He swept the room dispassionately, his head swiveling in the leatherneck collar like a tank turret. Then he racked his shoulders back and let his hands dangle at his sides near the broad red stripes running up the legs of his trousers. The tinkle of his decorations as he adjusted his uniform blouse sounded like the roll of a snare-drum.

His voice was throaty and deep but he pronounced each word clearly and distinctly as though he were on an instructor's platform teaching bored boots.

''I have never wanted to be anything more than a professional soldier, the best Marine it was in my power to be. I have sacrificed a lot to achieve that goal. I have never married. I have never owned any trappings that might distract from my duty as a United States Marine.

''I got through the hard times by believing in our military system, by believing with all my heart that the service repays loyalty, dedication, and leadership by giving a man pride and a sense of self-worth . . . a genuine meaning to his life. It wasn't easy, but no one ever promised me a light pack or a downhill grade.

''Unlike many of my shipmates, I never worked for or sought material gains. I wanted nothing more than to share the tough times—the life-and-death situations—with men who would care for me as I was honor-bound to care for them. I knew all along I was in the minority. Some Marines thought I was a dinosaur and some civilians thought I was nuts. That didn't matter. To my way of thinking, I was living life the right way, the way a real Marine should live it.

''Suddenly, I discover I'm wrong. I see that service, sacrifice, and dedication are not enough. You have to give your heart as well as your soul and shame on you if you offer part of that to someone you love. Shame on you if loneliness pushes you down a dark alley. Shame on you if love for another person suddenly comes bubbling up from somewhere down inside and leaves you blind.

"I will not apologize or beg for mercy because I finally fell in love with a fine woman. After all these years and all these wars, I owed it to myself."

Becker flipped open a file folder and spun it around to face the board members.

"These are my formal retirement papers. Take it or leave it. I want nothing further to do with you."

Major Rodney Claiborne's hand was sticky as he gripped the receiver and he felt the prickle of sweat beading through his double-strength antiperspirant. His assignment monitor in Washington was playing it cool, but the message cut through his casual tone like a sharp bayonet.

"What's the problem? I won the case, for Christ's sake!"

"Yeah, you won . . . but I gotta tell you, Rod . . . you didn't score any points doing it."

"How about precedent? How about that? This is one that's going into the books. It'll be cited in case law for years."

"Hey, Rod . . . what can I tell you? You wanted a transfer out of Camp Lejeune . . . you got one."

"But Okinawa? Holy shit, I . . ."

"Hey, we need good lawyers out there, man."

"Listen, there was every indication when I started this case that I'd be transferred to the JAG staff at headquarters if it went as expected."

"Rod, no one on the JAG staff expected it to turn into a shit sandwich . . ."

"I'm not gonna go to Okinawa and waste my time and talent!"

"That's right, Rod. You're gonna go to Okinawa and be a good Marine Corps lawyer. Or you're gonna get out. Let me know by midweek."

Becker was stuffing a seabag when Kramer arrived at the BOQ bearing a raft of formal documents. They stood for a moment, letting the smiles build, mold, and match. When all the emotions were conveyed, Kramer found himself speechless. He swept his eyes around the bare room, searching for a cue.

There was not much stimulus. The room was naked and dingy, featuring only Becker's battered shaving kit on the washbasin and a single unadorned winter service uniform hung in the clothing press.

"Going somewhere, Buttplate?"

"Yeah. Soon as they announce the sentence."

"Gonna spend some time with Becky?"

"Maybe. It's up to her. I'm through tryin' to influence other people's lives, Leon. If it's real between us, if all this shit was worth it, she'll find me."

Kramer sat on the springs of Becker's bed, flipped his briefcase over into a lap-desk, and opened the folder containing a stack of neatly typed forms.

"We still got the appeal, buddy. These are the papers you need to sign."

Becker toyed with Kramer's pen but made no move to sign the documents. Kramer stared up at him and chewed on his lip.

"Tell me something. Why'd you do it? We had it locked up. Until you stood up and made that speech, we had a guaranteed letter of reprimand. There was no way they were gonna vote for anything more."

Becker shrugged and sat beside his friend. "You got me. Some kinda sudden brain fart, I guess. I really don't give a shit. They'll either kick me out or they'll let me retire. Either way, I'm history. They won."

"It's the Corps that lost, Buttplate! Not you. Now what would you rather have as a consolation prize? A cheap suit and a bus ticket or a retirement parade and a pension?"

Becker grinned and bent to the business of signing forms. When he was finished, Kramer wrapped Becker in a bear hug. He could not stop the tears rolling down his dark cheeks.

"No matter what happens, you always got me and Tubes.

Don't forget that! I love you, man, and I'll always be there when you need me.''

Becker backed out of the embrace and smiled through his own tears. ''That's all a man needs, Leon. As for the rest of 'em . . .''

''Fuck 'em! All but nine . . .''

''Six for pallbearers, two for road guards, and one to count cadence . . .''

Kramer picked up his briefcase and headed for the door. Over his shoulder he saw Buttplate Becker standing uncertainly behind two battered seabags and a footlocker, the sum total of his material existence, minus what might be salvaged of a brilliant, selfless career.

He drove slowly across the base and marveled at the bustle of intense, driven activity. Marines scurried, sweated, strained over typewriters, trucks, and tanks. They grinned and grunted under howitzers and heavy packs. They shouldered empty weapons and leaned forward to absorb imaginary recoil, training; yearning for the inevitable day when something besides Carolina pine trees would pop up in their rifle sights. It was a different world. It was Buttplate Becker's world . . . and he should be welcome in it.

No matter what sentence was announced by the courtmartial board—stern scolding or banishment with broken sword—Buttplate Becker and a few—too damn few—others like him would always live in this world. The appeal was prepared, cogent, airtight, and incriminating.

Do your damnedest, Kramer thought as he walked into the packed courtroom to hear the sentence, you can't beat the best.

XVII.

Dismissed . . .

Buttplate Becker stood tall and steady in the gusty wind pushing an Atlantic storm toward North Carolina's Outer Banks. It would be raining hard by nightfall. He stared straight ahead, seeing nothing on the grassy plain below his perch, thinking of the mud Marines who would shake and shiver under leaky ponchos when the squall swept over them.

Tubes Douglas jabbed him painfully in the ribs. "Get yer head outta yer ass," he whispered. "Here comes the colors."

Becker disengaged his hand from Becky's and popped a rigid salute as the color guard leading his formal retirement parade passed for his review. He watched as the tall corporal carrying the Marine Corps colors struggled against the breeze and tried to see around the wind-driven swirl of battle streamers.

Good man, Becker thought, as the color-bearer smoothly, unobtrusively swept the streamers away from his face. He'll continue the march. He'll carry on . . . he'll carry *me* on. And that's all I can ask.

There was a long line of back-slappers, well-wishers, and hand-shakers at the end of the parade. Leon Kramer was there, gloating over his easy victory and vindication at the Court of Military Appeals. Tubes Douglas was half-drunk but dignified and resplendent on his last day in dress uniform. He was headed home to Ceiling, Oklahoma, but he showed Becker an open plane ticket and promised not to unpack until he got a wedding announcement.

Becky Campbell stood at his side for a long moment when the parade field was empty. Her world was round again, spinning in the right direction and keeping her locked to Becker's side. The Marine Corps let her go without a squawk. John Stewart wrote her a cryptic note from Cyprus and enclosed the necessary paperwork to cut her free.

She wrapped an arm around his waist and squeezed until he grunted in surprise. "I am so proud . . ."

Buttplate Becker took her in this arms and stared into her eyes. "Proud? How come?"

"Because I'm about to spend the rest of my life with the man I love . . . and he's the finest fighting Fleet Marine there is."

"Nope, that's wrong. You're gonna spend the rest of your life with me . . . just another lifer . . . ree-tarded and ree-tired."

She kissed him then, hanging on tightly until he pulled her arms from around his neck and squinted up at the glowering sky over Camp Lejeune.

"Gonna rain soon. Let's go on up to the Club and get a beer."

**A Triumphant Novel of
War Through the Ages—
Bound by
One Family's
Blood Code of Honor**

SONS OF GLORY

Bound by blood and honor, they have fought the greatest
battles of all times—and survived. A glorious family of
fighting men and women, the Gallios are descendants
of a legendary general, sworn to a timeless tradition of
strength and courage. Their military heritage is their
pride. They live and die by the words: "For the greater
good, the greatest glory."

Turn the page for an exciting preview of

SONS OF GLORY

by Simon Hawke

Coming in May from Jove Books!

PROLOGUE

Afghanistan: August, 1986

The name Hindu Kush meant "Hindu Killer." The Pathan tribes who lived in this forboding mountain wilderness called it *Bam-i-Dunya*, the Roof of the World. To Tony Gallio, the terrain seemed majestically surreal in its savage beauty, a rock-strewn, broken landscape of jagged, 20,000-foot peaks that seemed to stretch into infinity. Rushing torrents of ice-cold snowmelt roared through its steep defiles. Twisted scrub pines and cedar trees grew out of nearly vertical rock walls. The days were mercilessly hot. The nights were biting cold. It was a brutal, unforgiving land that had defied the armies of Darius the Great and Alexander. The hordes of Ghengis Khan and Tamerlane had stormed through its precarious mountain passes, but had ultimately failed to conquer it. The British Empire had experienced some of its worst defeats here, humbled by the untamed land and its indomitable people. And now the Soviets were floundering in this fierce and primitive country, throwing everything they had against the freedom fighters of Afghanistan and failing to subdue them. The Hindu Kush killed those who did not belong here.

Tony Gallio was no stranger to harsh, inhospitable country. He had survived the steaming jungles of Vietnam and Cambodia. He had slogged through the dense under-growth of Nicaragua. He had returned unscatched from covert missions in such places as El Salvador and Lebanon, but he had never before encountered country quite like this. The rocky path they followed was barely a foot wide, with a sheer drop of several thousand feet directly to his left. One false step could prove fatal. Despite being in superb physical condition, Gallio was breathing like a spent mar-athoner and his clothes were soaked with sweat. It was all he could do to keep up with the seemingly inexhaustible *mujahidin*, the holy warriors of the *Jihad*.

The days stretched into weeks as they continued on their trek. The Panjshir Valley, 70 miles long with an elevation of 7,000 feet, was a three-week journey from the border. Located 40 miles to the north of Kabul, it was a valley of mud and stone villages, vineyards, wheatfields and fruit orchards, with one main entry road to the south flanked by steep escarpments. It was controlled by the Russians, inasmuch as they controlled anything in Afghanistan. They had a base there for the Hind helicopter gunships. It was a place that Gallio thought should provide some fine target practice. He was looking forward to shooting one down himself. It was, of course, strictly against orders. He wasn't even supposed to be here. He could imagine what would happen if it ever got out that a colonel in the American Special Forces, working for the CIA, had shot down a Russian helicopter with a Stinger missile. But there was no way he was going to miss this chance.

Along the way, they frequently saw flights of MiGs passing overhead. Several times, they observed groups of four or six helicopter gunships. They remained out of sight, hidden in the rocks, despite the mounting enthusiasm felt by the *mujahidin*, who were anxious to try out the Stingers. They had heard about them, because the forces in Pakistan had been equipped with both Stingers and Sidewinder air-to-air missiles. There were F-16 jet fighters in Peshawar, provided as part of the military aid by the United States, to protect Pakistani airspace and prevent the MiGs from

attacking the refugee camps. The temptation to fire on some
of the helicopters they saw was great, but it was essential
not to give themselves away before they reached their
destination. To ease the tension somewhat, Gallio unpacked
one of the Stingers and gave them dry run instructions in its
use, all without ever actually firing it. Soon, he told them,
the time would come when they would get the opportunity
to use them.

As they continued on their journey, they encountered
several groups of *mujahidin*, as well as Afghan villagers.
The people were dirt poor, living in simple, thatch-roofed
houses with dirt floors, but always, their hospitality was
effusive and they shared what little they had. They lived by
their code of *Pakhtunwali*, unwritten laws of social conduct
composed of three main dictums. *Melmastia* demanded that
anyone who crossed the threshold of their dwelling be
treated as an honored guest, even a sworn enemy. *Nanawa-
tai* dictated that asylum must be granted to anyone who
sought it and *Badal*, the strictest commandment of them all,
demanded remorseless revenge, payment in blood for any
personal affront. *Mordabad Shouravi*, Gallio thought. These
were people who believed that it was better to die in battle
than in bed. A *Shahid*, a martyr, who was killed in battle,
gained admittance through the gates of Paradise. No wonder
the Soviets couldn't crush these people. Death held no fear
for them and they didn't know the meaning of surrender.
They found freedom in death as well as life.

Gallio was unable to keep his group from talking excit-
edly about the Stinger missiles to those they met on the trail.
He tried to caution them, but it was no use. They were like
children with new toys. For all he knew, anyone they met
could be a spy for the Karmal regime. For that matter,
despite all his best efforts, word of what they carried might
have leaked out before they had even crossed the border.
However, in a very real sense, the operation was no longer
his, but theirs. They would get the missiles to Massoud, but
if they met the enemy along the way, they'd fight.

They were about five or six days' journey from their
destination when they ran into an ambush. A group of

Afghans approached them from down the trail, but something in their manner had given them away before they got too close. Whatever it was, Gallio hadn't spotted it, but the others had and almost before he knew what was happening, he found himself in the middle of a firefight. The ''Afghans'' were Soviet Spetsnaz commandos in disguise.

The *mujahidin* reacted quickly. Half of them rushed forward and took up position to cover the retreat, so the others could escape with their precious cargo of Stingers. But the Russians had prepared for that. The previous night, a flight of helicopters had passed by overhead, an occurrence that had become so common, Gallio hadn't paid much attention to it. The choppers had dropped off several squads of commandos to their rear and they had moved up during the night, setting up a hammer-and-anvil assault to hit them from both sides.

As bullets struck the rocks around them, Sikander shouted, ''*Boro! Boro!*'' (Let's go! Let's go!) He grabbed Gallio's arm and tried to pull him back out of the way, but Gallio shook him off and took up a position to return the fire with his AK-47, covering the others while they quickly started taking the missiles off the frightened pack animals. They shouldered them and began to scamper up into the rocks like mountain goats. Bullets whined off the rocks around them. Gallio felt a sharp pain as his cheek was lacerated by a stone chipped off by a round from a Kalashnikov. Adrenaline surged through his bloodstream as he returned the fire.

Cries of ''*Allah o Akbar!*'' and ''*Mordabad Shouravi!*'' echoed over the sharp, firecracker bursts of the automatic weapons. Then, suddenly, another sound was added to the din as the loud, staccato clatter of helicopter blades filled the air. The Hind helicopter gunships swooped down like screaming pterodactyls, raining a deadly hail of bullets into the mountainside. One of the panicked mules was cut completely in half as the chopper ''walked'' its fire up the trail and Gallio heard a scream as Sikander's body was reduced to bloody pulp in less than two seconds. He huddled behind the rock outcropping where he had taken shelter, trying to become a part of it as bullets spanged into the mountain all around him, sending dust and stone fragments flying in all directions. Then he heard a loud *whoosh* and a concussive *whump* as the helicopter blossomed into a bright orange fireball.

He glanced up and saw Daoud, the little thirteen-year-old who had paid such close and rapt attention when he had explained the function of the Stingers, lowering the tube from his shoulder, raising his fist and shouting out triumphantly. He had downed the first Soviet helicopter gunship in the Afghan War.

"Awriight!" Gallio shouted, with elation. *"Yeah, Daoud!"* The boy waved at him, a wide grin on his face. Then his small body jerked convulsively and fell as it was struck by a bust of machine gun fire. Gallio screamed hoarsely as he emptied the magazine of his AK-47 into the commando who had killed the boy. He jacked out the clip and slapped a fresh one in. But before he could raise the rifle, he felt a sledgehammer-like blow to his head and everything went black.

He woke up to the jouncing of a truck careening down a rutted road. He was lying on a bloodsoaked truckbed, surrounded by the dead bodies of the freedom fighters. The Soviets had knew it had a demoralizing effect on the *mujahidin* when they took away the bodies of slain freedom fighters, thereby denying them a Moslem burial.

Gallio was surprised to discover he was still alive. His head was throbbing. The bullet must have only grazed him. He no longer had on his turban, but his head was bandaged. The side of his face felt sticky, but he couldn't tell if it was from his own blood or the sticky gore on the floor of the truckbed. He couldn't raise his hand to feel it. They were tied behind his back. His feet were tied, as well. He was trussed up like a roped calf, a short cord running behind him from his hands to his feet, arching his back painfully. He was hemmed in by bodies and he couldn't move. The stench was awful.

He had no idea how long he had been out. He had no idea what time it was, whether it was day or night. He heard only the roar of the truck's engine and felt the jarring impact as it bounced over the road. He tried to think. There hadn't been a road close to where they were when the ambush had gone down, so they must have carried him out and loaded him onto a chopper, then transferred him to the truck along with the bodies.

"Well, son," he mumbled to himself, "you finally did it. You really screwed the pooch this time."

The truck braked to a stop. He heard doors slamming and the sound of running footsteps. A moment later, the back gate of the truck was lowered and the tarp was pulled aside. Two men jumped up into the truckbed, walking over the bullet-riddled bodies of the *mujahidin*, and Gallio felt himself lifted painfully and tossed out on the ground. He fell on his side and grunted. His head felt like a thousand hangovers. Someone leaned down and cut the cord running from his wrists to his feet, then cut the cord around his ankles.

"*Vstavai! Vstavai, svolotch!*"

A booted foot connected with his ribs.

Gallio grunted with pain and awkwardly lumbered to his feet. Every muscle in his body felt cramped. It was dusk. The sky was a wild orange-purple as the sun set. The wind blew gently on his face. He was in a valley, possibly the Panjshir, though he had no way of knowing for sure. The mountains rose majestically around him. As he quickly glanced around, he saw large tents and rows of corrugated iron huts. A hundred or so yards in front of him was a supply depot, with several trucks parked alongside it, as well as four BMP armored vehicles with 30 mm cannon. Farther off, he could see a line of BM-21 rocket launchers positioned near the perimeter of the camp, aimed to fire salvos at the mountain slopes. Nearer, a line of APCs, a couple of fuel tankers, and a row of T-64 tanks. To his right, there were several rows of Hind-24s, huge, ugly-looking choppers with stubby wings and weapons pods. Someone gave him a hard shove and he almost lost his footing.

Four men marched him around the front of the truck and he saw a sight that was right out of *Gunga Din*. It was a huge adobe fort, with thick, thirty-foot walls and gun towers. A gun barrel prodded his back as he was marched through the large, heavy wooden gates. They marched him down a series of dark and narrow corridors, illuminated by lights strung on wire. He heard someone screaming. They brought him to a room and shoved him inside, then tied him to a wooden chair placed behind a folding table. One of the soldiers struck him hard across the face, drawing blood. Gallio spat at him and received a gun butt in his stomach for his trouble. As he fought to get his breath back, the door opened and a colonel in the sand-colored uniform of the Spetsnaz commandos entered.

He was tall and muscular, with dark, curly hair and deep-set brown eyes. He was about forty years old, deeply tanned, with sharply chiseled features. Behind him came another man, a swarthy-looking Afghan in the uniform of the Karmal regime. He came up to Gallio and asked him something in Pushto. Gallio didn't understand a word. He simply stared at his interrogator belligerently. The man struck him in the face and repeated his query. Gallio said nothing.

One of the Russian soldiers raised his rifle to strike Gallio in the face with the gun butt, but the colonel quickly said, *"Nyet!"* and the rifle was lowered. *"Ostavteh nas."*

He jerked his head toward the door and the others left, leaving him alone with Gallio.

He took out a silver cigarette case, snapped it open, took one for himself, then held out the case to Gallio and raised his eyebrows. Gallio nodded. The Russian took one out and placed it between Gallio's lips. He lit it, then lit his own and exhaled the smoke through his nostrils.

"My name is Col. Grigori Andreyvitch Galinov," he said, in excellent, though heavily accented English. "What is your name?"

Gallio gazed at him with an uncomprehending expression and shrugged his shoulders.

"Your pretence at ignorance is pointless," Galinov said, matter-of-factly. "I will ask you again, what is your name?"

Gallio did not reply.

"You know that we can make you talk," Galinov said. "You are, no doubt, familiar with our techniques of interrogation. Why put yourself through unnecessary pain?"

Gallio said nothing.

The Russian officer stared at him thoughtfully. "Very well. You do not wish to tell me your name. In that case, I will try another question."

He leaned forward across the table, close to Gallio's face, staring at him intently. He held up a gold signet ring.

"Where did you get this?"

Gallio recognized his own ring, a gold signet inscribed with the symbol of a *gladius*, the Roman short sword, surrounded by the letters P.B.M.M.G. He had not realized until that moment that they had removed it from his finger. And as the Russian held it up before him, Gallio saw, with a shock, that he was wearing a ring that was absolutely identical.

Galinov saw the expression on his face and his eyes narrowed. He took the cigarette from between Gallio's lips and tossed it aside.

"Where?" he repeated.

"It belonged to my great grandfather," said Gallio, staring at him with astonishment. "Where did you get yours?"

"It has been in my family for generations," said Galinov. He placed the ring on the table before Gallio and straightened up. *"Pro bono . . . ?"* he said, watching Gallio with an anxious, intense gaze.

Gallio felt a fist start squeezing his insides. He swallowed hard. *"Pro bono maiori, maxima gloria,"* he said, completing the Latin motto that the letters on the ring stood for. He felt suddenly lightheaded.

"So you know the words," Galinov said, slowly. "But who was the first to say them?"

"Marcus Lucius Gallio. My ancestor." He moistened his lips. "And who did he say them to?"

"To Hanno, son of Hannibal," Galinov replied. He exhaled heavily. *"Chiort vazmi!"* he swore, softly. "Who *are* you?"

"Col. Anthony Mark Gallio." Suddenly, it hit him. He couldn't believe it. He felt as if he had been gut-punched. "Gallio? *Galinov?*"

"We are kinsmen," said the Russian, staring at him with awe.

"Jesus Christ! I can't fucking believe it!"

"Your shock is no greater than mine, I assure you," Galinov said. He shook his head. "If this were any other regiment than Spetsnaz, that ring would surely have been stolen."

He took his knife out, went around behind Gallio's chair and cut his bonds. Then he opened the door and called out, *"Suvorov! Prenehsi butilku vodki."*

A few moments later, a sergeant entered with a bottle of vodka and two shot glasses. Galinov nodded and dismissed him. The man left and shut the door. As Gallio massaged his wrists, Galinov opened the bottle and poured them each a shot. "What the devil shall we drink to?" he asked. "You have children?"

"A son."

"I, also. To the children, then."

"To the children," Gallio said, softly. They drank.

"Of all the places in the world to meet," Galinov said, offering Gallio another cigarette. He took it and Galinov lit it for him. "You are Special Forces, of course. Yes, you would be." He snorted and shook his head. "You son of a bitch."

Gallio said nothing. He was still in a daze. Galinov refilled their glasses.

"I had thought that my branch of the family was the last," he said.

"So did I," said Gallio.

"A colonel in the United States Army Special Forces, working for the CIA, of course," Galinov said. He shook his head. *"Yob tvayu maht."*

Gallio had some knowledge of Russian. He was familiar with the Russian equivalent of motherfucker.

Col. Galinov stared at him for a long moment, a strange expression on his face. "What is your son's name?"

"Tony, Jr."

"Mine is Alexei," Galinov said. "He will be six years old now. I have not seen him since he was four."

"Mine's eight."

Galinov nodded. "I hate this lousy war."

"I hate the way you're fighting it," said Gallio.

Galinov nodded again, his gaze distant. "Yes. So do I. This is not a war for soldiers, but for butchers. I can no longer sleep without nightmares. What we are doing here fills me with disgust. May God forgive us."

"God?" said Gallio.

Galinov smiled, wryly. "You are surprised? Did you think that all of us were atheists? I am Russian Orthodox. And when I return home to Novgorod, if I should return, I shudder at the things I must confess."

"Why?" asked Gallio. "Why kill innocent civilians? Why the atrocities, Galinov?"

"The United States has never committed atrocities, I suppose?" Galinov said, sarcastically. "What of your Lt. Calley? What of your support of the Nicaraguan Contras?"

"I won't deny the Contras commit atrocities, but we don't control the Contras and Calley was prosecuted. What he did wasn't our policy, as it is yours. You people are committing genocide."

"And your hands are so clean?" Galinov said. "Your country's history is without blemish? What about your American Indians?"

"That was in the past," Gallio said.

"So shall this be, one day," said Galinov. "But whether you believe it or not, I don't like it any more than you do." He refilled their glasses again. "For the first time, there are demonstrations against the war back home. Such a thing has never been before. Our young people do not wish to go. It is like your Vietnam. They injure themselves to get medical exemptions, some even pretend insanity and go to institutions rather than serve in the army." He shook his head. "There is talk we may be pulling out soon. I hope to God it's true."

He shoved his chair back and got up. His manner seemed

to change. He drew himself up and looked down at Gallio. Without warning, he punched Gallio in the face, knocking him back over his chair and breaking his nose. As Gallio struggled back up, Galinov hit him three more times, powerful, punishing blows that bloodied his mouth and cut the skin over his left eye. Gallio collapsed on the floor.

Galinov opened the door and shouted something to the men outside. They came in, picked Gallio up, and took him to a cell. They shoved him in and he fell sprawling on the dirt floor. There were rats crawling in the corners. The door was slammed and bolted.

"SHATTERING." —*Newsweek*

PLATOON

They were the men of Bravo Company.
Officers and grunts. Black and white.
Americans. It was war that

5:30 - 10:00 - 2:30 - 4:15 - 7:00

THE BEST IN WAR BOOKS

DEVIL BOATS: THE PT WAR AGAINST JAPAN
William Breuer 0-515-09367-X/$3.95
A dramatic true-life account of the daring PT sailors who crewed the Devil Boats—outwitting the Japanese.

PORK CHOP HILL S.L.A. Marshall
0-515-08732-7/$3.95
A hard-hitting look at the M

All of them Am...
brought them together — and it was war
that would tear them apart.

A novel by Dale A. Dye
based on a screenplay by Oliver Stone

___ Platoon 0-425-12864-4/$4.50

...ing look at the Korean War and the handful of U.S. riflemen who fought back the Red Chinese troops.

"A distinguished contribution to the literature of war."—New York Times

__THREE-WAR MARINE Colonel Francis Fox Parry
0-515-09872-8/$3.95
A rare and dramatic look at three decades of war—World War II, the Korean War, and Vietnam. Francis Fox Parry shares the heroism, fears, and harrowing challenges of his thirty action-packed years in an astounding military career.